Creeps,
Cache,
& Corpses

Mary Seifert

Books by Mary Seifert

Maverick, Movies, & Murder
Rescue, Rogues, & Renegade
Tinsel, Trials, & Traitors
Santa, Snowflakes, & Strychinine
Fishing, Festivities, & Fatalities
Diamonds, Diesel, & Doom
Creeps, Cache, & Corpses

Visit Mary's website and get a free recipe collection!
Scan the QR code

Creeps, Cache, & Corpses

Katie & Maverick Cozy Mysteries, Book 7

Mary Seifert

Secret Staircase Books

Creeps, Cache, & Corpses
Published by Secret Staircase Books, an imprint of
Columbine Publishing Group, LLC
PO Box 416, Angel Fire, NM 87710

Book layout and design by Secret Staircase Books
Cover images © Marcel Pelz, Svetolk, Miruna Niculescu, Dmitry
Kalinovsky

First trade paperback edition: March, 2024
First e-book edition: March, 2024
* * *
Publisher's Cataloging-in-Publication Data

Seifert, Mary
Creeps, Cache, & Corpses / by Mary Seifert.
p. cm.
ISBN 978-1649141712 (paperback)
ISBN 978-1649141729 (e-book)

1. Katie Wilk (Fictitious character). 2. Minnesota—Fiction. 3.
Amateur sleuths—Fiction. 4. Women sleuths—Fiction. 5. Dogs in
fiction. I. Title

Katie & Maverick Cozy Mystery Series : Book 7.
Siefert, Mary, Katie & Maverick cozy mysteries.

BISAC : FICTION / Mystery & Detective.

813/.54

You don't choose your family.
They are God's gift to you, as you are to them.
—Desmond Tutu

ONE

I read Pete's text, and just like that, my awesome spring break plans imploded.

Six days after my boyfriend, Pete Erickson, surprised me with plane tickets to California for our spring break getaway complete with a biking-through-wine-country itinerary, one of the other emergency room physicians announced his retirement, effective immediately, due to serious health issues. Pete's vacation went up in smoke and vacuumed mine right alongside.

That left me four days to find something to keep me busy during my week off, hopefully something with pizazz.

For the remaining twenty minutes before the deluge of students poured into my classroom, I scribbled my list of possible engaging break activities. The choices dwindled as I dismissed alternate proposals by running a black line through each—the lost trip to Sonoma first.

My phone buzzed again. I read 'The Inimitable Harry Wilk' and reluctantly accepted the call.

"Hey, Dad. Looks like you've been playing with my contact list again."

"Hi, Darlin'. Pete called." I groaned inwardly. "The offer to join us skiing is still on the table. Our Minnesota peaks might not be gargantuan, but winter could last forever."

"Thanks. I'll get back to you. Gotta run." The pencil swung like a pendulum over the idea as I considered the three strikes against his suggestion.

First, it hadn't snowed in two weeks, and, though man-made snow often covered the hills, temperatures hovered close to thirty-two degrees, and the condition of the ski slopes would not be optimal. I drew one line through Ski Trip to Duluth with Dad and Ellen.

I nibbled on my lip while I thought. Second, most of the state's schools had spring break at the same time and rooms proved difficult to find. The semi-primitive lodging Dad secured boasted accommodations for ten: one queen-sized bed in each of two bedrooms, two pull-out couches, blowup mattresses to toss on the floor—sans bedding … bring sleeping bags, a tiny kitchen with a microwave and mini-fridge, six place settings and a dinette, one bath, men's and women's communal showers available in the lodge, and access to the slopes—transportation provided by retired school buses. It added up to a disaster in the making. I pressed the tip of the sharpened pencil into the paper repeatedly, not intending to carve the lines into the pages beneath.

I eyed the clock. Third, I hadn't yet forgiven him for dropping the nuclear bomb on my definition of family and blowing up my neat and ordered life. I stabbed the pencil point below the 'D.'

For as long as I could remember, Dad had said my mom was gone. I thought she'd died, and he never corrected my assumption. She'd left me as an infant, but for twenty-seven years, my mother had been alive, somewhere. I just hadn't been good enough for her.

Dad drummed into me, "Honesty is the best policy." Although he never lied outright, I fueled my anger with the knowledge he could have shared what he knew. My heartrate picked up in a bit of a panic. I wasn't ready to listen to his excuses, and I reeled every time the thought came to mind. I just met a half-sister I never knew I had, and she wanted to go skiing. I couldn't go with them. The word Duluth disintegrated beneath the lead.

I loved my dad. I would forgive him eventually, but for the time being, I would feel sorry for myself and let him fret.

I clenched my fists. Straightforward numbers and facts calmed me. I tugged a puzzle page from the emergency folder I kept tucked between my textbooks. The first Plexer fell easily. JOANB translated into AN inside JOB. I rewrote STTHEORY as THE inside STORY and began to breathe more easily.

My phone chirped. I combed my fingers through my flyaway hair. "Hi, Jane."

"Hey, Katie. Now that you'll be around over break—"

"How did you find out so soon?"

"There are no secrets in Columbia. You should know that everybody knows everything in small town Minnesota." I could almost see her toss her blond curls and roll her twinkling brown eyes. I envied her natural beauty and confidence. "And ..."

"Spill, girlfriend," I prompted.

"Pete told Drew about his partner leaving, so Drew transferred the Sonoma tour into his name." Her voice softened. She added the last part in a giddy rush. "We're taking the bike tour in your place. Sorry."

I started to laugh. "I'm glad someone will be going, but Pete's going to owe me big time."

She breathed a sigh. "Before we go, maybe you can help me nail down a few more wedding details."

"I thought you had everything under control, control being your middle name, of course," I said.

She'd been planning the wedding of her dreams her entire life. Until recently, the only piece missing was the groom.

"My big day could be here sooner than we realize, and I paid a hefty deposit and finally finagled a phone call with the fabulous photographer, Kimber Leigh, on Sunday afternoon. I don't know what I'll do if she doesn't fit us into her hectic schedule."

"Isn't she the eccentric curmudgeon that absolutely everybody wants? I heard she's booked out a year in advance. And you arranged to talk with her? That's great." I turned her words over in my head and tapped the pencil against the desktop.

"Can you join the call?"

"I suppose if I don't find anything better to do." I

stopped smiling and dropped the pencil as understanding dawned. "But won't you be on a plane to California? What time do you land? Are you thinking you'll be unable to take the call, and you want *me* to talk to Kimber Leigh? Alone?"

Her voice sounded chipper. "Maybe. Would you? Pretty please? Just in case. Then if I'm unavailable, I'd be covered?"

"Like no Wi-Fi on the plane? Or are you thinking you'll be busy with dinner? Or basking by the pool? Or visiting that next winery?"

"Or a flat tire or a bad connection." She sounded a tiny bit defensive, as if she almost believed the alternatives herself. "That would take a load off my mind. I'd really appreciate it. I haven't decided on when or where the wedding will take place yet." She hemmed and hawed. "I need to make a location decision soon and line up my vendors. I'll plan around her, but I really could use your assistance."

I couldn't help but smile again. My best friend, Jane Mackey, said yes to the love of her life, Drew Kidd, and asked me to be her maid-of-honor, but I hadn't anticipated the smorgasbord of plans necessary for her wedding bliss—flowers and showers, menus and venues, dresses and suits, shoes and ties, not to mention guest lists, cake, and a photographer. Years of watching classic television shows recording transformations of the captivating brides made me squirm as I considered a Jane-style *Bridezilla* or *Say Yes to the Dress*.

"Katie, are you still there?"

"Hmm. Yes. Imagining your super special day."

"Would you ask her …"

Her words sounded less distinct, and I began to dream.

Helping Jane provided a great excuse to avoid skiing with Dad and my half-sister. As she droned on, I observed the second hand of the clock lurch its way around three hundred sixty degrees. I'd worked hard to rein in my recent chaotic, anxiety-riddled student lives and keep them on track. To aid my students' retention and hone their math skills, I required daily homework. Not much, but enough to continue strengthening and building on prior skills. Lately, my subtle reminders went unheeded. My ten measly problems were no match for visions of photo-worthy spring break vacations and often got lost overnight or eaten by the proverbial dog.

Jane brought me back to the conversation with an abrupt, "Katie, what do you think about a black bridesmaid dress?"

She didn't need me to answer—she went ahead and itemized her own list of pros and cons while I concocted arguments in defense of assigning homework to my high school pupils. For some of my students, visions of slaloming through the sand dunes on a beach or attempting to soak up the sun through layers of coconut-scented sunscreen slathered on their winter-white skin clouded the importance and thrill of finding the solution to an integral or derivative even if it would be on the Advanced Placement calculus exam. One of my students mentioned shopping the Miracle Mile in Chicago. Another would attend a show at the Orpheum in Minneapolis. And yet a third asked what I thought of wearing souvenir Mickey Mouse ears to prom.

My dad and I purchased numerous boxes of fruit and frozen bread braids from students in the music and foreign language programs to help fund their travels to new locales. Caught up in their excitement, my dependable math students, with images of those new and exotic places on their minds, ceased to complete homework.

My thoughts wandered to a possible mathematical escape I could host for my students next year: determining windspeed and arrival time of an airplane bearing as far south as we could go, computing statistics at a sports competition or square footage of an arena, and uncovering the math used for designing and manufacturing in a factory which made an item the kids would want to know more about. I sighed, realizing how difficult it might be to raise the positively prohibitive funds needed per individual.

"Katie? What do you think?" The voice on the phone broke into my contemplation.

"What do I think about what?"

"You didn't hear a word I said. Pining your lost March getaway, I suppose."

"I'm going to enjoy watching my to-be-read stack of books shrink to nothing. I owe Maverick a few long walks and practice retrieving and finding. He's going to make a great search-and-rescue canine."

"Anything else?"

"The usual. I'll eat my veggies and workout two hours a day." Jane snorted and I giggled. "And I'll binge watch some cooking shows."

She stopped snorting. "The last time you made toast, the smoke detector scared Ida half out of her wits."

Known for her prowess in the kitchen, my landlady, Ida Clemashevski, had never heard the sharp, high-pitched beeps before I set it off, and she'd lived in her Victorian home for decades.

"I'll give you my list of questions and responses for

Kimber Leigh. We'll talk later." She ended the call.

I added 'Kimber Leigh' to my ravaged list and shuddered. Maybe something else would come up, and I'd have to bow out and run a dismissive line through her name too.

And then I got an offer I couldn't refuse.

TWO

My forehead dropped into the palms of my hands as the shallow well of entertaining ideas dried up. I breathed deeply, still wallowing, until I heard a knock on the door jamb.

"Ms. Wilk?" My gaze shifted toward the door at the unexpected arrival.

I pulled a smile onto my lips, retrieved a pencil, and pretended to be busy. "I'm back here, in my classroom." I sat up straighter.

Carlee's straight ebony hair swung like a full-length curtain in front of her face as she rounded the corner. She came to a halt and lifted her gray eyes. "Am I bothering you?" She reached for the pendant hanging around her neck and polished the calming talisman. I knew the gesture—Charles' wedding ring suspended from the chain around my neck had been rubbed smooth too.

I shook my head. "No. I'm woolgathering."

She looked down. Her sneaker became the most riveting item in the room, and she tormented the industrial carpet, drawing semicircles with her toe.

"Carlee?" Her eyes met mine and twinkled.

Her toe stopped. "I'm going to meet my maternal grandparents next week. They're coming from North Dakota." Her face broke into a huge grin, and her beautiful bright smile lit the room.

Carlee and her dad had been recently reunited, but, like me, she never knew her mother.

"Oh, my goodness. That's wonderful." I studied her face. One side of her lips formed the beginning of a frown, and her brow furrowed. "Isn't it?"

"It is, but I'm nervous as all get out. My dad's been in contact with my grandmother since he found me."

She chewed on her bottom lip. Her smile contorted into a grimace of sorts. "My grandfather finally consented to meet me, but even after all this time, he still can't forgive my dad."

"Your mom was only trying to protect your dad."

"I know. She wanted him to stay safe. Those SEAL guys can get into some dangerous situations, and if their minds aren't focused, bad things can happen. Dad said half the time he couldn't tell her when he was gone, let alone where." Her hair slid forward, and she whispered, "She never told him about me." She tucked the strands behind her ear.

Her lip protruded and she hiccupped a sob. Her dad, CJ Bluestone, barely made it home after he sustained a nearly fatal injury in the line of duty, and his limp reminded us daily of the frailty of life. He had no idea what he'd missed. The woman who'd raised Carlee had been present at her birth but had also watched her mother die.

Carlee's eyes brightened, remembering. "If we hadn't done the blood typing experiment for science club, and you hadn't come to find me, and if —"

"And if you hadn't worn the lapis lazuli necklace—"

"That Dad made with his own hands for their engagement—"

"In your mom's favorite color. If everything hadn't aligned—"

"We might never have known." Her eyes sparkled. "Grandmother has been teaching me a few words. Hidatsa is a beautiful language. She admits my grandfather is an ornery old coot, but he's warming, and if he'd have known about me, he might've softened a lot sooner." She looked at the floor. "Dad's trying to get along with them, but he finds animals easier to deal with than people."

"I agree. He's nurtured Maverick's use of a great nose."

"Maverick proved it when he found me," she said and raised her chin, grinning.

"It's difficult training next to your dog though. Renegade is by far the more serious student. We're still only a probationary canine search-and-rescue team, but your dad says the trick is using positive reinforcement to communicate expectations and rewarding correct behaviors," I parroted. "Although I could do with something other than Maverick's favorite—hugely stinky, tiny salmon treats." I pinched my nose.

"Positive reinforcement works on people too." She giggled. "Dad is still trying to figure out parenting, but he buckles nearly every time I call him Daddy." At first, she sputtered, and then a hearty belly laugh erupted. "I figured out how to wrap him around my little finger."

I chuckled. "I've known my dad my entire life and he caves the same way." I sobered, thinking of the secret he'd kept from me. "You two are doing great."

She wiped away happy tears and said, "Do you want to come with us?

I didn't answer immediately.

Her eyes widened. "You don't have to, but I thought since your plans fell through and if you hadn't figured out anything else to do next week, you could join us."

My jaw dropped. Everyone knew my business.

"It's a trip to memorialize my mother. Would you mind acting as a buffer and ease the meeting with my grandparents?" Pink flushed her cheeks, and she stammered. "Never mind. I'm sure you can find something better to do." She turned to leave.

"Carlee," I called. She stopped and glanced back at me. "It would be my privilege."

She took a measured breath. "We're going to find where my mom's buried. Dad's certain a town the size of New Prague can't have too many unmarked graves from seventeen years ago. He's hoping holding a service will bring us closure."

I thought of my own wound torn open when I learned about my half-sister. Knowledge could be a double-edged sword.

"I need details." A sly grin inched across my face. I wanted to let Jane down gently. I grabbed a notebook and jotted down the information.

She recited as if reading from a well-curated list, "It's

a two hour and twenty-two-minute drive. We have rooms at a ninety-nine-year-old five-star bed and breakfast called White Star Inn. On Saturday morning, Dad has an appointment with an administrative assistant at the hospital where my mother's …" She gulped. "Body was left. They should be able to tell him where her remains might be. After Mass on Sunday, we're meeting with the parish priest to finalize the service." She picked up her pile of books and headed out the door. "Thanks, Ms. Wilk."

I attacked the final item on the list with an exclamation point. I had a spring break plan.

THREE

Chattering usually ceased when the president of the after-school science club officially struck the block with her gavel, but at the final meeting, one day before break began, Ashley Johannes requested order four times before reining in most of the enthusiasm bubbling in the room. She shook her blond hair and squinted her sparkling blue eyes. "We're not going to get anything accomplished today so we may as well provide details about all our spring break plans."

Lorelei Calder pulled a pencil from a tight chignon and tapped it against her palm while she paced. "My mom scheduled college visits over spring break, and my head is spinning."

Galen Tonlenson brushed back his light-brown hair.

He cracked his knuckles and groaned. "Brainiac," he kidded. "Any school would be lucky to have you, and you know it."

"But I don't know which school I want to attend."

Galen shook his head. "Me? My season's over and I'm eating everything in sight." He patted his flat wrestler stomach.

"*Me voy a* Costa Rica with the Spanish students, but don't worry. I won't forget you plebes," said Brock Isaacson. "I'll send photos from the beach.'"

"How generous of you, Brock," said Ashley, cooing and rolling her eyes. "But next week our band is going to Nashville. By the way, Ms. Wilk, thanks for supporting our trip with your purchases, but what are you going to do with two cases of grapefruit?" She giggled, not really listening for the answer I couldn't even dream up. "What about you, Kindra?"

"Dairy cows don't take a vacay you know, and we usually have chores, but ..." She squealed like a little girl at Christmas. "Mom's boyfriend, Ransom, hired a few day laborers and arranged for us to take a long weekend at a spa. It's a surprise for mom, and Patricia and I can't wait. And she promised to teach me how to sign more phrases." She finger spelled as she said, "Improve my ASL fluency."

Her head fell forward, and she took a deep breath before looking around the room. "I'm really glad Patricia came home from that school. She kind of had a chip on her shoulder, but the transition could've been so much worse. Thank you all for making it easier for her, for helping her. She tries so hard to retain her ability to speak. I don't know what I'd have done if I'd have lost my hearing." She snorted. "Yeah, I do. I'd have been the biggest pain in the neck ever." She turned her attention to her friend. "How about you, Carlee?"

Carlee lit up. "I'm researching my family history and meeting my grandparents." When the hoots and hollers quieted, she winked at her tall guy leaning against the wall, his arms crossed over his broad chest, one foot braced as if to help him shove away, a hank of hair hiding his grin. "And Galen's parents are taking a cruise so he's coming with us. I promised I'd feed him."

The rumble of conversation began. Before Ashley pounded her gavel again, she wrapped her neon yellow nails around the handle and pointed it. All eyes followed the end and its trajectory to me, and they quieted. "Ms. Wilk, what are you doing next week?"

Happily, I had plans. I cleared my throat to answer, and my phone buzzed. "You start your meeting, and I'll take this out in the commons."

'Dr P' glowed from the display. I answered, wearing the most flirtatious smile no one would ever see. "Hello, Doctor." I sighed. The thought of his gorgeous chocolate brown eyes never failed to make my knees wobbly and my heart thump in my chest.

"Hi, Katie. We're still on for dinner at Santino's at 5:30?" I hummed. "But I wanted you to know, the OR manager reorganized the schedule and I'm on call, so we'll have to drive separately tonight."

Bummer. "That's okay," I said in a singsong voice. "I'll see you there."

"Duty calls."

I turned back toward the classroom, holding a silent phone in my hand and a ditzy smile on my face and met the entire crew wrapped in their coats. Their expressions indicated they'd been standing there long enough. I could feel the tips of my ears and my face heat up. "What—"

"We're heading out to determine what difference color makes in the temperature around it," Ashley said, ignoring my stammering. "Brock wants to know which swim trunks to wear to stay cool." She fanned squares of colored tagboard like a deck of cards.

"'Course, I know I'm too cool already, but I'm asking for a friend," said Brock.

Ashley ignored him. "We're using the flat thermometers, and we're trying black, white, and red backgrounds first time around. We hypothesized the coolest will be white, but you never know. If we have time …" She threw her head toward Brock. "He'd like to try blue and green too."

Brock batted his eye lashes. "I need to find the best color to bring out the suave in my baby brown eyes."

Lorelei swatted his shoulder. Ashley strutted at the front of our line like the Pied Piper of Hamelin, leading the children out into an afternoon of bright sunshine, cornflower blue skies, and a breeze. I shivered in the gentle wind, slightly chilled as it caressed what persisted of the small mounds of white, gray, and black ice.

Lorelei aligned the three paper squares on the concrete walkway and placed each of the thermometers dead center. With all eyes riveted to the gauges on the ground, ZaZa Lavigne's sudden presence startled me.

"Wear white," she announced. The awestruck faces turned and gazed at her. One by one, as recognition dawned and memories of her well-meant but poor advice interfering with their latest mock trial competition surfaced, the same eyes rolled and went back to observing the thermometers. I gaped at her three-inch blue heels and shook my head.

"Manolo Blahniks," she said, lifted her nose as if I smelled distasteful, and strutted to the black sedan idling at the curb—the only cab in town, and one she treated as her personal chauffeuring service. She stumbled on the uneven surface but caught the arm of the unfortunate driver waiting for her.

ZaZa had been a team leader at the Royal Holloway where she and I had studied cryptanalysis. We'd been friends until the man she thought she wanted to spend the rest of her life with fell in love with me. For a moment, memories assailed me and took my breath away. I missed Charles' all-encompassing, vivid blue eyes and gentle smile. When he died, he took a piece of me with him.

ZaZa had accepted a teaching job in west central Minnesota, far from Paris, under the guise of *my* wanting to work with a familiar face. I shook my head. I'd never understood her and avoided her whenever possible.

"The gauges have stopped, and Ms. Lavigne predicted correctly," said Brock. "But I'd like to include a bit of color in my wardrobe."

"I'll take the thermometers inside for a few minutes to let them reset," said Carlee.

Lorelei exchanged the colored squares and neatly lined them up on the sidewalk. While they waited, the students dropped onto makeshift seats and benches, phones came out, and talking ceased.

I looked over my charges, quiet and busy. I loved my job.

Before I could finish my thought, the metal fire door banged open and drew all eyes like a high-powered magnet.

Kindra hopped off the short brick wall, ran to her sister and held her shoulders, watching and listening as Patricia's fingers flew and her words tumbled one over the other. She said, "Not so fast. I can't understand. What happened? Are you okay?" She enunciated the words slowly—Patricia read lips and had great skill and dexterity communicating with hearing and deaf alike.

Kindra drew back and looked into Patricia's brown eyes, alight with fire, as she spoke and signed emphatically, "Our break plans fell through. One of Mom's biggest clients is being audited, and she had to go to Chicago." I watched her hands, fascinated by how much I understood in her expressive body language.

"Is that all?" Kindra sighed and let her hands drop. "You scared me."

I shuddered—no one could mistake the sign for afraid. My students circled the girls, a show of support.

Kindra's face relaxed for a second. "You brat." Her features hardened. "I thought something really horrible happened."

"It did." Patricia's words rumbled deep in her throat. I strained to understand. "I don't know if he thought he was trying to be thoughtful, but Ransom spilled the beans about our weekend."

The disappointment on Kindra's face lasted a few seconds. She lifted her chin. "The surprise is on us, I guess. We'll have to find something else to do. Let's go home now." Kindra shrugged. "If I don't see you all again, have a great week."

She tossed a three-finger wave, and they flew past Carlee returning with the thermometers. "What's with them?" she said, nodding over her shoulder.

Galen took the gauges and hurriedly placed them on the colored squares. "Their spring break plans fell through.

It's too bad. They had a rough winter, and it would have been a great pick-me-up."

Galen gave Carlee a questioning look. Her mouth formed an O and she turned and jogged after Kindra and Patricia. The other girls raced after her.

Brock looked on, disheartened. "Hey, what color do I wear?" he whined.

"You'll look good in any color," Lorelei called over her shoulder.

"I know but ..." he began, shook his head, and took off at a trot. Galen shrugged and brought up the rear.

After collecting our gear, I had just enough time to race home, change out of my school duds and into something with more color. Ida hinted I looked best in blue to match my eyes. I brushed my unruly flyaway light-brown hair, touched up my lips, and drove to Santino's, arriving precisely on the half-hour.

Mr. Santino met me at the door with a frown on his face.

FOUR

I'm sorry, Miss Katie, but Dr. Pete said you didn't pick up. He has a patient, and he won't be able to join you tonight."

I pulled out my phone and sure enough, through the small drama at school and concentrating on getting ready for the evening, I'd missed four calls and two texts. "That's okay, Mr. Santino. I knew it was a possibility. May I get my order to go, please? And could you double it? Dad loves your lasagna."

I waited on a chair by the entry, absentmindedly swiping through pages on my phone when the door dinged. Kindra and Patricia sauntered up to the hostess desk.

Kindra nudged her sister and pointed. I waved. They completed their order and joined me as Mr. Santino carefully set the large, tomato, onion, and garlic-scented white paper bag upright in my hands.

I understood Patricia's signs for 'smells good,' and I signed one of the few words I'd learned. "Yes."

Kindra nodded her approval. Kindra's mom requested me for Patricia's math instructor, and I vowed to make it my mission to help her in whatever small way I could, which included learning signs.

"Carlee didn't even have to ask her dad if it would be okay," Kindra said. "The owner of the bed and breakfast reserved the entire residence for their family and friends, and Dr. Bluestone offered to take us with. It'll be Galen, Dr. Bluestone, Carlee, Patricia, you, and me until Carlee's grandparents join us." The smile stretched across her face. "It's not the same as the weekend we had planned, but Mom won't have to worry about us because we'll need to behave."

Patricia nudged her. "Never," she said and plopped onto the bench.

"It's going to be tough, and I'm glad Carlee will have a few friendly faces with her," I said. "Have a great dinner."

"No doubt."

I dragged myself out to my car. Panic set in for a moment as I glanced down the row of vehicles. I still looked for my Jetta, but it had lost a battle with a buck in October. It took me a moment to remember the Ford Focus Dad purchased as our everyday vehicle. I clicked the lock button on the fob and followed the chirp.

Before I could set the bag on the floor in front of the passenger seat, my phone rang.

"Hi, Jane. What's up?"

"I will not allow myself to be let down. I'm not angry.

I'm merely frothing at the mouth because there's nothing I can do under the circumstances." She held her breath and released it slowly, air whistling as if from a birthday balloon. "Drew got a new assignment. Even if we can go west, it won't be until midweek at the earliest, and that's highly unlikely."

I caught myself before I snickered. "I do know what it feels like. Drew does his job so well you'd better get used to it. I don't imagine his hours will change much when you're married." As a highly sought after undercover agent for state law enforcement, he worked whenever the need arose.

"I know you're right. I promised myself I wouldn't vent to him, so is it okay if I use you as my sounding board?"

"Only if it works both ways." I chewed on my bottom lip. "I've been meaning to talk to you about Kimber Leigh. I can't take the call."

No reaction.

"Jane? Are you still there?"

She sighed. "Are you sure? I've never even talked to her, but her texts give off massive scary vibes. I could use the support."

Happily, I had a good excuse. "Carlee Bluestone asked me to accompany her to meet her grandparents and look for her mother's grave." I waited, cringing. "Jane?"

"I'm thinking about how very lucky I am. Some of our kids have gone through so much more in life than I ever will. Please don't let me ever forget."

"The same goes for me." Life might not always have turned out the way I'd hoped, but I thought again of Charles and smiled. At least he'd been part of my life for a little while. And now I'd found Pete. "Jane, you could come with us. I'd love the company, and you could use the diversion. We're leaving tomorrow after school. We could talk to Kimber Leigh together. And if things work out in Drew's schedule, we can make sure you catch a flight to California."

She took extra time to answer. "Maybe, but I heard your dad invited you to go to Duluth. What happened with that?"

I massaged the spot between my eyebrows. Another case of everyone knows everything in a small town. "I'm not ready to spend a whole week with her." Jane understood my hesitation.

"If you're going with Carlee, and your dad is going to Duluth, what are you doing with Maverick?"

"He's staying with Ida."

"Are you sure there'll be room for me?"

"There's always room for a five-foot nothing bundle of energy, and it would be nice to spend relaxed time with my friend. Carlee said we have the entire inn."

"If you say so. I'll try to make arrangements, but no promises." She ended the call.

Pete stopped by in the evening for a few minutes, just enough time to tell me he'd miss me and to have a good week, before the ER called him back. They needed to hire another doctor soon.

I packed my bags, researched not-to-be-missed highlights of the New Prague area, and prepared for a frenzied Friday. Fortunately, I woke refreshed. The day turned out to be grueling.

FIVE

The chapter tests and section quizzes elicited groans, but assigning no homework, for a change, garnered grateful applause from every class and elevated my rank to two notches above the teachers who tended to overload with spring break assignments. ZaZa peeked in and raised her eyebrows as my happy students scoured the white boards, spritzed lemon-scented cleaner, and swiped desktops to ready the classroom for a fresh start to the year's fourth quarter upon our return.

The final bell rang. Students scattered, leaving no trace they'd ever graced the halls. I mentally checked what remained on my vacation to-do list. CJ and Carlee would pick up Galen and meet Kindra, Patricia, and me at my humble abode so I could say goodbye to my dog. The thought tugged at my heartstrings. We'd been together every day since he'd arrived, and I missed him already. As I flipped the light switch off, my phone chimed.

"Hi, Ida."

"Katie? My cousin fell and broke her hip. I'm running up to Fargo, so I won't be around to look after your precious puppy. I'm sorry."

"I understand. We'll be fine."

I couldn't moan, even though I wanted to. Another plan went up in flames. Ida absolutely needed to take care of her family, but I'd have to spend my break in Columbia after all. At least I still had a good excuse to opt out of the trip to Duluth.

I pulled up contact information for CJ. My finger hovered over the keypad, and I hesitated for a few seconds before I pushed 'call.'

His mellow baritone held an unusual undercurrent of nervousness. "We will be there shortly. Are you ready?"

I hated to disappoint him. "CJ," I began.

"That does not bode well. What is the difficulty?" His intuitive nature allowed him to easily read vocal subtleties and language nuances in me and just about everyone else.

"Ida's cousin needs assistance so she can't take care of Maverick. I don't have anywhere for him to go."

"Is that all?" He chuckled. "That is not an insurmountable obstacle. I believe we have accommodations at the only pet friendly establishment in town. Renegade is coming as well. Bring Maverick and we can work on cues with both dogs. See you soon."

I released a breath I didn't know I'd been holding. *My big boy would be going with me.*

My cheeks ached as I drove home wearing a Cheshire-cat grin and pulled up in front of the grand Victorian structure I called home. I collected my thermal mug, briefcase, notebooks, and satchel and, with full arms, lumbered to the door. It swung open and Dad stood, holding it, wearing a timid smile. "Hi, Darlin'."

"Hi, Dad." Maverick circled in and out of my legs, and I tripped.

Dad grabbed my arm. "Steady there, girl."

Oh, how I loved that man, even when discombobulated with undeniable facts about my childhood I couldn't yet rationalize. We'd never discussed Ellen's declaration of sisterhood, but by the look on his face, he hadn't been surprised. I'd closed down and let my anger simmer. Jane, however, was right. I could never discount my good fortune. I owed Dad my life—first growing up as the daughter of a loving parent who supported every good decision I made, and of course letting me take the heat when making a poor choice, and secondly, when he took a bullet I think was meant for me.

My belongings scattered as they dropped from my hands, and I wrapped my arms around him. "I'm sorry, Dad."

"Me too, Darlin'." He rested his chin on the top of my head and patted my back. "You're still invited to Duluth."

The tender moment lost, I pulled back and caught the twinkle in his eyes.

"Nope, not happening." My heart sank as the twinkle dimmed a bit. "Yet," I added as much for my benefit as for his.

Maverick sat still, tongue hanging out, and I could've sworn he smiled at the turn of events he may well have orchestrated. *You scamp.* I shook my head. *Nonsense.*

Maverick rose and barked before four loud raps sounded on the door.

"Coming," Dad said.

Patricia and Kindra stood on the top step with beseeching eyes. Dad signed a lengthy set of words and Patricia responded, grinning broadly, beginning a dialogue. Kindra's eyes widened, a baffled expression on her face.

Silent waters ran deep, I thought. I had so much to learn about my dad.

Kindra looked at me, shrugged, and said, "Here we are." They stepped inside onto the rag rug, and the duffle bags they shrugged off their shoulders pounded the floor.

"What do you have in there?" I asked.

"We're ready for anything," Kindra said, squinting sneakily. "And everything."

Maverick yelped once and took a step toward the door. His tail beat a steady rhythm against the frame, marking time. I glanced past Dad and walked onto the stoop. Four heads bobbled in the cab as CJ's white veterinary truck rocketed down the drive and jerked to a stop.

The driver's door creaked. Fancy-tooled, worn cowboy boots came first, one at a time, followed by a cane and a tall broad-shouldered man in faded jeans, a red-plaid flannel shirt, and a fringed beaded leather vest. He removed his black felt hat and shook loose his straight blue-black hair. It hung to the middle of his back. With his high cheek bones and copper skin, there was no mistaking his Hidatsa heritage. He turned as the passenger door opened and beamed at Carlee.

She hopped out of the passenger seat. Side by side I noted her resemblance to CJ in the set of their jaws, the shape of their eyes, and the ease of their smiles. She tugged on a leash and out hopped Renegade. At the same time Maverick hurdled Kindra's bag and bolted through the door, Renegade tightened her leash and pulled, yanking Carlee off balance, barreling toward her friend. CJ snapped his fingers, and Renegade sat, prim and proper, eyes glued to CJ.

Maverick immediately did the same. My eyebrows crawled to my hairline. *Incredible.* CJ had a magic I couldn't reproduce, but I promised to work on it.

CJ limped to Carlee. "Okay?" The love in his eyes took my breath away. He'd missed watching her grow up, not knowing he had a daughter. For a brief moment, before Pete and I became a couple and before he found Carlee, I harbored a teensy thought about being more than this man's friend. Now he channeled all his energy into their relationship, and we were all better for it.

"Fine," she giggled.

A voice called from inside the truck, "Hey, what about me?"

CJ lifted his hand, and with a sly smile, pressed the key fob. The lock clicked. The door opened, and Galen slid from the back seat, groaned, and stretched.

"How are you ever going to last for the two-hour trip?" Carlee's eyes lit with mischief. "You've only been back there for six minutes, tops. Guess we'd better get this show on the road." For an instant, I thought I saw anxiety flash in her eyes. She took a breath, and it disappeared.

I turned back to the house. Dad lugged the kennel down the steps with Maverick's travel pack slung over his arm and a favorite chew toy bravely fighting gravity from his side pocket. Dad glanced over his shoulder at Ida. She waved a soggy handkerchief and wiped the tip of her nose.

Kindra and Patricia hopped after him and snapped me out of my thoughts.

Dad headed for the car, and I raced up the stairs to gather my luggage when my phone chimed again. Breathless, I answered, "Hey, girlfriend."

"Can I still come with you?" She sniffled. "I don't want to hang around Columbia by myself."

I tucked the phone under my chin and grabbed my bag and backpack. "If you can be here in five minutes, and ..." I inhaled. The pitch of my voice raised to pleading. "Can you drive? Maverick is coming too, and it would be so much less crowded."

"I'm already here, standing behind CJ's truck in your driveway." I slid the curtain panel to one side and peeked out the window. She pulled her phone away from her ear and waved. Her quilted down coat flapped like wings over a winter-white silky suit. Dazzling red gloves, fur-trimmed bombardier cap, and scarlet sky-high boots completed the trendy ensemble. She pointed her keys, and her lift gate rose. Dad stowed the kennel securely in the storage compartment with the rest of the luggage. Maverick hopped in and curled up, ready for the trip.

If I couldn't be with Pete or Dad, I would celebrate time away with the next best—friends.

SIX

I dug my toes in the warm sand, appraising my lilac nail polish, sipping an ice-cold piña colada, and relishing the crash of the waves lapping in my ear. *My ear?*

I yanked my eyelids apart to find Maverick licking the drool from my cheek, dragging me back from a wonderful dream, and I blinked as we pulled in front of a massive shape towering over the entire area. A smattering of clouds drifted past a narrow crescent moon peeking out from behind a chimney. Spindly trees, just waking from their long winter's nap, scratched the night sky.

"Wake up sleepyhead," Jane said in her soft Georgian drawl and patted my arm. "We're here."

I struggled to sit up, bending and flexing my neck and stiff joints, gently nudging Maverick's tickling tongue away from my face, and glanced around. "Where's CJ?"

"He told us to go on ahead. He stopped for gas and burgers, but the inn's owner will only be on site until eight before we'll have to get our registration figured out some other way. That detour held us up for a good thirty minutes or we'd have had plenty of time."

"What detour?"

"The Minnesota River banks are swollen this spring and we added a slow-going fifteen miles to our trip."

"Sorry. I didn't mean to fall asleep on you like that. Why didn't you wake me?""

"To be honest." Jane looked sheepish. "Kindra practiced her signing, and Patricia assessed the attempts. The silence was therapeutic. But they're so excited to be here, they jumped out the minute I set the parking brake." She pointed up a steep bank of cement steps dug into the tall hill. Lights blazed from all the windows like a homing beacon in the middle of nowhere.

"Is this it?"

"It has to be. It's the only building anywhere near the address CJ gave me."

I smiled and watched the girls as they mounted the stairs to the entry but frowned as Patricia slammed into Kindra's back. Kindra spun around, dragging her sister behind her. Even in the gloaming, I could make out their forms bolting back the way they'd come.

I checked my watch as I exited Jane's Edge and looked up in time to catch Kindra's shoulder to keep her from tumbling. "What's wrong?"

Between gasps, she said, "I heard fighting up there." Patricia read her sister's lips and her eyes grew round.

"Stay here." I stomped my way up the stairs and heard

shouts coming from a slightly opened window as I neared the front.

"You are not to be seen or heard. Do you understand? I won't repeat myself again. I don't know why I put up with your incompetence." A door slammed.

"Auntie, be reasonable," said a male voice. "It's impossible to do all you ask and remain unseen every minute of the time."

"I told you nothing good would come of it. You invested all that money and still need more. I'll not have it."

"It'll bring in four hundred dollars a night, Auntie."

"Not if it's the last room available for a hundred miles. And stop calling me Auntie. Put that bottle down. You can't afford it."

"This Macallan is a birthday gift."

The voices became indistinct, but I knew I had to get us checked in. With my fist poised to knock, I heard the whiney male voice say, "Auntie? Edith, I love her."

"You only *think* you love her. I tell you who to love."

"I'm going to marry her."

"Over my dead body," came the reply and what sounded like a slap.

I heard a crash and rethought my rapping when the door in front of me swung open. I came face to face with a blustering woman, who scrunched her black eyes and puckered her scarlet lips. She gasped, startled, and sucked in her mottled cheeks. "What do you want?"

I inhaled, trying to act as any innocent guest might, one who hadn't just overheard an argument, and said with a cheeky smile, "I'm here to check in as part of CJ Bluestone's party. I apologize for our tardiness, but there was an unexpected detour. I'm Katie."

She ignored my outstretched hand but forced the deep angry-looking lines around her eyes and on her forehead to relax. When she raised her chin, she said, "Follow me, please."

I looked over my shoulder and down the hill, motioning for everyone to join me, then turned and walked into a home designed to look as though it came out of a history book.

"What a ..." I struggled to find a word I could use and not lie. "What an unusual home." It felt like I'd stepped back in time. The woman's heels clacked in a contrapuntal rhythm with the tick-tock of a giant grandfather clock rooted in the corner. Wide, ornamented baseboards edged the dark wood floor in front of a broad curving staircase. The filigreed crown molding drew my eyes to the mural of yellow stars on a deep blue background painted on the ceiling. A pattern of dancing rainbows emanated from prisms dangling from the crystal chandelier. A large mirror hung in just the right spot to make the room appear twice its size.

The woman opened curtained French doors and revealed a living space decorated with striped wallpaper and packed with furniture covered in pink floral chintz, a buffed roll-top desk, and a rocking chair with plush red padding. Tassels dangled from the glass lamps sitting on the end tables. The space housing the old-fashioned furniture bore the newish smell of a showroom in the mall. Tags dangled from some of the lamp knobs. I peered closely and frowned at the prices scribbled there.

She reached beneath the counter and lifted a creaking, hinged flap. She stepped through and onto a platform, closed the access hatchway, and dropped it back into place.

Standing behind an antique registration counter lit by low wattage bulbs, the woman's haughty face took on a sickly yellow hue. She peered down at me from a six-inch vantage point. I felt small, even at my five feet six inches. I finger-combed strands of hair away from my face. When she craned her neck and turned her head at the noises from the girls and my dog as they climbed the hill, not one white-blond hair moved, cemented in place with some kind of product. The comfy sweatshirt and jeans I wore looked even more worn and faded next to her dark-gray three-piece skirt suit embellished by a string of pearls and matching earrings. Gently touching the ring I wore on a chain around my neck gave me courage. "CJ Bluestone will be along shortly. Could we begin the registration process, please?"

Without a word, she opened a thick registry book to the first page and handed me cardboard forms and pens. "Fill in the blanks and leave them on the blotter." She handed me seven key rings. "The room rate is $159 a night. We lock up at ten, but the small key fits the outside door. The rooms upstairs use the skeleton keys. If you need anything tonight, press help on the house phone."

Sparks flew when someone kneeling at the base of the fireplace deposited a log on the already roaring fire. I flinched, and my shoulders shot up as a shield against the flames. A nondescript, thirty-something-year-old man rose and the tension in my shoulders eased. He brushed debris from his hands and dusted off his trousers. He strode across the space, and parked himself next to me, lounging cockily against the counter. "Reginald Farthington, at your service."

One appraising eyebrow arched over a cool blue eye,

causing the hairs on my neck to stand at attention. For me, eyes provided a glimpse into a person's soul. "Good evening," I croaked.

The noises grew louder, and Maverick dragged Jane through the doorway. He barked and strained at the leash. She stumbled and dropped the two bags from her shoulder in a lame attempt to plant her feet and steady him next to her. "Maverick, heel," she cried, lurching as he lunged across the floor toward me. Reginald stumbled back, startled. His face turned red, and his pink scalp shone through his thinning blond hair. He retreated to a bay window surrounded by a wall of potted lilies wrapped in sparkly green paper. He snatched a spouted can and began to water in earnest and deadhead the blossoms.

"Maverick," I said with as much force as I could muster. He tugged again, and I stepped toward him. "Maverick." I lifted my hand, palm up, our sign for him to sit. He stubbornly resisted, wrestling back and forth, until a faint whistle sounded, and Maverick lowered his backside to the floor.

All eyes turned to CJ as he stepped through the open door. He dropped a bulging black duffel from one hand and hiked up the gray backpack slung over his broad shoulder. In his other hand he held the tether to a rich warm yellow Labrador retriever with mischievous eyes. The cane he used on rare occasions dangled from his wrist. CJ removed his hat and his hair cascaded over his shoulders. He tilted his head to the dogs and they both went down into an alert sphinx pose.

Reginald slammed the watering can on the windowsill, huffed, and crept out the door, eyeing the dogs warily.

"We spoke on the phone. I am CJ Bluestone. I

apologize for the lateness of the hour. I hope we are not inconveniencing you." His backpack slid from his shoulder and thudded to the floor. "My friends and I encountered a long detour."

The woman behind the counter bowed her head. "Welcome to White Star Inn. I'm Edith Farthington."

"Mrs. Farthington—"

"Mr. Bluestone, call me Edith. My husband's been gone a long time."

I took a breath to correct her, adding his professional veterinary honorific, but his chin came up. "And I am CJ." He nodded toward the kids entering behind him. "This is my daughter, Carlee and her friend, Galen." He identified each of us.

Her finger wagged between CJ and me. "So, you're not ..."

I shook my head, and he laughed. Edith's face took on a slightly hungry look. Her demeanor changed. A bowl of what looked like saltwater taffies magically appeared from beneath the counter and landed in front of him. He declined, but Carlee plucked a green and pink one from the dish.

"Ah, my favorite too," Edith said and stepped out of the cubicle, wearing the smile of a woman on the prowl. After she shook his hand, she bent at the waist to peer more closely at our canine companions. "What beautiful dogs you have. I'm glad they were able to join you." She stood and crossed her hands. "What brings you to our humble abode?" Although her voice seemed sincere, that smile didn't quite reach her eyes.

I plied everyone with registration forms and pens and parked myself near the pristine fireplace. I slid my fingers over the smooth white painted surface of the face and in and out of the carved frieze, and skimmed the warm polished marble surrounding the firebox, listening to CJ tell his story, not just to Edith, but to the kids, Jane, and me too.

"Seventeen years ago, my wife gave birth to this beautiful child." He wrapped his arm around Carlee's shoulders, and she blushed. "She died giving birth. The woman who delivered my daughter left my wife's body at the hospital in town and kept this one as her own. We are here to put my wife to rest and hold a memorial service."

"Oh, my," Edith said and leaned back. "What a tragedy. I don't mean to offend ..." She looked exactly like she meant to offend. She sniffed and asked, "But why did it take you so long?" She accepted his credit card and ran it through her machine.

"Fortune smiled on us. Carlee and I have just recently met." They read each other's faces, and unheard messages passed between them. CJ turned again to Edith. "I never knew Danica and I had a child."

Edith's eyebrows rose, and she stretched her neck. I thought I read the word scandal in the set of her mouth and the indignation that passed behind her eyes. She squinted at the credit card, holding it as though it might burn her hand. "Well—"

Before I could form words of explanation, a boisterous, "Helloooo" cut her off. "We're here. Where is everybody?" The speaker stumbled into the registration annex. He tossed a forelock of long blond hair to one side. "People," he sang exultantly, as if, until that moment, he'd been stranded alone on a deserted island for his entire life. He yanked a slim cross-body bag forward, held up his arms in a long stretch, and yawned open-mouthed.

"What do you think you're doing?" Edith said.

His arms slowly returned to his sides and his lips stretched into a leer when the college-aged man caught sight of the girls, my girls. I stepped in front of them. One sniff and I cringed at the yeasty smell of beer wafting around the man like a cloud surrounding Charlie Brown's friend Pigpen. I widened my stance to enlarge my presence and bumped into Galen doing the same thing.

The man's grin fell away. "We need someone to take care of our luggage. Where's your bellboy?"

"No bellboy." Edith never looked away from CJ, finishing his transaction.

"What kind of place is this, anyway?"

"A fully occupied place. We have no rooms. We're booked all week. Now if you'll excuse me, I'm checking in a registered guest."

"We made reservations." He flashed a pearly-white fake smile at us. "We're here to fill your last two rooms. But no worries. My man, Reggie, told us all about the other guests." He held his right hand out to Edith. "Ryker Chesterfield." She ignored it, and he retracted his hand. He dug deep in his pocket and pulled out a phone. He pressed some buttons and said, "I have an email receipt for two rooms at $399 each per night for the week. These were the last two rooms in town. We came for the brewery fest. Its rep is getting around and we want to be in on the ground floor."

He held the phone screen for Edith to read. "We're here for the duration," he snarled.

Her eyes widened. White lines formed around her jaw, and I could almost see smoke coming out of her ears.

Ryker smirked and eyed Edith as he dug in the leather

pouch slung over his shoulder. He retrieved a plastic bag and held it out. "Sunflower seeds?" he said, baiting her.

Before she could form any retort, three more men trucked into the foyer, laughing and nudging each other. "One heck of a trek. But we couldn't find any closer parking, Ryker."

"Reginald," Edith raised her voice. "Get in here right now."

SEVEN

As quickly as he appeared, Reginald must've taken a position immediately outside the door and heard the exchange. "You rang?"

For a moment, the air sizzled. Our party settled near the fireplace where there was less chance of getting burned than being caught between the fierce glares passed between Reginald and Edith. Chesterfield's gloating added fuel to the fire.

"Mr. Chesterfield, glad you could make it." Reginald said. "I haven't had time to share the good news, but …" He turned to Edith. "We finished the renovations of the rooms on the third floor today."

The daggers in Edith's eyes receded when CJ said, "We will not mind the company, if there is room for all."

Edith looked down at the registry and said sarcastically, "Reginald. Help with their luggage and take your lodgers to your guest rooms on the third floor …" She glanced up and gave him a scathing look. "That is if you think the rooms have been prepared to my standards."

Reginald ushered the young men outside, using a soft ingratiating tone, cajoling, laughing, whispering. Ryker brought up the rear and the sneer on his face he thought no one caught sight of made me shiver.

Edith searched CJ's face. "I apologize. I didn't know Reginald readied the third-floor rooms to open, but we have plenty of space. Do you still have two more guests arriving on Monday?" CJ nodded and she took a ragged breath before reciting, "Complimentary beverages and snacks are available in the kitchen at any time. A three-course gourmet breakfast is served from seven until nine. There will be a charcuterie board available from eleven until one, and happy hour …" She turned her head to check out the kids. "… with sodas and snacks begins at four every afternoon." She plastered on a grin and returned his credit card. "You're all set. If anything comes up, please let me know. Reggie is working the hospital information desk tonight. We take turns volunteering, but he'll be available the rest of the weekend."

CJ lifted a bulging white paper bag. "If we promise to clean up after ourselves, may we use the dining room? I am starving, and the placard at your local bar and grill advertised their Juicy Lucie burgers as the best."

Edith took so long it seemed she tried to come up with a good excuse to say no, but instead, she smiled a real smile and said, "Those burgers won the state competition four years running. Of course, you may use the dining room.

You'll find paper plates and silverware in the sideboard. If we can help you any other way, please don't hesitate to ask."

At that moment, my stomach growled, and the aroma of the burgers took up residence in my head to the exclusion of every other scent. Burgers and fries on a Friday night at the start of spring break. Who could ask for anything more? Except maybe a bike trip to Sonoma with Pete. A sigh escaped. Jane stepped to my side and threaded her arm through mine, reading my thoughts. She squeezed and I returned the gesture.

We schlepped the luggage to our rooms on the second floor. The girls took the mustard-colored room with two four-poster queen beds and a large armoire. Patricia flopped onto the frilly white comforter covering the bed, acting exhausted, and let out a huge breath before sinking into the puffy pillows.

Kindra flipped a light switch on the attached bathroom. "Whoa. Is this just for us?"

Fancy bottled soaps and lotions lined a delicately carved shelf above a large whirlpool. Fluffy creamy-white towels hung from the rack in front of the walk-in shower and smelled faintly of lilies of the valley.

CJ commandeered the dark-green two-room suite with a Jack and Jill bath for himself and Galen—the better to keep his eyes on his daughter's boyfriend.

The light-blue walls in the third room complemented the intricate pattern on the multi-blue-hued-denim hand sewn quilts topping the comfy looking canopied twin beds. With the books and vintage toys occupying the shelves against one wall, our room could have been a nursery at one time. Jane and I would share the large full bath in the middle of the hall with Carlee's grandparents.

Jane hung her garments in the narrow closet, and I unzipped my duffel. At first, I thought I'd grabbed the wrong bag. Glittery red paper winked at me. I checked the ID tag. Carefully, I removed the box and untied a sheer red ribbon. A thick card dropped from the bundle. I bent to pick it up. My name filled the front of the envelope.

I slipped my finger beneath the flap, slid it open, and wriggled out a stiff folded tagboard bearing two words. "Miss you."

"Awww. Isn't that sweet?" Jane cooed, and I lightly swatted her away. She giggled shamelessly.

I flipped the card, hunting to be certain of a name, and when I didn't find one, I peeled the paper away from the package, revealing a precise pencil portrait of Maverick. Thousands of short black lines covered the page and looked so real, I wanted to pet the hair. The dark, intelligent eyes spoke volumes. The signature in the corner, although very small, read Pete.

"Did you know he could draw?" Jane asked, standing on her toes and looking over my shoulder.

"No." My voice caught. My head cocked to one side as I stood the drawing on the nightstand against the wall. Maverick yipped, then spiraled twice and dropped onto a beautiful rug.

"Classy," said Jane, kneeling down and running her hand over the woven floor covering. "An Aubusson. I love the colors and texture."

Maverick's head came up when he heard the clicking of Renegade's nails outside our door. He jumped to his feet, whimpered, and nudged my thigh, urging haste.

After the dogs dismissed me and snuggled on the

carpet, CJ led the herd of hungry teenagers, trampling down the stairs to the dining room. The wide mahogany table easily seated twelve guests. A skimpy chandelier attempted to light up the dismal room papered in dark gray and white paisley. The brown crown molding and double-sized mopboards added weight to the already heavy room. Two portraits hung on opposite walls, and although wearing Edwardian attire, the cheerless faces staring at us looked an awful lot like they belonged to Edith and Reginald.

Jane lugged the heavy pocket doors closed, turned her back and sagged against them, taking a breath. She pushed herself away and made straight for the seat next to me.

I unwrapped my burger and studied the work of art dripping juices and cheese and took a picture. I sent it to Pete with 'thanks for the portrait' and 'wish you were here' messages. Jane nibbled fries bathed in ketchup and surreptitiously eyed the kids, trying to figure out the least messy way dig in.

I took a small bite, catching the exploding juices with my knuckle, when the doorbell rang. I glanced at my watch. Mickey Mouse's hands read nine.

The doorbell sounded twice again, followed by heavy pounding.

"Hurry up. Let me in." The loud voice carried throughout the ground floor.

Carlee's silver-gray eyes locked on CJ. The legs of his chair screeched as he pushed away from the table and stood. "Excuse me," he said. Galen popped up and followed CJ to the door.

Jane and I flanked CJ and Galen as each slid one door to the side, revealing Edith, striding angrily across the foyer. She yanked open the front door. "You're late," she said gruffly.

"Let's get this over with."

The tall, balding man tugged at his walrus moustache with one hand and thrust an ornate wooden box at Edith with the other. He cast his eyes to the dining room doors, and Edith followed the wag of his bushy eyebrows. Her head jerked back, realizing she'd been caught by our curious, prying eyes.

"I apologize for disrupting your meal, CJ," she said with less vinegar. Her hand hovered over the knob, and she inclined her head our way. "I have urgent business."

CJ returned the nod and pulled the dining room doors closed but paused to listen. "In case she needs our help," he confessed. We heard unintelligible mumbling and then nothing. After a few seconds passed, we resumed our seats, and concentrated on finishing the fabulous feast.

Galen picked up the four-inch-high sandwich with both hands, firmly holding the tomato, bacon, lettuce, and onion fixings together. He had no neatness qualms. "Here goes." He took a humongous bite, groaning in pleasure. As he pulled his hands away, the melted yellow cheese oozed from the center of the burger, hanging in strings down his chin and onto the table. He wound the sticky stray strands around the bun and laughed so hard he almost choked when he swallowed. "This is so good." He took another huge bite. If someone wanted to know the meaning of mastication, Galen provided a spot-on visual. He gulped and furrowed his brow. He wiped his lips and licked his fingers. "Are there more?"

CJ made a conspicuous show of digging in the large bag, tapping his hand against the sides, pretending to find nothing, and surprisingly extracting another burger. He set it in the young man's greedy outstretched palm, shaking his head. "Just in case," he said.

After watching intently, Jane daintily cut her burger in half and pouted in dismay as the gooey golden center spurted onto her designer shirt. All chatter and movement ceased, waiting. She snorted and it morphed into a chuckle as she wiped her front. The napkin shredded with the grease. She shrugged a 'what can I do.'

The kids resumed their chatting and promptly ignored us.

I unfolded my well-curated list of recreational activities, and Jane snatched it. Her lips moved as she silently read the suggestions, featuring geocaches in the area, the local historical museum, and the chamber of commerce map of businesses, highlighting an ethnic bakery and several nearby restaurants.

The conversation at the adult end of the table turned to CJ's morning visit with the person in charge of records followed by his initial call on the parish priest.

"Would you chaperone Carlee and her friends?" CJ asked earnestly.

Jane raised an eyebrow, incredulity written on her face. "You mean these sixteen- and seventeen-year-old mini-grownups?"

CJ flushed, a novel occurrence. "Then they will have an adult if they need one," he stammered.

I gave Jane the evil eye and responded, "We'd love to. Wouldn't we, Jane? It isn't every day we take on the sights and sounds of a new community."

She complained. "You can see both ends of downtown at the same time no matter where you're standing. What trouble could they possibly get into?"

I didn't know how she could have gauged the length of main street. She hadn't seen it yet. Maybe the disappointment of lost time with her fiancé manifested in displeasure. I patted her hand. She pouted then looked down at her lap. She inhaled, exhaled, and forced her lips into a smile.

"We'll give it our best shot," she added apologetically, rapidly scrolling through pages on her phone. The browsing stopped and her face relaxed. "But only if I get to pick the first place to visit."

It appeared she found something she thought she might like.

The kids filtered from the room, thoughtfully piling their garbage in the squat black trash can on the floor next to the door. By the time I reached the exit, the stack of plates teetered. I wiggled the waste sack from the container, stuffed my own leavings in on top, and went in search of a replacement. We hadn't been given an authorized tour, but I figured I'd find some plastic bags in the kitchen near a trash receptacle.

I slid the first door to one side. It opened into a parlor. A tall lamp topped with a linen shade illuminated the elegant space, crowded with a forest-green loveseat, a plush yellow couch, two warm brown leather wingback chairs, a glass-topped coffee table, a matching end table, and multiple panoramic paintings adorning the walls. I took an appreciative glance inside, then closed the door.

The knob on the door of the next room rotated, but it stuck. I jiggled the handle, thinking how a closed door shouldn't be enough to deter me. There'd been a time when I would've passively backed away, but no longer. Helping Dad recover from his gunshot wound and working through my own grief had taught me resiliency and given me a more immense well of strength. The meaning of life had changed. I no longer thought about my losses every day. I wished I hadn't had to go through Charles' death and Dad's traumatic brain injury, but then I never would have met Ida, Jane, Drew, CJ, all of my students. My intake of breath hitched, and my heart stuttered, thinking about Pete.

'Promise me you'll live a good life.' Charles' words gave me more and more strength each day, and I clutched at the ring on the chain around my neck.

I pressed down, jiggled the knob, and pulled up. The door opened.

The dark night sky didn't penetrate far into the room and the blackness hid its contents. I ran my hand lightly over the wall on the left side of the door. Nothing. Just as my right hand connected with a switch, I heard muffled voices. I almost cleared my throat, but before I flipped the switch, I strained to hear.

"You get one chance," said one deep churlish voice, dripping with contempt.

"Is that an ultimatum?" another answered.

"Take it any way you want."

"I promise we'll have it. I just need a little more time. Try not to mess anything up."

"Or what?"

I leaned forward and the floor squeaked.

"Shh. I heard something."

I froze, looking down at my shadow backlit by the lights in the foyer.

EIGHT

Two faint woofs sounded. The deeper voice hissed. "It's just those nuisance dogs upstairs." Prickly bumps crawled up my arms at the suggestion my dog could be a nuisance. After a short pause, he added, "You have until tomorrow."

I tiptoed out, holding my breath, and pulled the door closed without even a snick.

Thank you, Maverick.

I stutter-stepped; my knees gave out in relief. As I searched for the kitchen door, I contemplated the credible topics of their conversation, rationalizing the tone and the words with a number of innocuous explanations. Maybe someone was buying a lottery ticket. Maybe someone had a bread recipe to try out. Maybe someone needed a car fixed.

Then why did I sneak out of the room?

I shrugged a silent answer. It wasn't any of my business. I was on vacation. I opened the next door. The overlarge spotless cook stove, walk-in cooler, fingerprint free double oven, and up-to-date appliances in the industrial kitchen seemed excessive even if guests filled every room. After topping off the garbage bin, I yanked free a new plastic bag and shook it open, intending to replace the one in the dining area.

A whimper sounded behind me.

My head swiveled, looking side to side. I thought I was alone. I peeked under the prep table, next to the refrigerator, and behind the door to the pantry.

A small woman with short curly pink-and-white streaked hair, elfin features, and blue eyes rimmed in red stood between the shelves of canned goods and appliances. Her hands covered her mouth. She adjusted the starched white apron worn over her dark clothes.

"Goodness. Am I … I'm sorry if I'm bothering you." She swiped at her eyes. "May I help you?"

I shook my head. "Is there anything I can do for you …"

"Lauren. I'm Lauren Trnka." Tears flooded her eyes again. "Don't tell Mrs. Farthington. She'd never give me another chance." Her hand flew to her mouth and her eyes went wild. "Please don't tell her I said anything. Please." She pleaded.

"Of course not." She hadn't said anything, and the moment felt like the right time for a subject change. "I wanted to replace the trash bag in the dining room. We pretty much filled it to the rim." I held up the new bag as evidence.

"Let me do that." She seized it from my hands and fled the kitchen.

I wonder what that was about.

Returning to the foyer, I rounded the corner and found the four late-arriving guests surrounding a twisting, turning figure. "What's going on?"

Lauren squirmed. Ryker Chesterfield held her elbow tight for another moment, looking down into her terrified eyes. He gloated when she wrenched free and pushed her way through to the dining room.

I put on my best teacher face, turning over in my mind what I could say when Maverick bounded down the steps and slid to a stop at my side, reading my expression expectantly. We all looked up at the form clomping down the stairs.

The sneer on Ryker's face shifted into something more benign.

"May I be of any assistance?" Even from behind the cane, CJ's intimidating figure silenced the four men. Renegade sat next to him, watching.

"Just came in from a little jaunt downtown." Ryker snorted and tried glaring. "Isn't it past your bedtime, Gramps?"

CJ had maybe a dozen years on the idiot, but the wisdom of the ages. So out of his league, Ryker gave up on the staring contest and jerked his head. His henchmen turned simultaneously with the precision of a synchronized swim team. CJ stood his ground on the steps and slowly nodded at each as they trundled past him, hugging the banister.

Maverick rose to all fours and stood facing me, panting. "A trip outside is in order, I believe," I said. Renegade's paws clambered the rest of the way down, and we headed out the front door. "Thanks, CJ."

"I released the dogs when they would not settle, Katie.

What did the wayward youth want?"

Maverick read me from a floor a way. A warm feeling flooded my insides in opposition to the cool air, or something, that caused me to shiver at the same time. "I'm not sure. I don't know about those other guests."

"Do not look for trouble." CJ's bright, laughing eyes belied his serious tone.

"This inn isn't what I'd been expecting."

"It has surprised me as well."

When the dogs finished their romp in the yard, we strode up the stairs and inside. CJ threw the bolt on the door. "My hospital appointment is after our breakfast."

"Do you want me to go with you?"

"Galen is coming. The girls made plans to which he is not privy." CJ's eyes lit up. "And I will get one-on-one time to learn more about him."

As we cleared the last few steps to our floor, I locked eyes with Ryker, standing amid his chums outside my door at the end of the hall. He scoffed, pointed a finger, and closed one eye as if looking down a scope. After he mimed pulling a trigger, he and his pals beat a hasty retreat up the remaining steps to the third floor and vanished. CJ and Renegade escorted Maverick and me to our room at the end of the long dark hall. As we passed, he twisted the knob of the girls' room, testing to ensure their safety.

My hand hovered over the knob to our room. "Goodnight, CJ. See you in the morning."

CJ bowed and turned. He tapped his thigh and Renegade pranced after him.

I slid into the room. Jane's head rested on the pillow. Her right hand held her phone to her ear. She smiled and spoke softly. When she completed her call, she set her phone on the table next to her, and Maverick jumped on her bed. "Oh, you big burly boy, you." She sat up and scratched behind his ears. He leaned in for as much as he could wriggle out of her.

"How's Drew?"

She answered, all dreamy-eyed. "He misses me." She twirled her blond curls around her finger. "Have you heard from Pete?"

I shook my head. "Being on call has been a bear since his partner resigned." I dragged on my sweats and pulled my hair into a ponytail. "I doubt I'll hear much from him all week. The admin is working on hiring a locum or two. Pete wasn't the only doc to have scheduled a vacation, but we talked it over. One of the other physicians has kids, so spring break week worked better for him. We'll be able to figure something out. In the future. Sometime. Your job is to keep reminding me how lucky I am and how good I have it."

"Ditto, girlfriend." She smiled and collapsed back onto her pillow.

I stretched out on my bed. We kept to our own thoughts, and, within minutes, she rolled on her side. Her even breathing became my mantra. In and out. In and out. My neck muscles relaxed but before I could allow my eyes to close for the night, I made one last trip down the hall. Toothbrush and toothpaste in hand, I focused on the nightlight, and crept into the bathroom.

A soft, haunting melody played on a low-pitched flute and reverberated through the vent in the ceiling. I closed my eyes and listened, swaying to the gentle sounds and slowly washing my face. I dragged my lids open. After wangling a curlicue of toothpaste on top of the bristles, a work of art, I brought the brush to my teeth, and my phone pinged with a selfie of Dad attached.

Have you settled in, Darlin'?

I bit down on the brush to hold it in place and answered the text.

Yup. It's a swell place.

Swell? I know you. What's wrong with it?

Nothing. But you're not here and Pete's working. How's Duluth?

We found a great pizza place. I'm sure you'd like it.

And?

I didn't see his answer because I dropped my phone when my shoulders involuntarily rose to protect me from the distant screech which set my nerves on fire.

NINE

Luckily, my phone missed the sink full of water. I grabbed it off the floor and gripped it in one hand. I thrust my head out of the bathroom doorway, holding my toothbrush in attack mode in the other hand. The silent hall unnerved me almost as much as the squeal had. Surely someone else would have heard it, but the doors in the hall remained closed.

I doubted my faculties for a second and stepped back in to finish my nighttime routine. I rinsed my mouth with my familiar minty mouthwash, rotated my shoulders, loosening the kinks, and glanced at my phone screen. Dad hadn't added anything to our exchange. Stifling a yawn, I collected my belongings, quickly organizing my small cosmetics pouch, and stiffened when I heard the piercing noise again. It resonated as if it occurred in a large space far away.

I pinpointed its source—the vent.

The high-pitched cry sounded less like a scream this time and more like a musician breathing full force into a hollow tube, overblowing to generate harmonics. A goosebump-inducing melody of sorts pierced the air. Mystery solved unless I wanted to know who made the noise, why, and how.

I checked the time. Those answers would have to wait.

The door barely creaked as I eased back into our room. The clock showed midnight. I plugged in my phone and settled in.

My eyes slammed shut but as much as I wanted to sleep, it proved difficult to achieve. The hours-long nap I'd taken during the afternoon drive had removed slumber from my personal arsenal. I looked up at the ceiling and recited the first fifty digits of π, doubled the number one thirty times, recalled the state capitals, and silently sang the alphabet song in reverse.

When I couldn't lie there any longer, I rolled off the narrow bed. I carried the water dish, and Maverick followed me downstairs. Warm milk had a reputation as a sleep aid.

Maverick hurried us through the kitchen door, and we came face to face with CJ and Renegade. The dogs sniffed, happily circled, and flopped onto the floor. CJ pointed to the stool next to him, a cup of something steaming in front of it.

"How did you know?"

"Renegade gave every indication she awaited her friend."

I shook my head and took a long slurp of hot chocolate hidden beneath a cloud of marshmallow cream. I set it on the counter, wiping the white fluff from the tip of my nose. "Are you worried about tomorrow?"

He answered without looking in my direction. "I am hoping we will achieve peace, but what will be, will be."

If I told him of the strange noise I thought I'd heard, his peace might be elusive. He didn't need another disruption. His calming presence and the warm drink took the edge off. I took a more encompassing glance around the kitchen, reconciling the troubled space where I'd met Lauren with the tranquil spot in which I found myself now. The room boasted a high-tech beverage dispenser available to use all day long with its comprehensive book of directions attached to the side. I confiscated a soft, sweet bread from a two-tiered carved wooden tray standing next it. I'd had one before. Father Steve Anderson introduced me to kolaches in November while we waited to be selected or rejected from a jury pool, though he might have been disappointed in the absence of his favorite, poppy seed. Raspberry filling squirted from the center at first bite, and I hummed in satisfaction.

We finished our beverages in silence.

"Has the warm milk worked its magic?" he asked.

I yawned, certain I'd imagined the haunting noise earlier. I didn't know how he did it, but my arms and legs felt heavy. "I think so." I rubbed my eyes. "How about you?"

"I think we will make it through the rest of the night." We rinsed the cups, put them in the dishwasher, and headed up the stairs.

He walked me to the door of our room yet again. "Goodnight, Katie. Stay." I wasn't certain if the last comment was made to me or Maverick. Renegade trailed him, looking back once to check on us.

This time, Jane's rhythmic breathing took us with her.

* * *

Maverick's slobbery kisses rescued me from a dark dream before the sun rose. If I went back to sleep, the rest of the day would be shot. I picked up his food dish and squeezed today's baggie of kibble into the pouch of my sweatshirt. We padded downstairs back into the kitchen.

I opened the door and the air gusted as if I'd uncapped a wind tunnel. Quickly checking the space, I glimpsed a figure exiting through a door at the rear of the room.

"Sorry, I didn't mean to chase you out …" I delivered my last two words more slowly, and they were barely audible. "Of. Here." The person had disappeared amid a flurry of royal blue.

Maverick gobbled his food and looked to me for possible extra. "Sorry, Mav. But let's make a trip outside." The second door from the kitchen delivered us to a small, divided alcove. One branch led to a narrow passage filled by a circular staircase. Maverick pushed down on the handle of the other branch to escape outside. After he performed his little doggie dance, he barked at a hawk, answered a few goose honks, took second place to a devious squirrel, and we snuck back inside.

Words froze on the lips of the fearsome foursome seated at the island as we walked into the kitchen. Their demeanor changed from surprise, perhaps at being caught, to superiority. Ryker's shifty eyes sought his companions, and he said with saccharine sweetness. "We were just leaving."

They each plucked a flaky chocolate pastry from the restocked trays, avoiding the hidden treasure of puffy fruit-filled bread, leaving more for me. They rose from their stools, but before they slipped from the room, Kindra, Patricia, and Carlee bounced in, ready to take on the day. Their eyes locked on my young women and the men reseated themselves. Their rude exchanges made me cringe.

Lest the lecherous louts forget themselves, I corralled the girls with large arm movements, inviting them to take seats at the banquette, as far away from the stools as possible. I lifted the entire tray of pastries and presented it to the table, extolling the spectacular taste of each of the choices. Maverick eyes drifted between the pastries and the men.

Jane joined us, perfectly made up. Under her critical scrutiny, Ryker shoved one of the cads off his stool. They retreated, and I breathed more easily.

Patricia signed, and Kindra interpreted. "Yes," she said. "They are creepy."

Okay, no worries on that front.

Jane brewed a creamy coffee for herself and recited instructions so the girls could make their beverages.

"I've got the day planned, Katie. I made spa appointments for our nails in thirty minutes." Jane's eyes twinkled. "Think you can make it?"

I looked down at my comfy loungewear, mortified. "I'm on it. C'mon, Maverick." We raced up the stairs. Maverick settled into his spot on the rug with a large dog chew.

Seven minutes later, the door sprang open, and Jane flounced in, glancing at the time. "You'll do." Renegade peeked out from behind Jane, her curious doggie eyes begging. "Do you have another treat? We can leave her with Maverick."

I dug in my backpack as Jane unleashed her wriggling ward. "Do we need to check on our boys?" I asked as I made for the stairs.

"CJ and Galen have already gone. We wished them luck."

With all my heart, I also wished them success.

TEN

We might not have been able to see all of Main Street from one end as Jane had said, but I chuckled because we could see almost the entire charming downtown from the entryway of a well-concealed spa, Polished Perfection, in the heart of New Prague. We stepped inside, and the serene atmosphere provided a welcome diversion from the task which brought us to town.

The light, fresh scent of lavender and the calming sway of waves washing onto a beach floated on the air. Jane took the reins and, in a voice as soothing and smooth as silk, ordered us to choose colors and follow the technicians assigned to each of us. Amid our feeble attempts to dissuade her, she provided a credit card. "My treat," she said in a near-whisper.

Exiting the locker room, Jane sighed. "We've so needed this. Right, girls?"

Kindra steeped a soothing herbal tea. Patricia and Carlee poured ice water in tall glasses, showcasing a rainbow of citrus slices. The exotic oils they tested on their pulse points left a gentle fragrance in the air. Their infectious chuckles smacked of feel-good hormones as, pampered by the amenities, they fished for favorite snacks from the basket on the table.

Swathed in a robe fresh and warm from the dryer, I wriggled into an oversized tan leather recliner, facing the wide archway leading to an adjacent hair salon. A number of patrons, in varying states of hair finish, moved swiftly and quietly from reception to chair to sink to coffee machine to dryer back to chair and to check out, white fluffy terry cloth oscillating in efficient assembly line fashion. Glad for a reprieve from the bustle of school, I leaned back and closed my eyes and immediately opened them to find Jane adjusting the massage vigor and temperature of my chair. My warm backside melted under the rhythmic kneading.

Our technicians held us captive, as we were mesmerized by the array of instruments used to soften, clean, trim, file, shape, and decorate with a wide assortment of colors, nail art, and glittering gems. My focus, blurred by the comfort of the chair and the gentle hand massage as I sat at the end of the row of plush chairs closest to the salon gateway, sharpened when I overheard two women discussing Edith Farthington and that "no good sleazy lawyer."

"Ex-cuuuuse me but I was his law associate for four years. I should know. I had to fend off his advances almost every day."

"Willy Zasko is a philandering Lothario," a woman with short dark hair agreed. She dabbed at her forehead with the end of the fluffy white towel draped over her shoulders.

Riveted by the mention of Edith Farthington, one of the few names I knew in this town, I leaned toward the speakers, my curiosity piqued.

Jane tittered and coughed into her hand to hide it. She must have heard them talking too and seen my reaction. She caught my eye and raised a perfectly arched brow.

"You can't be serious," said the short squat woman with tight blond curls. "With all her money, why would she choose Willy?"

"How do you think Edith got all that money?" replied a tall slender woman whose jet-black hair color didn't come close to matching the lighter shade of her eyebrows.

"You're just jealous," came a voice from the other side of the room.

"I don't have to be jealous. I have Reggie right where I want him." The bright pink of her fingernail flashed as she tapped her ruby red lips.

The blond said, "I think Zasko might know Reggie's father. Maybe he *is* Reggie's father and she's been blackmailing him all this time."

"But he's married and has about a dozen other kids. And he's an elder at our church." A woman with a high squeaky voice and a head full of twisted foil strips stepped to the circle and joined the conversation.

"That's another Zasko, one more concerned with propriety. Willy and his ex-wife never had kids."

"You mean *other* kids, don't you?" The blond woman grunted. "I think Reggie looks a lot like him."

"There are about a dozen Zaskos in town—the barber, the sheriff, the manager at the pizza parlor … and not many of them are related." A new husky voice entered the rumor-ring.

"Reggie's not related to Willy." The tall woman swung her head from side to side, eyeing her hair in the mirror, checking the color as dark as pitch. "And that's a fact. He's Edith's nephew."

Had these women nothing else to do but gossip? I hadn't meant to eavesdrop, but they spoke so clearly, I could hear every word.

The blond noisily slurped from a steaming cup and cleared her throat. The words carried clearly across the room. "Her of all people. I mean, really. It's not like anyone cares."

"She makes Reggie call her Edith as if we didn't already know how old she is."

"How old is she?" called a husky voice from somewhere out of sight.

"Edith?" the black-haired woman answered. "Old enough to know better. Even though she won't let Reggie call her Auntie, she dangles all that money in front of him. But I won't say another bad word about her. She likes me, and I don't want that to change. Word has it she's even chosen his wife for him." She gave a self-satisfied purr.

"About time, I'd say. He's old enough."

Trying to direct my attention elsewhere, I surreptitiously glanced past Jane to watch the girls. Carlee and Kindra appeared to concentrate on their nail procedures, until Patricia said, a bit too loudly, "What's going on?"

You could have heard a pin drop. Having been caught faking rapt attention, Kindra's head jerked up. With the forefinger of her free hand in front of her lips, she quieted Patricia, but if we could hear them, the taletellers could certainly hear us. The women in the room next door caught the commotion, drew their heads together, and finally limited their conversation to their immediate and private circle.

After the final swipe of color and a clear topcoat, my nail stylist placed my hands under a UV light. I ignored the piercing eyes of the busybodies in the next room and said, "I can't remember when I last had my nails done. Thanks, Jane. What's next?"

"After we pick up the pups, we're geocaching."

A super surprised 'Oh' left my lips. I searched Jane's face.

Her eyes gleamed as she mocked my disbelief. "Your vacation wouldn't be complete without one, would it?"

"It will be another highlight, that's for sure."

"It's a two-part puzzle cache marked as a favorite by seventeen searchers and it's only two miles from town."

We leisurely ambled from the exit, rubbernecking and appraising our varied colors, ranging from bold chartreuse and scarlet through royal purple and neon green. On the short drive to the inn, I admired my more sedate Café au Lait, hoping I wouldn't ruin the manicure before we returned to Columbia.

We picked up the enthusiastic dogs. They hurled themselves into the Edge's cargo space, panting and drooling in anticipation.

"Did the bedmaking leprechaun hit your room too," Carlee asked, adjusting her seatbelt.

"Do you mean the housekeeping service?" Jane asked.

"Our room looks even better than it did when we moved in last night. I had a watermelon taffy on my pillow and an origami towel in the shape of a swan on my bed.

"We had a banana and a chocolate taffy and an elephant-shaped towel," said Kindra, and Patricia signed a long swooping trunk.

I gave Maverick the side eye. By the time I'd seen them, the unremarkable towels had lost their shapes and lay crumpled on the bedspread.

"And wrapped caramels. Yum, the perfect treat." Jane said.

"We had caramels?" I asked.

"Maybe." Jane smacked her lips. "If we're ready, I'll send you the link, and after we find the cache, we can do a little shopping."

Jane forwarded the puzzle description to the girls' phones and pulled around a small, red disaster on wheels I hadn't noticed before. The right rearview mirror hung on by a mere silver ribbon of duct tape and the streaky do-it-yourself paint job on the front right fender needed a touch up.

As she drove in the direction dictated by her GPS and specified in part one of the cache, I took in the patches of snow lingering on the dark soil in the vast fields and skeletal forests in the landscapes of the family farms, blurring as we whizzed by. The girls tossed around ideas for the solutions.

"What's a Code Talker?" Kindra asked.

The pretzel contortion I performed to face the back seat caused them to laugh. "Code talkers were Native American United States servicemen who used their indigenous languages to send secret, encrypted messages. In World War I, Choctaw, Cherokee, and Lakota soldiers trained to send encoded radio and telephone transmissions. During World War II, the Navajo, Hopi, Meskwaki, and

Comanche United States Marine Code Talkers relayed communications the enemies never understood."

Kindra continued scanning the cache description. "Who's Winnie Breegle?"

"Wow. That's a blast from the past."

"Do you know who she is?" asked Carlee.

"In one of my classes, I watched a video she headlined. Winifred Breegle enlisted in the Navy as a WAVE in World War II and trained as a cryptographer."

Patricia touched my shoulder. "Like you," she mouthed.

"Maybe in my dreams." A snicker escaped and I added soberly, "More than four hundred bilingual Marines used the Navajo language to exchange messages indecipherable to the enemy." Patricia watched my lips and I articulated carefully. "Winifred was one of the women who learned the skill and, in her way, helped win the war."

Carlee's fidgeting stopped.

Kindra tilted her head and handed me her phone. "How does that help with this cache description?"

I read the name of the cache, 'Yá'át'ééh,' the blurb, and the hint. "Good one." I searched for the Code Talker dictionary on my phone and handed both phones back. "What do you think?"

A pencil and paper appeared from Carlee's backpack, and the girls bent over the screens, pointing, scribbling, signing, and whispering.

As we crested a large hill, I sucked in a breath at the magnificent sight of the mirrored surface on a large body of pewter-colored water surrounded by rolling hills. We drove under a hanging wooden county park sign, the painted words peeling in chips of black and white.

"What a view," Jane said. Gravel crunched under the

wheels as she pulled into the empty lot. "We're here." She shifted into park. One hand released her seatbelt and the other popped her door.

Carlee jammed her index finger into the air. "One sec."

Jane unlatched the tailgate and clipped a leash on Renegade. As I lassoed Maverick, the girls jumped out.

Patricia lifted bright eyes and a beaming face. "C-U-L-V-E-R-T." she pronounced the letters as she signed.

Scraggly trees, just coming awake from their winter dormancy, formed a channel we navigated to the water's edge. Trickling rivulets of melting ice ran off the stones and splashed to life in the lake. Bird song gave a suggestion of warmth to the crisp air, hinting at spring.

We untethered the dogs, and they raced back and forth, down to the water and up into the gentle hills, tracking unknown scents, zigzagging in and out of sight. When they were gone too long, I trekked off the path to get their attention and called them back. Maverick returned from one excursion, dragging a narrow, pointed branch. When I envisioned the sharp end impaling him or Renegade or someone else, I ordered him to drop it. Thinking it was a game, he played keep away until I latched on to the sharp tip. Immediately forgotten, he dashed near the girls and the charred end crumbled in my hand, dusting my pants with steel gray ashes. I tossed the offending stick over a tiny ravine and into the trees beyond, bringing to mind a javelin or flaming arrow.

"I'd call that about a two," Jane said, laughing at my extreme lack of distance.

I brushed my dirty fingers on my pants, leaving dusky smudges, and we continued onto the grounds. The coordinates brought us to a small boat landing. Fifty yards south, a narrow car path crossed over corrugated steel.

Their eyes met, and the girls bolted to the possible hiding place, legs churning, hair flying, arms flailing, giddy and giggling.

Jane held tight to Renegade after seeing Maverick lurch from my grip. He barreled after the girls, loping and barking, overtaking them. Carlee reached the spot right after he did and bent over at the waist, panting. Maverick snuffled the ground, occasionally yapping. Kindra followed closely, nabbed the end of his loose lead, and waited for her sister. Patricia jogged into position. Maverick continued woofing. Still breathing heavily, Kindra tightened her hold on Maverick's leash and gave Patricia the go-ahead.

Patricia briskly rubbed her hands together and grinned. She knelt, examined the opening, and reached in. The tube devoured her arm up to her shoulder. Patricia burrowed deeper. Still unable to find anything she leaned away and peered into the pipe. We heard a plaintive cry. She rolled back and quickly crab-walked away, her face wearing a mask of horror.

ELEVEN

Thirty minutes later, I stood beneath a wooden shelter answering official questions, shivering.

"These aren't ideal conditions for hiking the county park trail." The thin, nervous, young officer had introduced himself as Deputy Gray. He jotted another note on his electronic tablet. "Tell me again what you were doing out here."

"Geocaching." Nothing but his intense eyes moved, shifting to look at me. I shuddered, remembering the first body I'd found while geocaching. "The coordinates took us to the boat landing, and the hint brought us to the culvert where we found the body."

"Which one of you called 911?"

"I did," said Jane, standing guard over the girls.

He went back to his notes. "Did you know the victim?"

I breathed deeply. "It's Edith Farthington."

He stopped writing. "Do you know anyone who would have wished her dead?"

I didn't appreciate the look he gave me and shook my head. "We just met her last night. We're staying at the White Star Inn." I straightened and willed myself more backbone. "Ask Mr. Farthington."

"You do know you've compromised the crime scene."

I let out an exasperated sigh. "How else could we determine if she needed help?"

The collapsible metal gurney rattled across the lawn. Two EMTs transported the remains to a black bag, hoisted it to the gurney, and tightened the straps before rolling the body back the way they'd come. Jane wrapped her arm around Patricia, hugged her, and continued to console her as Kindra signed calming words. When they'd clattered out of sight, I turned to the young man. "What else can I tell you? Deputy Gray, I need to get the girls out of the cold."

Renegade and Maverick curled up next to Carlee. Her eyes scanned the road, waiting for a response to the text messages she'd sent her dad and Galen. When a giant truck barreled into view, kicking up a plume of gravel, Carlee pulled her coat tighter, and her voice hitched. "Dad."

Before the dust settled, CJ dropped from the cab. Under duress, his limp was more pronounced, and he hobbled to Carlee, wrapping her in a huge embrace and planting a kiss on the top of her head. Galen stood tall, a foot behind CJ in unparalleled support.

CJ drew himself to an imposing height. "Officer—"

"Deputy Gray."

"Deputy Gray." Gray shook the hand offered. "Dr.

Chantan John Bluestone. This is my daughter." He tugged Carlee closer. "And these are her friends. Why are they being kept outside, in the cold? If you need to talk to them, surely you have an office. We can meet you there."

Deputy Gray closed the cover on his tablet and said, "You're all free to go but please don't discuss anything that's happened here with anyone else. We haven't yet notified next of kin." He pivoted with military precision and then turned back and added, "It's crucial you stay in town. Sheriff Zasko will be stopping by the inn later."

Jane whistled. I saw her astonished recognition of the name we'd overheard in the salon, Zasko, and she tried to conceal it by talking animatedly to the girls.

Kindra, Patricia, Maverick, and I filled Jane's seats and trailed CJ, Carlee, Galen, and Renegade to the inn. The silence in the vehicle allowed for terrible thoughts to swirl in my head. I couldn't believe Edith was dead. Murdered. Edith hadn't crawled into the culvert herself.

Dry grass clung to the front of my jacket. I brushed at my muddy knees, further fixing the damp dark stains in the denim, and I wrinkled my nose. I scraped light colored dust from beneath my ruined nails and chewed the inside of my cheek. It had been quite a job for Jane and me to dislodge Edith from the pipe, hoping for a chance to save her. But the bloody wounds on her head and in her chest had done their deadly deeds. It hadn't been self-induced.

"Who could have killed her?" Kindra asked in a soft voice.

"That's not our job, hon," said Jane. "Let the sheriff and his fine deputies figure this one out." She gave me a side glance and said softly, "Do you think we're safe at the inn?"

I thought for few seconds before answering. "No one here knows us. I can't imagine anyone wanting to hurt us, but we'll discuss safety with Sheriff Zasko. Dr. Bluestone will know what to do."

We pulled up behind CJ. In the light of the day, the fresh paint on the Tudor revival and meticulously cared for yard would have given the inn welcoming vibes if I hadn't known better.

I breathed in and opened my door. We had to do more than make the kids feel safe. We had to ensure they were.

The nine of us trudged silently up the hill. Galen opened the door and we entered, following CJ to the dining room. He gestured for us to take seats around the table.

"This is not turning out to be the week we had planned."

So caught up in the death of Edith, I'd forgotten for a moment the real reason we'd come. "What did you find out about Danica?"

CJ's chin rose and his black eyes went flat. "I met with the head of the department who assured me, even though the hospital changed hands, they kept meticulous records. They searched three years before and after Carlee's birthdate for any female bodies left at the hospital, identified or not. There were none. We do not know where Danica is."

He cleared his throat. "It seems Edith worked evening admissions over the six years we searched, and if anyone would have known about Danica, it would have been Edith Farthington."

"Dad, now we'll never know." Carlee burst into tears and buried her face in Galen's chest.

When Carlee's sobs eased, CJ said, "My initial meeting with the parish priest, Father Svoboda, was cut short. I have another appointment with him tomorrow afternoon.

He believes a memorial Mass will give us the peace we seek, and I concur." He touched the tip of Carlee's nose. "We will hold the service on Monday afternoon after your grandparents arrive. You …" His open-handed gesture circled the table. "You mean the world to us, and Carlee and I invite you to share in the preparations, in whatever manner you choose."

He forced out his next words. "After we talk to the sheriff, we should be free to come and go as we choose."

The dining room door banged open. Ryker and his cronies tumbled into the room, laughing and jostling each other. They seemed surprised by our presence. "What's going on here?" Ryker said, haughtily. "It looks like you're holding a funeral."

Galen rose so quickly, his chair screeched across the floor and slammed into the paneling behind him. In three strides, he had reached out, gripped Ryker's collar, and lifted him to his toes.

"Hey man, what's your problem?" Ryker whined and looked to his pals for support. They backed away when CJ rose.

"You're my problem." Galen twisted the collar and Ryker squeaked. "Man."

"Galen." At the staid sound of CJ's voice, Galen conspicuously released his hold on Ryker and raised both hands. He patted Ryker's chest with exaggerated movements, smoothing the fabric, and stepped back. His body language relayed a truce, but his eyes flamed.

Ryker straightened his shirt and snickered, suggesting he had not been impressed, but his words came out an octave higher than expected. "It's been fun, folks." He and his buddies turned and fled under CJ's scrutiny.

"I think it would be best to avoid that crew whenever possible," I said. "They're on their spring break and know no boundaries." Our kids nodded solemnly.

"We're on our spring break too," Galen muttered.

Lauren rushed in at the back of the room, arms laden with trays of fixings for sandwiches. "Sorry. I didn't know anyone was waiting." She slid the trays onto the sideboard and disappeared in a whirl. We looked at each other in confusion.

"Kids, remember what we were told at the lake." I touched my lips and hoped they understood my inference not to say anything until Sheriff Zasko arrived,

Time had smashed together, and I hadn't registered hunger until the soup tureen she brought back landed heavily on the countertop. "Help yourselves to *Vomacka* and my special pickled banana peppers." She raised the lid on the soup and inhaled. "One of my best, even if I do say so myself." She replaced the lid, and, before anyone could ask 'what's *Vomacka*?' she vanished again.

Jane said, "Even if you don't feel like it, I expect you all to fix yourself something. It's noon. We don't want anyone collapsing from starvation. Galen, why don't you lead the way?"

Galen kept his eating eagerness in check and assembled only two sandwiches before returning to the table. I urged the girls to follow. They each put together a small lunch. "I know you probably don't have much of an appetite, but you need to eat. Then maybe we can, parroting my dear friend, Ms. Mackey, do some retail therapy." I filled cups with vegetables swimming in the rich, creamy broth, wafting with dill, and delivered them.

Galen left nothing on his plate nor in the cup but didn't

go back for seconds. The girls picked at the sandwiches, nibbling at the edges, but the warm, tangy soup was comfort food for us all.

Their troubled faces morphed into inquisitive expressions, and my students converted Edith Farthington's tragic murder into an urgent discussion. They approached the issue with logic and detachment. Unfortunately, they'd had practice.

Concentrating on what had happened during the day and listening intently to each other, we never heard the front door open.

TWELVE

Carlee said, "I've been thinking about Mrs. Farthington. We didn't know her long, but we saw how prickly she could be."

"What about the fight we heard when we arrived last night?" Kindra said, slurping. "Someone didn't sound very happy. You heard them, Ms. Wilk. Did you recognize the voices?"

"One was definitely Mrs. Farthington, and the other was probably Reggie. I had a feeling there might have been a third individual, but I couldn't say for sure. I never saw who was arguing." I shrugged.

Carlee cleared her throat. "The women in the beauty shop didn't have very nice things to say about Mrs. Farthington. They were downright mean. I'm sure the hairdressers would know the women. And what about that philandering Zasko guy?"

Before I could direct the colorful conversation in a new direction, Jane sat back and said, "There was also that man who came to the door last night while we were eating supper."

Patricia's head flew side to side, catching the volley of hypotheses. Jane put a calming hand on Patricia's shoulders and waited for her to catch up. "Mrs. Farthington didn't seem pleased with him either." She looked up at a corner in the room, contemplating. "I guess it could've been Zasko."

Patricia signed the words and said, "Mrs. Farthington acted inconvenienced and not happy when Ryker and his friends arrived last night."

Out of the corner of my eye, I noticed CJ's shoulders tightened. He placed his hands on the table, on either side of his plate, and rose.

"That is enough speculation. We cannot make assumptions. We will not get involved …" His eyes fixed on me. "… again."

No one moved until a soft knock on the jamb broke the stillness.

A round-faced, portly man with a bristly pate stuck his head around the corner. "Excuse me, but I need some help."

CJ stood. "Come in. We are guests here but will do what we can."

"I don't mean to be a bother." He stepped into the room. "I'm Sheriff Zasko." The uniform and badge were a dead giveaway, and my heart quaked, the nervous flutter that happens when I see a police car pointing a radar gun even when I'm cruising at the speed limit. "You found the body of Edith Farthington," he said. "I have a few more questions. Would you mind sharing your observations with me?"

CJ stiffened. Even though his October encounter with police in Columbia resolved in his favor, I imagined he might still be wary of officers of the law. He and the sheriff faced off, gauging the other's weaknesses or strengths. Eventually, CJ relented. "Please, take a seat." CJ introduced us and explained our mission in town.

Sheriff Zasko nodded. "After I read the statements you gave Deputy Gray, I checked you out. Columbia's Chief West was reservedly complimentary." His tone was slightly accusatory, very much like Chief Amanda West's might be. I'm sure she had plenty to say. He ran a hand over his face. "Murder is a dreadful occurrence in any community, but this one is personal. I've known Edith since first moving here. I'm sorry your plans in our town have been disrupted." He finally sat and pulled out a small notebook and pen. We stared at him. "Can you take me through it again?"

* * *

Sheriff Zasko identified the women in the salon; apparently everyone knew everyone in this town and the Saturday clients never altered their beauty makeover schedules. He showed us a photo, and we readily recognized Willy Zasko with his bushy eyebrows and shaggy moustache. He'd met Ryker and crew last evening when they had words at the festival, following a complaint by one of the customers.

"Have any of you seen Reginald Farthington this morning?" the sheriff continued.

Jane wrinkled her nose and glanced at me, and I said, "Mrs. Farthington told us Reggie would be at the hospital overnight, but he'd be our contact today."

"Try to make the most of your stay here. If you need anything or think of anything let me know. But do not interfere." He thanked us, handed us each a card, and left with the same admonition as Deputy Gray—we shouldn't leave. We hadn't planned to return to Columbia yet, but revoking permission imposed a prison-like sentence all the same.

Jane, thinking positively, said, "Let's all take a break and regroup in an hour. Okay?"

While our charges and Jane retired to their rooms. CJ and I leashed the dogs and headed out for a walk.

After a mile, CJ cleared his throat, and I looked into his dark, troubled eyes. "How could this happen again, Katie?" He rubbed his forehead. "Trouble seems to follow you."

Guilt wrapped itself around my heart. I had no grounds for protest, and I swallowed hard. "It might look that way, but I hope you're not right."

"I should not have said that. My emotions are a bit out of control. I missed Danica every day for seventeen years and now I see her in Carlee's eyes. I hear her in Carlee's laugh. I cannot allow anything to happen to our daughter. Today, I felt Danica's presence more acutely."

I held his arm, and we walked in silence, allowing the dogs to do their doggie things. I breathed in the fresh air and put away thoughts of Edith Farthington until we concluded our walk, climbing the cement steps to the inn. The sun furiously shook the winter doldrums away and shone so brightly I had to shade my eyes to identify the man lounging against a pillar on the porch.

We had ten steps remaining when I heard footfalls behind us. Someone elbowed me aside and clattered in front of us on obscenely high heels.

"Oh, Reggie," said the black-haired woman from the salon. "What's this world coming to?" Her arms snaked seductively over Reggie's shoulders, and she interlocked her fingers behind his neck, bowing her head and sighing into his chest.

We reached the bottom step as she said, "You need to find someone who understands you and can help you run this lovely inn."

Reggie wrenched her hands free and clasped them together in front of him, drawing them down and strongly passing them back. She caught herself before tipping over.

"Irinia, what have you done to your hair?" Reggie said with a hint of disapproval.

Irinia retreated a step and smoothed the black locks over her ear. "Do you like it?"

He ignored her question. "Why are you here? What are you prattling about?"

"Poor Edith, of course."

"I haven't seen her yet today." He glared at Irinia.

"The rumor mill has been hard at work. News of her murder is all over town." She twisted her body right and left, like an innocent toddler.

Reggie's eyes widened. "What?" he stammered. "Edith? Auntie is …" His face contorted in anguish, and tears clouded his hazel eyes.

"You didn't know? I thought you'd be the first to be notified. Unless of course—"

A deep voice growled from the street below. "Holocek. Leave him alone."

She turned her head toward the order and hissed, "I will not leave the poor man alone, Mr. William Zasko. What are you doing here?"

Willy Zasko slammed the driver's door on a shiny black Range Rover. He trudged up the steps, one at a time, as if he held the weight of the world on his shoulders and came face-to-face with Irinia Holocek. "You'll have to excuse us. Reggie and I have a lot to discuss." He looked pointedly at CJ and me, and then back at Irinia.

"What happened to your beat-up old pickup, Willy? Did you get a windfall of some kind?" Irinia said smugly, checking out her hot pink nails.

"We're sorry for your loss, Reggie," I said. CJ and I backed away from the simmering exchange and headed to the kitchen entrance. I winced, remembering the words I'd overheard in the hair salon, but knew I shouldn't believe anything said without solid proof.

"Leave now, Irinia." Willy's ominous warning carried around the side of the inn. "Before I get angry. You wouldn't want to see me angry, would you?"

We heard heels tramping away, down the porch steps.

The dogs pulled us into the alcove entry, stopping at the full water dish on the floor by the back door to slobber water on themselves and the rubber mat. Maverick's ears pricked up.

"I hear it too," I said.

My dog scratched on the kitchen entry and the female warbling stopped. The door opened and Lauren greeted us, beaming.

THIRTEEN

Y ou look …" I said.

"Ecstatic?"

"My thought exactly." She obviously hadn't heard about her boss, I hoped.

"I'm thrilled. I spoke to the doctors this morning and they told me Davy is being released today." Her incandescent smile covered her entire face.

"Davy?" asked CJ.

"Davy's my boy," Lauren's gleeful eyes shined almost as brightly as the sun. "They finally got everything under control, and I'm picking him up after I set out the happy hour spread."

A throat cleared. Lauren turned around and I glanced over her shoulder. Reggie filled the doorway, his face downcast. He clenched and unclenched his big hands. "I'd like a word with you Lauren. I have some bad news," he said, haltingly.

She gasped and smacked her chest. "It can't be Davy," she cried in a panic-stricken voice.

"No, no. It's Edith." He sagged a bit. "Could you excuse us, please?"

"Of course," CJ said. He snapped his fingers and the dogs jumped to attention and led us to the foyer.

The anxious dogs tugged as we made our way up the stairs. When we walked by the girls' room, CJ turned the knob, and the door opened. He stopped and peered inside. The room was empty, but we heard voices coming from down the hall.

Renegade rarely misbehaved, but she pawed our door, scratching the wooden surface. CJ whistled and both dogs took to their seats. Jane peeked through a narrowing opening and then pulled the door wide, revealing Carlee and Kindra on Jane's bed, Galen at the desk, and Patricia sprawled on the floor.

"Where've you been?" Jane asked.

"We've been waiting like forever," said Kindra.

"We've got so much to tell you." Patricia articulated with care and proceeded to watch the conversation.

"We called mom. We didn't want her to find out about Mrs. Farthington's death from someone else. At first, she was going to come right home, but we talked, and she said the only person she trusted more than you three was Ransom." Kindra screwed up her face. "He's okay, but Patricia and I trust you way more." Patricia nodded emphatically. "Mom said she'd support our staying here for the memorial service as long as we keep her in the loop and Ransom on speed dial."

"I'm glad you called her." Their mom, Debora, had a tough year and didn't need more to worry about.

"We met the mysterious housekeeper too." Carlee said.

I raised my shoulders in a 'who's that' sort of way.

"You know. The origami fairy. Her face was so flustered when we caught her cleaning the bathroom. She apologized for letting down her guard. Mrs. Farthington likes, ah, liked the help to be invisible."

Patricia's hands released of flurry of motions, echoed by the words she spoke. "She signs, Ms. Wilk."

"She signs?"

"Like Patricia, only she isn't deaf," said Kindra. "She just doesn't speak. She uses American Sign Language and signed 'sorry' when we walked in on her. Fortunately, Patricia noticed and signed in return. Their hands were spinning and twirling like storm clouds, and we were so lost until Patricia interpreted for us."

Very tiny warning bells increased my heart palpitations. Wasn't it bad enough the girls had discovered a dead body? Now there was an adult nearby I hadn't met, and I had to worry about stranger danger too.

"I'd like to meet your new friend," I said.

The girls glanced at one another. Carlee spoke up. "I think she left for the day. While we were talking to her, she got a text and said she needed to finish up, but she'll be back tomorrow. She prepares the breakfast. We can go down early and introduce you."

"What's her name?"

"Nicki," Carlee and Kindra said at the same time and giggled.

"Nicki what?"

The girls looked at each other with confused

expressions. Patricia shrugged and said, "Just Nicki."

Kindra furrowed her brow. "She's uneasy because the only job she's ever had was working for the Farthingtons. We told her about the geocache and finding Mrs. Farthington's body at the park—" Kindra caught my sharp intake of air. "She'd already heard about Mrs. Farthington, but she's worried about her future here."

"How long has she worked here?"

"White Star Inn? It just opened. We're the first guests."

CJ's face showed signs of confusion, which never happened. He removed his phone from his back pocket and viewed the screen. "It is a five-star inn," he said.

"Yeah, Dad, but how many reviews does it have."

He read from the site. "Two," he said, and his eyes widened. "One from RF and one from EF."

Jane murmured, "Reginald and Edith."

"I'll bet that's why price tags are hanging from some of the furniture." Carlee walked over to a lamp and lifted a rectangular piece of cardstock tied with a red string. "They haven't gotten around to removing them. Nicki doesn't know if Reggie has the wherewithal to keep the inn going, and she's a little nervous."

"What did Nicki do before tending to this bed and breakfast?

"Mrs. Farthington has, er, had other properties, and Nicki's worked at many of them, but this one was Reggie's brainchild. Mrs. Farthington merely footed the bill."

"How do you know all that?" My voice sounded a bit harsh, and the girls quieted, glancing away. "Sorry. But you really don't know Nicki very well. Be careful."

Jane gave me the you-should-be-the-one-to-talk look and pulled herself up to her full almost-five-feet. The watch on her wrist beeped. She checked it and said, "Let's not waste the next sixty minutes. Who wants to go shopping?"

The tension eased. CJ and Galen begged off, hinting that almost anything would be preferrable to exhausting themselves, traipsing from one store to another on a secret mission no one understood, to discover the best deal with the least cost, taking the most amount of time in order to avoid meaningful conversation or healthy activity, and doling out cash by the handful. They promised to play with the dogs and find a great location for dinner. I wished I could stay with them.

Kindra and Carlee rolled off the low bed. Kindra teasingly tapped the top of Patricia's head to drag her attention from her phone screen before she yanked her sister to standing.

Jane tied her hair back in a ponytail as if she was getting ready for a serious workout. Her jaw was set as was her determination to lead us to the very best shops New Prague had to offer. She pocketed my prepared list from the Chamber of Commerce and followed the girls down the hallway. Her thick golden ponytail swung back and forth as she marched on a mission. "We've got a job to do."

Patricia stopped abruptly. She turned to Jane and displayed her phone screen.

"The temps are milder than yesterday, but if Patricia's right, you'd best bring jackets. It's going to rain."

I dragged my feet for fifty-five minutes, silently objecting to the onerous undertaking, but happy Jane effectively diverted the girls' attention away from the death. Her easy, effervescent smile signaled her delight in the shopping process. We were so different. How could she be my best friend?

FOURTEEN

We returned to the inn. Galen waited at the front door decked out in a light-blue button-down shirt, a navy-blue sport coat, and khaki pants, subtly hinting that perhaps upgrading from our standard T-shirt and jeans would be a good idea.

A pang of regret hit me when I realized we wouldn't be able to flaunt the graphic on our new matching tees: a tall multicolored stack of books, a library card, and the slogan, Czech'n out.

This was a quaint town. What could possibly be the height of elegance?

I donned black leggings and a simple red-and-black sweater and joined Galen in front of the fireplace of the living room. He leaned against the registration desk, his chin in his hand, until something drew his attention to the doorway.

"Hey, handsome, how do I look?" Carlee asked, playfully batting her sultry silver eyes while inserting a bobby pin to secure her elegant updo. The short mahogany dress clung to her waist, and she spun on her heeled boots.

Galen's eyes lit up. "You look fantastic."

He stopped narrowing the gap between them when CJ spoke up. "Carlee, do you have anything else you can wear?"

"No, Dad." Her teasing voice carried a hint of exasperation, suggesting this conversation might have occurred a time or two before. "This is the style." Kindra breezed in, wearing a similar frock—short and flared—forest-green with miniscule yellow and white blossoms. "See?"

Patricia dressed in a flowing light blue pantsuit dolled up with chunky silver jewelry.

Amazed at Jane's ability to ambulate in four-inch heels and fleetingly blinded by the light reflecting off the sequins in her little black dress, I failed to notice Maverick before he slobbered on my pants. I had a pang of awkwardness and a spot of envy. My fashion-forward friend turned heads wherever she went. If I didn't clean the drool off my pants, I'd turn heads for quite a different reason.

The four-and-one-half-star establishment had over eight hundred reviews and its premium reputation seemed slightly out of place amid the town's relaxed ambiance. Five-foot-high partitions sectioned off semi-private dining compartments. Fresh flowers and glowing candles topped each linen-covered table. Taking cues from CJ and the waitstaff assigned to us, Galen held out Carlee's chair.

When we were seated, the extraordinary dining experience began.

We savored each morsel of our delicious multi-course meal, and, by observing our plates when we'd finished, you'd have thought none of us had ever eaten a hanger steak before. (Jane had, but that's beside the point.) There wasn't a speck remaining. We'd scraped the bottoms of bowls of green beans almondine and garlic smashed potatoes. I even spotted what might have been a leftover crumb from one of the dinner rolls, but I could have been mistaken. Despite eating more than we ever anticipated, we still managed to demolish two pieces of lighter-than-air turtle cheesecake and two towering slices of the Czech delicacy, *Medovník, a layered honey cake with caramel cream filling.* Galen raised a hand in surrender, indicating even he couldn't possibly ingest another bite.

Kindra, Carlee, and Galen slowly rose from the table and made their way to the piano bar guy who played requests in exchange for tips. As Patricia savored the last few bites of her cake, I hung back, letting CJ and Jane haggle over the bill.

That's when I heard the commotion in the adjacent cubicle. I craned my neck and peeked over the short partition, spotting Willy Zasko. He took measured sips of a clear liquid from a martini glass, ignoring the pudgy salt-and-pepper-haired woman wringing her hands and wagging her finger at him. A few of the louder words drifted my way. I heard, "You think I'm going to let you get away with this," "My fair share," "I'll get what I have coming to me," and "You owe me."

Zasko regarded the woman as if she were invisible. He drained his glass, plucked the cherry off the cocktail skewer, and popped it in his mouth. He adjusted his moustache with his knuckles, tossed a handful of bills on the table, and stood. He gestured to his server, pointed at the payment, and pivoted on his heels. I ducked and quickly averted my gaze, not wanting to be caught eavesdropping again. The woman chased him, weaving through the tables, trying to keep up, though her efforts came to a halt as the hem of her shabby fur coat caught on the back of a chair. She struggled to disentangle herself as he marched through the exit doors and never looked back.

Before I could process the scene, I looked around the room. Irinia Holocek sat at a small table, close enough for her to witness the strange exchange as well. Our eyes met and recognition flashed over her features. She lifted her highball glass in a mocking toast, nodded curtly, and sneered. Disturbing.

I turned my attention to Patricia, concerned she might be bothered by all the fuss, and discovered she'd disappeared. After a quick scan around the restaurant, I spotted her standing at the server station, her eyes trained on her friends, wearing a huge smile. A surge of emotion caught in my throat. She couldn't hear the exquisite rendition of "Perfect," but seemed to revel in their joy of hearing it. What a girl.

I sidled next to Jane at the reception desk. "Did you hear them?"

Jane slashed her autograph on the receipt, stowed her credit card, and arched a sculpted eyebrow. "Hear who?"

I leaned in and whispered, "Willy Zasko and that woman?"

"What woman?"

I gestured to the front door and then rapidly spun

three hundred sixty degrees. "She's gone. But I heard them arguing."

"What was Willy saying?"

"Nothing. He just sat there and ignored her."

"Ah."

"It's true. And she kept shouting at him, pointing her finger."

"Do you know who she was?"

"No, but …"

"Leave it, Katie. We can't get any more tangled up in this. We've got to think of the kids." She squeezed my arm and dipped to see up into my face. "It's alright. Really."

"You're right. It's just … I don't know …"

"I do. Drop it." She stood as tall as she and her four-inch heels would get her. "I need a love song." She fished a ten-dollar bill from her Yves St. Laurent bag and linked her arm with mine, dragging me to the piano bar. "I'm thinking *Do You Believe in Magic*. What about you?"

The piano player nodded farewell after rewarding our tips with his great musical skill.

The temperature had plummeted, and the predicted rain had already transformed into snowflakes, dusting everything. The expected accumulation was negligible, but in the dark, even a little snow could make the roads slick and treacherous. We inched our way safely back to the inn.

Singing along with the radio at the top of our lungs helped the long minutes pass quickly. We'd been gone for two hours and that provided ample time for two rambunctious dogs to land in a heap of trouble, but the sight of the sheriff's car was entirely unexpected.

"Good evening, Sheriff." Jane greeted the man sitting on the porch steps, bundled up as if prepared for a blizzard.

He was stuffed into a black duty jacket and wore a fur-lined trapper hat. "What brings you here?"

He rose and shivered slightly. "Good evening, folks. I was hoping to have another little conversation with the elders in the group."

CJ opened the door, and we filed inside. The sheriff and CJ briefly engaged in a 'you first' standoff, but this time CJ emerged the victor in the battle of wills. Sheriff Zasko stepped through the doorway and had removed his furry cap when scraping, banging, yelping, and whining noises echoed from upstairs. He reached across his rotund form for his firearm, and CJ gently pressed a hand on the man's shoulder, calming his movements. CJ lifted a warning finger and motioned for us to follow. I removed my shoes and crept up the stairs.

FIFTEEN

We traced the noisy yips to our lovable furry friends. They'd toppled their kennels and had skidded along the floor to the door, anxiously anticipating our reappearance. With a nod from the sheriff, Galen unlatched the grates. Maverick zoomed through the open door, knocking the sheriff off balance, and streaked down the hall. When Renegade trailed after, yapping with excitement, CJ caught Sheriff Zasko's arm, helping him regain his footing.

"Thanks," the sheriff mumbled, looking a bit dazed.

CJ bowed slightly.

"Kids," Sheriff Zasko said. "If you need anything, we'll be in the dining room."

"Guess we know when we're not wanted," said Carlee,

winking. She palmed something from my pillow with a sly grin. I tried to look menacing. I still hadn't tasted any yummy treats. She pursed her lips, buttoning them up tight. We'd have a conversation later.

The sheriff snugged his pants over his belly and descended the stairs, gripping the banister for support. The dogs paused on the landing halfway down. Sheriff Zasko maneuvered around them just as the doorbell chimed. From our vantage point, we watched Reggie plod from the registration office and open the front door. Irinia stood on the front step under the dim yellow light.

Sheriff Zasko put his finger to his lips, signaling us to back up to the second flight. When I took a gander through the balusters, I had a clear view of the entire foyer reflected in the mirror on the wall.

"Reginald, darling, I was terribly worried about you," she cooed.

Sheriff Zasko shook his head and mumbled, "What a gold digger."

"You weren't out with your friends tonight and I have so much to share with you. I've come over to tell you now while I still have the courage." Irinia's irksome voice circled up the staircase and didn't sound at all like she lacked courage.

Willy Zasko emerged from the library, running sandpaper along the edges of a carved piece of wood, chewing on a toothpick. Irinia glowered. "It appears you still keep strange company. I won't be but a minute."

"Irinia, I told you to stay away from Reggie," said Willy.

"Since when have I ever listened to you?" Irinia ducked under Reggie's arm and brushed past him into the foyer, unbuttoning her coat.

"I can handle her, Willy." Reggie said.

"I bet you can," Irinia purred suggestively.

"You should leave, Irinia," said Willy. "You've been a pain in my side ever since we parted ways."

"Now's not the best time." Reggie held the door open. "I'll see you later, Irinia."

"The tigress is finally gone," Irinia pouted. "And you're all on your lonesome. I'd hate for anyone to take advantage of you in your time of sorrow." She shot Willy a withering glance.

Willy took an intimidating step toward her.

Sheriff Zasko cleared his throat. "Would you expand on that thought, Ms. Holocek?" All eyes traveled up the stairs.

Just then, Lauren strolled in from the kitchen, a tow-headed toddler with huge blue eyes perched on her hip. The little one clung to her neck while her gaze swept the room, nodding slightly as if tallying bodies. "Mr. Farthington, I can whip up some snacks for your guests. It won't take a minute." She hiked the little guy to her other hip. "We'll be right back, won't we Davy?" she said, nuzzling the child and giggling. She vanished before anyone could object.

"You're busy so I'll be seeing you, Reggie, sweetheart." Irinia slithered to the door.

"Please stay, Ms. Holocek. As long as you're all here, I have some questions, if you don't mind." Willy set the block on the entry table and stepped toward the closet. "Willy, I'd like to speak to you and Reggie too."

Willy bowed his head. "Of course, Sheriff."

"Ms. Holocek, join me in the living room." The sheriff descended a few steps, motioning us to follow.

We stepped into view, to the bewilderment of the three

in the entry.

"If you would wait in the dining room, I'd greatly appreciate it," said the sheriff.

A quartet of boisterous, inebriated men meandered into the foyer, tripping on the pattern in the carpet, caught the serious vibes, and stumbled over one another in an unsuccessful attempt to sneak back into the kitchen.

"Chesterfield, where do you think you're going?" said Willy. "You're fortunate I was able to negotiate your stay here. Reggie finished up the rooms just in time, but Sheriff, the gang's all here. They could have valuable information for you."

Sheriff Zasko's lips curled in what might have been a scary smile. "I would like to talk to the four of you. I'll join you in the kitchen shortly."

One of the four hooted, "Ry-ker."

Ryker rammed the man's shoulder, and the raucous bunch straightened up. Ryker raised his head, wobbled a bit, and threw his shoulders back again, pasting on a crooked grimace. "Sure, boss."

"Thank you. I'll be as quick as I can." Sheriff Zasko sounded conciliatory, but the immediate compliance of everyone made me imagine him as a pit bull in disguise, armed with magic powers.

Once we were seated around the dining room table, Lauren bustled in, carrying a charcuterie board stacked with enough to feed a dozen—cold meats, cheeses, bright red strawberries, and green grapes.

"Please help yourself to the snacks. I'll fetch the lemonade." She returned in a flash with a pitcher of frosty pink liquid.

"You've outdone yourself, Lauren. How's Davy

doing?" I asked.

"He's a champ. Thanks for asking. I just can't believe he's finally out of there." Her voice cracked as she lowered herself to her knees. Swinging open the cupboard door, she dug out tumblers for our beverages. She stacked them on the countertop, forming a makeshift pyramid.

Normally, she'd slip out of the room, but it seemed like she lingered, longing for a chat.

"May I ask, what is it that Davy had?"

She took a big gulp of air. "Food poisoning. By the time they figured it out, he needed intravenous fluids. I was scared to death." Her tone turned solemn. "What kid listens to his mom? And what does a four-year-old understand? He ate supper with Mrs. Farthington one evening last week while she had me polishing the silver service set, and during the night he got really sick. I had to rush him to the hospital. But we won't have to worry about that happening again, will we?"

She cocked her head, her eyes widening. "Oops, I guess I shouldn't have said it like that. You've got to know, Mrs. Farthington made sure Davy had excellent medical care. I think it was guilt. But I don't think Reggie will be of the same ilk. He's the one who told me I'd have to leave if I missed any more shifts. I never actually missed any. Once or twice, I came a few minutes late on account of visiting Davy." She found something fascinating on the floor at her feet. "Gosh, I'm sorry. I'm running at the mouth. If you need me, press the help button on the house phone. I'll get out of your way now." She dashed from the room.

I poured four lemonades, and we settled in, waiting for the sheriff.

"What else could he possibly want to ask us?" said Jane.

"We found that poor woman's body and that's it. The only person who knows what happened must have killed her."

"Remember, only answer questions asked. Offering extraneous information will solicit enquiries, complicate matters for Sheriff Zasko, and prolong our interrogation," CJ said. "Because I guarantee it will be an interrogation."

Practicing what he preached, he wordlessly fixed a plate of snacks for the table. We nibbled and remained silent until Sheriff Zasko entered the room. He sighed and quietly secured the door.

He shook his head and groaned. "Some folks."

Sheriff Zasko dropped into the seat indicated by CJ, raised the glass, examined the contents, and drained it. "Thanks. I suppose you're wondering why you're here. We're trying to pin down the timeline. When was the last time any of you actually saw Edith, Mrs. Farthington?" He extracted his notebook and pencil from a back pocket. He licked the tip of the pencil and said in a self-deprecating tone, "Don't ask me why I do that."

CJ's left eyebrow shot up. "You do it to make us think you are more of a country bumpkin than you actually are." Sheriff Zasko stilled. "I, too, talked to Chief West. She tells me you were an extremely successful Chicago detective before you met the love of your life and settled down here."

Jane and I snapped our heads from CJ to the sheriff and back again.

"Warn us next time you drop a bomb, CJ. Jane and I nearly had whiplash."

The sheriff chuckled. "Does it work?"

We glared at him.

He scrubbed his grizzled five o'clock shadow and wiped the grin from his face. "We know a bit about the murder weapon and hope we can determine how or where it was disposed of. Did any of you catch a whiff of smoke at the park this morning? A hint of a fire, maybe? Or notice ashes anywhere?"

Jane shook her head. She rolled her lips over her teeth and pressed them together, clamping down to avoid oversharing unnecessary information.

As for me? I cleared my throat and avoided CJ's reproachful gaze. I was more forthcoming.

SIXTEEN

I may have smelled something smokey this morning," I said and chewed on my lower lip. "I can't be sure."

"Ms. Wilk—Katie, I'm grasping at straws here." Sheriff Zasko leaned in, and his belt buckle clanged against the table. "What can you tell me?"

I turned to Jane. "Remember the 'two' you awarded my throw this morning?"

She nodded but her lips were pinched together, CJ's cautionary words having their desired effect. Then she relented and the words cascaded forth. "Of course, I do. You tried to throw that stick away to protect Maverick and Renegade from getting hurt." She addressed CJ. "We didn't need to generate more patients for you."

"And?" The sheriff's store of patience faded.

"Wait here." I dashed from my seat, accompanied by both dogs who probably thought I was playing an exhilarating game with treats or toys hidden in my clenched fists. They danced beside me, their infectious excitement mirroring my own as we ascended the stairs. I burst into my room and four pairs of eyes locked on my form, stunned by my surprising appearance.

"Excuse me." I pulled my suitcase out of the closet, dug around in the laundry bag, and wriggled free the pants I'd worn that morning. I took a cautious whiff. And sniffed again to confirm what I already suspected.

"Ew," Kindra said. "Guests do have access to a washing machine, you know. You don't have to rate your clothes to help you choose the cleanest ones to wear."

Patricia understood every word and smirked.

I smiled and said, "Always good to have options. Thanks." The suitcase closed with a definitive zip, and I cued the dogs with a firm, "Stay," before easing the door shut behind me.

I walked a little taller, rejoining CJ and Jane in the dining room, and deposited the damp, muddy-kneed, and yellow-streaked pants in front of the sheriff like a trophy. He sat back in his chair, turned his head a degree to his right and back. The faint odor of smoke wafted from the fabric. He inclined toward the jeans and raised a questioning brow.

Jane crossed her arms. "Maverick's version of fetch ended in a minor mishap this morning. Katie took away his unwieldy stick and her throw earned her a solid two out of ten on my scorecard. Maybe her choice of wearing last year's Walmart special this morning hampered her javelin toss."

I glared at her, miffed at her offhanded comment. How did she know my jeans were from Walmart?

"Katie, can you find this stick again?" the sheriff asked. "We might be able to track the source of the fire if indeed there was one."

Intrigued, CJ did not follow his own advice. "How can a burned branch help your investigation?"

"I don't think you're involved in the murder," the sheriff said boldly, making eye contact around the table. CJ straightened his back and lifted his chin, squinting. "Truly I don't. I've decided to take you into my confidence. It appears Edith was knocked out with a rectangular piece of wood, and there are slivers imbedded in the gash in her chest, implying she might've met her end when someone stabbed her with a very sharp tool—perhaps one used in woodworking. We didn't find anything near the body. If our murderer possessed any intelligence, he—"

"Or she." My interruption elicited a glare from CJ.

"Or *she* could've disposed of the weapon. Burning wood would be the easiest way to get rid of it."

A shudder rippled through me. "I think I can lead you to the general location, and I wasn't able to toss the stick very far off the path."

"You can say that again," Jane said softly.

"We won't be able to find it tonight," said the sheriff. "I'd like an early start. Ms. Mackey, Ms. Wilk, let's reconvene at say, seven?"

"I suppose I can be ready," Jane said, trying to sound annoyed, but I recognized curiosity in her eyes. "We're not bringing the kids. They've been through enough."

"Agreed," said the sheriff. He pressed his heft away from the table. "Good night, folks. See you in the morning."

As the sheriff retreated, my attempt at bravado slipped out, aimed at the vanishing form. "We are bringing the dogs." I shrugged at the puzzled looks. "Maverick might just rediscover his stick."

The kids appeared on the steps as the door closed and joined us for a tiny, totally unnecessary snack while CJ debriefed them. They knew what the sheriff wanted and were more than happy to let us handle it.

"Is there anything more we can do, Father?" asked Carlee, with levity, her eyes teasing.

The cryptic smile on CJ's face set us all up for a chuckle. "Your efforts have sufficed, thank you, Daughter."

Galen tapped Carlee's shoulder. "It's time." Patricia and Kindra nodded encouragingly. Carlee drew two small bundles from her voluminous pocket. She handed one to me and one to CJ.

"Go ahead," she said. "Unwrap them."

My eager fingers peeled away the sticky tape and I gasped when I unveiled an intricately carved three-inch high jet-black statue of Maverick, looking like he was ready to chase a squirrel. The feather-light carving made its way around the room, scrutinized like the precious piece of art it was.

Jane gingerly lifted it to the light. "He looks so real, his ears look ready to twitch, and these eyes have a mischievous glint. It's as though he was caught mid-bark." She turned it over in her hands before giving it back.

CJ ran his thumb over the warm, toasty brown likeness of Renegade, and his voice soft with reverence, he said, "A wonder."

"Where did these come from?" I whispered in awe.

"They're Nicki's creations," said Carlee. "She's an accomplished woodworker and completed the statuettes this afternoon. Isn't she great? She said our dogs are gorgeous animals and inspired her. She wouldn't let me pay for the carvings, insisting we keep them."

That name jolted me from euphoria and injected the feeling of unease. "She captured their personalities perfectly. Where is she? I'd like to thank her."

"She stopped by and dropped off the carvings right after you went downstairs with the sheriff. She didn't want to get in the way and left, but said she'd try to check in with you tomorrow."

CJ and Jane seemed unperturbed, so I attributed my disquiet to the fatigue of an endless day. Just as I was about to suggest turning in, Patricia said, "Let's play one of the old games from that collection in the library."

"Library?" I wondered about the undiscovered spaces in the inn. "Where's the library?"

"It's huge. How could you miss it?" said Galen. "It's right next to the kitchen."

The sinister late-night conversation I'd overheard returned and visiting the library might be enlightening.

We tiptoed into the stunning space.

Floor-to-ceiling bookcases lined the walls, and a maze of intersecting shelves formed an enigmatic center. We navigated the maze to a grand picture window, moonlight caressing a massive conference table encircled by ten leather-covered swivel chairs. Next to the cupboard of games stood an intriguing black filing cabinet and a vintage escritoire with three nested wooden bowls.

"Anyone here? Mr. Zasko?" Jane's voice resonated in the space Willy had occupied earlier in the evening. Fortunately, not even her echo answered.

Jane's fingers traced a pattern in the aged, dark wood of the desk as Patricia knelt and selected her favorite game from among the worn and tattered boxes—Clue.

It seemed too coincidental. My eyes went wide, and I said, "I'll take Maverick and Renegade for a walk. I'll be back in a jiffy."

CJ crossed his arms, surveying the scene, then turned and said, "Let me join you."

Jane's eyes stayed fixed on the gameboard as she pulled herself away, clearly wanting to play the game. But she exited with us.

The dogs trotted in tandem, not venturing out of sight. Jane cleared her throat and said, "You've got that look, Katie. What do you have brewing in that mind of yours?"

I brushed away the notion initially. "I haven't really thought about it much." CJ's amused snort drew a glare from me. "Edith Farthington has had her share of detractors. Take Willy Zasko for instance. He's been sticking around like pinecone sap, and the women in the salon seem to think Edith had him on the hook for something, or they were simply jealous he paid attention to Edith."

That brought CJ up short. "Blackmail?"

"They brought up the rumor about Reggie's parentage and suggested Edith might've been getting money from Willy for some indiscretion."

"That could be one explanation for his recent visit."

"Maybe Edith's will holds a few surprises. Willy could be presuming he'd receive a posthumous gift."

"If any of the rumor is true, Reggie might be expecting a windfall. Or not. Reggie and Edith seemed at odds when we arrived," Jane said.

"I'd forgotten about that fight. Reggie sounded disgruntled, but I don't know if that equates to murder," I said.

CJ continued listening to our commentary.

"But isn't Willy her attorney? He'd probably know the contents of the will."

"Maybe."

"And then there's Irinia," said Jane. "She practically danced on Edith's grave tonight. She sounded downright gleeful until Sheriff Zasko made his presence known."

After a few seconds of contemplative silence, I said. "The first night, I stumbled on Lauren crying in the pantry. She blamed Edith for Davy getting sick. But Lauren sounded more afraid than angry, like her job was on the line."

CJ's voice was sure and definitive. "We do not need to investigate. The sheriff is doing his job. Our time will be better spent on—"

"Oh, CJ, I'm terribly sorry. What can we do to assist with the memorial preparations?"

As we finished the walk, he rolled out his plan, assigning Jane to research scripture and me to explore music options. By the time we found the kids, they'd stashed the game and lazed around the table.

Kindra's yawn worked like dominoes, and we all felt the weight of the day catching up to us. As we tramped up the stairs, I asked, "Who won?"

Galen grinned in triumph. "Mr. Green used the candlestick in the library to commit the murder. I cracked the case."

If only every puzzle could be untangled so swiftly.

SEVENTEEN

The tranquil stillness carried us upstairs, but thoughts of contentedly curling up in our warm beds were shattered by a prolonged wail followed by a high-pitched lament. We froze in our tracks.

"Are you hearing that?" I whispered. No one answered. "I heard the same sound last night. The caterwauling sounds like someone in distress." Fourteen feet and eight paws thundered up the remaining flight, searching for the culprit. I dashed to the bathroom and pointed to the vent from which the sound reverberated like the final dying notes of a haunting scream.

"That is totally eerie," said Galen.

"You have weird looks on your faces. What's happening?" asked Patricia. She and Kindra exchanged a few signs, and Patricia took a step back.

CJ advanced four or five steps up the next flight and came face to face with Reggie.

Reggie cocked his head, listening. "I apologize. Typically, when the bathroom door is closed, no one can hear the music."

"Music?" I said, utterly perplexed as I tried to conjure an image of the instrument responsible for the spine-chilling cacophony and whoever created it.

"I'll get it stopped immediately." He spun on his heels, retracing his steps.

"Wait," I called, and Reggie turned back. "That might not be necessary." I searched the befuddled faces around me. "If we close the bathroom door, the sound is negligible, right?" I shut the door to demonstrate the soundlessness. "And you know what is causing the, ah, disturbance so it shouldn't bother us anymore."

Reggie looked like he mulled over my suggestion and finally nodded in agreement.

"I think they should be allowed to continue. Kudos to anyone practicing anything," Jane said. "I never heard a sound last night. It obviously didn't bother me. And our room is closest to the vent, so I'm okay with it."

Reggie heaved a sigh. "Thank you."

"Reggie, please accept our condolences once more for your loss," I said.

He gazed at the ceiling, a reflective expression dimming his features. "Edith was a force to be reckoned with and her absence leaves a void. However, she left her affairs meticulously organized. Your stay will not be disrupted." He lifted one corner of his lips in the semblance of a smile. "She was quite the taskmaster. Now if you'll excuse me, have a goodnight." He resumed his trek down the stairs and along the hallway.

For my final task of the day, I sent off three texts, one to Dad, saying goodnight, one to Pete, telling him I missed him, and one to Ida, inquiring as to the health of her cousin.

My heart skipped a beat when my phone chimed, but only to tell me home was two hours and thirty minutes away by car. No replies.

* * *

Mother Nature continued to unleash Minnesota's unpredictable weather, and we woke to a world smothered in a thin blanket of fluffy white.

Jane and I yanked on boots and bundled up in enough layers to rival an onion and, carrying cups of steaming liquid courage, climbed into Jane's Edge. The dogs sat bolt upright in the rear seat, observing the cold world come awake around us, conscientious judges presiding over the trial of winter. We covered all but the last few hundred yards before her heater coughed up its first puff of warmth. "Hang in there, Greenie," Jane said, stroking the dashboard, treating her vehicle like royalty. She cupped her hand in front of her mouth and whispered, "I might need a new car soon, but don't let on."

Jane got a little squirrelly if she didn't get enough sleep.

Sheriff Zasko stood amid a trio of official cars awaiting us in the parking lot. "You remember Deputy Gray?" he said.

"Morning," I said with exaggerated cheerfulness.

The sheriff introduced us to the other law enforcement

officers and said, "We have almost three hundred acres to investigate and not much manpower. We're hoping you can remember where you were yesterday and whittle down the possibilities."

Jane opened the geocaching app on her phone.

Sheriff Zasko shot her a questioning glance. "What are you doing?"

Jane took a deep breath and let it out slowly. "The breadcrumb detail of the app will allow us to follow the exact trail we used yesterday. Katie will have to remember where she threw the stick, but we can't get any closer than this."

If the technology could be trusted, we traversed the same path, and my heart thumped in my chest. Our surroundings morphed into a gray-scale painting of frosty brushstrokes and looked decidedly different today. The earth melded with the cloudy sky the exact same color and formed a dreary, unbroken tableau.

I hoped I could locate the stick and it would provide the information the sheriff was looking for. I unzipped the plastic bag holding the jeans I'd worn yesterday. Maybe Maverick would make the correct association. Maybe not. I held them to his brilliant nose and said, "Find."

Maverick and Renegade snuffled back and forth across the path, seeking a scent matching the black smear of ash on the jeans. As we moved forward, I kept my eyes on the lookout for landmarks I might recognize, and Jane directed us down the path.

The dogs' movements became more animated, their excitement palpable. Sweat beaded at the small of my back, and I unzipped my jacket. Patches of black dirt broke through as the temperatures quickly rose and the hard ground transitioned to mud, oozing around my boots. We hopped over a small stream running to the lake, fed by the melting snow.

"Sheriff, I think I stood here." I simulated an overhand throw. Maverick's head snapped up and his nostrils flared. He scrambled in front of me, navigating through the brambles, and emerged triumphant, brandishing the javelin-like stick, too unwieldy for him to carry safely.

"Here, Maverick." He sat in front of me and relinquished his prize. The sheriff picked up the piece of wood. I rewarded both dogs with tasty treats. They sat and their tails swept the ground with enthusiasm. "Good dogs. You couldn't have done any better."

The sheriff examined both ends of the tree limb and gazed over the expanse of land in front of him. "This branch is definitely charred, and it still smells smokey. Fan out, men," he said. "We're looking for the remains of a recent fire."

"What about us?" Maverick nudged my hand, bumping my fingers for more scratches. Renegade sat next to him and eagerly awaited the same from Jane.

"If you've got the time, you can check out the terrain as you head back toward the parking lot." He sent us off with a distracted wave of his hand.

"Do you just want to leave?" Jane whispered. "He'd never notice."

"No. Do you?"

"Nope."

We split up. Jane and Renegade tramped through the snow on one side of the path, and Maverick and I forged a parallel trail. I reveled in the peace and quiet, devoid of houses, cars, and people. The absence of animal sounds struck me as curious, but I attributed it to the hunting dogs wandering through their neighborhood. Jane drifted out of sight.

When Maverick took off at a trot, I jogged behind. After a short distance, a small bay came into view. Thin disks of ice floated on the placid waves near the shore. Twigs, decaying plant life, lake debris, and a modest heap of discarded plastic bottles littered the narrow strip of sandy beach. Determined to recycle, I marched up to the manmade mound, but before I plucked the first offender from the top, I stepped into a depression.

"Maverick, sit." I retreated cautiously as I made sense of the scene and called as loudly as I dared without causing alarm. "Jane."

That failed and I screamed instead. "Jane!"

She zipped through the trees, a coral-colored blur, Renegade bounding next to her, tongue lolling in anticipation of play. Maverick sat perfectly still. I knelt and held him close, my heart thumping in my chest.

Jane came to a screeching halt and snapped on Renegade's lead. "Katie?"

I leaned away for her to see behind me.

Jane retrieved Sheriff Zasko's card and punched in his number. When he answered, she pulled the phone away and I could hear him clearly from where we knelt. "What do you want now?"

"Sheriff, you'd better get down here."

EIGHTEEN

The sheriff groused about jittery women wasting precious time or nervous nellies afraid of their own shadows. He grumbled until I stepped aside and allowed the evidence to speak for itself. The pile of ashes and the remains of scorched pieces of finished wood along with natural branches punched holes in his skepticism.

He carefully examined our find, peering at the detritus. "Did either of you touch anything?"

"No, sir," I said, trying not to sound offended he'd even consider such a thing, although I easily could have.

"Did you hear anything, see anyone?" We shook our heads. "Then there's little more you can do here. You may leave, but don't say anything to anyone."

Jane's lack of sleep continued to make her fidgety and

none too compliant. She shifted from one foot to the other.

"What are you waiting for?" Sheriff Zasko said in a curt voice.

"I realize you are under a lot of pressure, Sheriff, but a simple 'thank you' would be appreciated," she said.

He stammered and growled a few words that vaguely resembled gratitude, then swiftly returned his attention to the investigation. Sensing Jane's frustration, I gently took her arm and let the dogs guide us to the parking lot.

Back in her vehicle, she gripped the steering wheel and turned to look at me.

"What? What's wrong?" My insides churned.

"That was it, right? No more snooping. You're out of it."

"Yes. That was it." I certainly hoped so.

"Good," she groaned. "I need coffee."

She swung by a local caffeine emporium, procuring two large black coffees and two pup cups of whipped topping for our canine companions. Happily sated, we returned to the inn just as the grandfather clock in the foyer struck nine.

The exhausted pups dropped onto the rug in our room. We changed out of our dirty clothes and met CJ and our troops in the kitchen. After indulging in soft, delicious bagels smeared with an assortment of fruit studded cream cheeses, CJ shared his plan for the morning.

"I would like to attend Mass at ten and meet with the priest afterward. You are welcome to join," he said and pushed away from the table. "I have preparations to make." He kissed the top of Carlee's head. "If you will excuse me."

Jane pressed all the right buttons on the high-tech brewing machine and set before me another creamy smooth hot chocolate topped with melting miniature marshmallows. I brought the cup to my lips and closed my eyes, inhaling the aroma of sweet warm cocoa. When I peeked through the steam, I caught the surreptitious looks among the kids. "What?" I asked and slurped my beverage.

The girls giggled. Carlee whipped out a piece of paper and waved it like a white flag of surrender. "We give up, Ms. Wilk."

"Give up?"

"We can't decrypt your code," Kindra said and put her fists on her hips. "We think it works like the puzzle cache, but won't you give us a clue?"

I knitted my brows. "May I see it?"

Someone printed the names of my students in bold letters at the top of the page. Unfamiliar words assembled to make what looked like a sentence in the middle of the page. 'Ishdáwiri mirúxi buuxága naxbicci áhba ágawidaba ishdáwiri áhba xarée arupi caráa …'The reverse side was blank.

"This wasn't from me. Where did you find it?"

Carlee said, "It was slipped under our door. Can you still help us figure it out?"

"A puzzle enthusiast like you?" Jane said. I'd been inclined to agree until she added, "That's probably why you get caught up in so many investigations."

I read the clock face and slid the message into my pack. I stood, urging haste, and promised to attempt a decoding after the service.

* * *

The final transcendent chimes resonated from the bell choir, bringing a serene conclusion to a beautiful Mass. As the congregation filed out of church, processing to a majestic Bach piece played on the pipe organ, curious parishioners scrutinized the unknown faces occupying the entire back pew.

I held my breath until the last triumphant swell of notes completed its trip around the towering ceiling, meandering through various alcoves, lingering, thrumming, and finally burying themselves in the very foundation of the church. I gawked and marveled at the intricate embellishments adorning the cavernous interior. In reverent stillness, my gaze drifted upward and traced the elaborate pattern on the molded tin ceiling.

Jane leaned in and whispered, "Those statues look scary real, don't they?"

Full sized figures occupied niches on three distinct altars at the front. Additional sculptures hung on the walls around the church, depicting the fourteen stations of the cross. Filigree decorating the tops of columns and the panels on the elevated pulpit attested to an artisan's skill and unwavering dedication. The detailed carving in the wood of the baseboards, headers, doorframes, and furniture further confirmed craftsmanship imbued with love.

The vivid stained-glass windows painted a fluid kaleidoscope of colors across the faces of our awestruck group as we awaited the priest.

With our eyes trained to the wondrous architecture, the man magically materialized next to me, and his voice echoed our amazement. "Lovely, isn't it? I believe a tour is in order." As the tall, white-haired gentleman rolled down the cuffs on his black shirt, he led us to the front altar.

He eloquently narrated the tale of Minnesota's oldest Czech church. The explanation included how the

Romanesque Revival and Georgian architectural elements represented logic and order, reminiscent of the houses of worship back in the old country. Father Svoboda proudly pointed out the church's distinguishing features and strategic use of color.

We exited the vestibule past a stone baptismal font, through arched heavy double doors Father had difficulty latching, and silently collected our thoughts, standing on a meticulously crafted tiled motif. Jane took my arm, and as we began the long descent, a comforting warmth enveloped me. I glanced over my shoulder and met the compassionate eyes of the golden-hued statue depicting a youthful warrior leader, offering us courage though powerless to lend a hand.

"St. Wenceslaus," said Father Svoboda raising his face to the skies. He drank in the air for a moment, then shifted his gaze to CJ. "Follow me."

We gathered in the church basement. CJ related all he knew of Danica's tragic death and shared his thoughts on the fate of her remains. Carlee gave no visible sign of distress, but when she squeezed my fingers, I could feel the pulse of her heartbeat. I held tight.

Father Svoboda's tawny eyes blinked with empathy. He placed a reassuring hand on CJ's shoulder. "I'm sorry, my son. I can sense the storm of emotions brewing deep inside." He lightly tapped CJ's forearm. "Let us offer assistance."

CJ glanced at me, pleading. I extracted my notes. "We hope to incorporate this music during the memorial, if you find it appropriate," I said.

The priest reviewed the selections. "These are perfect."

Jane fidgeted in her seat, and her eyes locked on mine.

She recited Bible chapters and verses she believed carried significance. Father Svoboda concurred, seeing the depth of feeling in her words.

"What time suits you for the service? Our schedule is open from ten, following morning Mass, until five when bell choir practice begins."

Carlee had been watching the proceedings with eagerness. "My grandparents are due to arrive mid-morning. How about one o'clock?"

"Splendid," replied the serene priest. "While I may not have known the young woman personally, I am prepared to deliver a holy message. However, if one of you would like to share some thoughts, it would be most fitting."

CJ gazed off to some distant place, his eyes reflective and contemplative. "I will speak."

"Done," said the priest.

Father Svoboda escorted us outside and wished a blessed day. The sun had burned off the clouds, and puddles were all that remained of the snow. The tolling bell in the church tower pealed twelve times.

"Where has the time gone?" Galen said. "I'm starving."

"You're always hungry," said Carlee. "I had enough at breakfast to last until supper."

We wandered the enchanting Main Street and found a small café serving pizzas and burgers. Fifties music blared from the juke box. CJ unclenched his fists and some of the tension seemed to ease, replaced by a blooming smile as he watched his daughter. Jane typed a few words on her phone and watched for a response. After a moment, she tucked it away and joined in the mirth, grinning like a Cheshire cat.

Irinia Holocek and two of the other newly pampered

women from the spa paraded by the large window and came in the front door, picking up what looked like a takeout order. My thoughts drifted to Edith. Behind the smile I fixed on my face, my mind cataloged what I knew of her death. I couldn't seem to get it out of my head. When did Edith meet her end? Why was she at the county park? What killed her? Who harbored ill intentions toward her? Did any of the suspects possess alibis?

I sometimes thought CJ could read my mind. He eyed me guardedly, so occasionally, I'd concentrate on the conversation long enough to add an appropriate comment, and he wouldn't catch me ruminating.

I'd made a few observations. We still didn't know why Edith and Reggie argued Friday night, if it had been a recurring discussion, or if it had been Reggie at all. The unexpected appearance of the four insolent college guys, however, had Edith visibly perturbed and she seemed equally upset with Reggie usurping the opening. She'd opened the door to Willy Zasko late on Friday during our supper, and local gossips painted him as a roué with an unusual connection to Edith. Could he have killed her? Could one of the voices I heard in the library have belonged to Willy? The conversation carried a threatening undertone and although they didn't mention Edith, the word 'ultimatum' dangled in my memory.

Irinia Holocek calculated her best shot at Reggie's affection occurred after Edith was out of the way, and she was sticking to him like sand to wet feet. Lauren held Edith responsible for her son's illness yet praised her for providing medical coverage. Edith employed Nicki, whom I'd not yet laid eyes on. The kids had received an encrypted message or maybe it was simply a mishmash of nonsense, although it began to burn a hole in my pocket and my fingers itched to examine it more closely. And a cranky unidentified woman had tried unsuccessfully to confront Willy at the restaurant. Too many questions niggled at my brain.

"Katie?"

Those thoughts scattered like confetti and my attention whipped back to the table. "Sorry. Thinking about ..." What could I be thinking about? "Pete. I haven't heard from him, but it's only been two days and I know he's swamped."

"Of course." Jane winked. "Joining us for some retail therapy?"

An embarrassed giggle escaped. The last thing I wanted to do was shop. "Maverick is accustomed to roaming our house and yard. I need to walk him, or he'll be climbing the walls and anyone near him."

"Give me a call when you finish your daily constitutional, and we'll meet up. Let's get a move on, kids. We've got a lot of territory to cover. Coming, Galen?"

"This I've got to see," he said, and hurried after his friends.

CJ and I retraced our path to the inn, walking through downtown, past a thriving barber shop, a furniture store advertising its huge spring sale, a bustling bakery, a decrepit photography studio, and the post office.

I sighed and he said, "You cannot leave this alone, can you?"

"No one deserves to die like that, CJ. What should we do?"

"Be careful."

NINETEEN

The entry door on the big house opened with a squawk, and the stairs to our floor creaked, protesting our intruding footfalls.

"I believe I will use this time to collect my thoughts about Danica," said CJ. "I want to make certain her parents know what she meant to me and how much she loved them. It will be difficult. They have never forgiven me."

"Carlee will be here to help with that."

A wan smile worked its way onto his lips, and he shook his head. "It will either be correct, or it will not, but thank you. You are a true friend."

I hugged him tightly, long enough to blink away the hint of tears in my eyes. "The right words will come to you, Chantan John Bluestone." I took a cleansing breath.

"Is there anything I can do?"

"Would you mind filling the truck?" He handed over the keys. "Still a manual transmission, though," he quipped.

"Ha, ha, very funny." I could manage the stick shift. More or less.

I dashed to our room to pick up the dogs. The housekeeping fairy had come and gone, leaving another round of towel origami on beds made with military precision, but this time I snagged the candies. I stowed the saltwater taffy on the closet shelf to keep it away from the drooling pets and checked out the room. The windows gleamed. The carpet had vacuum tracks, and I'm sure the white-glove test would have proved fruitless. However, I'd missed Nicki again.

No amount of coaxing could raise an exhausted Renegade from her appointed spot on the carpet, but Maverick half-heartedly accompanied me downstairs, although the deliberateness in his steps indicated he might be just trying to humor me.

Drawn by the sounds of the crackling fire, I stuck my head in the living room. It really was most welcoming. Burning wood scented the air and warmed the space, but the lovely lilies appeared ready to wilt in the window niche, so I filled the watering can from the cooler and doused the pots before checking out the next room.

The library door stood ajar. I treasured libraries, brimming with the scent of paper and faint traces of ink, the varied textures of the bindings and the weight of the books in my hand, the mosaic of colored spines snugly pieced together on the shelves. I stepped inside and followed the rustle of papers around the stacks to where Reggie sat huddled over the desk, flipping pages in a three-ring binder.

Before I could rap on the bookcase nearest my knuckles and make him aware of my presence, Maverick barked. Reggie jumped in response and hastily covered the papers with his large hands.

"Sorry, Mr. Farthington." I said, "Sit, Maverick," and tried our new cue, "Eyes on me." That lasted about a second. I tried to look contrite. "I didn't mean to startle you."

"It's Reggie, please, and I'm fine. I was concentrating so hard I didn't hear anyone come in." He snagged a short thick glass from the desktop and swirled the smoky-smelling amber liquid. He sniffed and took a swig. "Ah. Nectar of the gods." Then he downed the remains and set the squat tumbler on the desk.

"It's a birthday gift to myself. I'm an April Fool's baby." He glanced at the half-empty bottle of eighteen-year-old Macallan. "Would you like one?" I shook my head.

"Is there anything I can do for you, Reggie?"

He closed the binder and rested his elbow on top. "There's nothing anyone can do now. I miss her. I came here ages ago, and she let me stay, teaching me about the hospitality business. She took care of so many details. That falls to me now, and the sheriff left our records in shambles." He drummed his fingertips on the desktop. "I just found out you're here for a memorial, but my aunt never mentioned that to me."

I recounted the same story CJ shared with Edith. His eyes grew round and sad. "What a tragedy. Mr. Bluestone never saw her again?" I shook my head. "What happened to the woman who said she left … Danica, wasn't it?" He stood and waited for me to agree. "Danica's body at our hospital?"

"She's in custody but that's another story." I shuddered

at the thought of the vile woman who raised Carlee. Maverick's nose brushed my hand, reminding me all was now well. "The service is scheduled for one o'clock tomorrow."

Reggie stepped closer and put his hands on my shoulders. "I'm sorry for your loss too."

I held my breath and tried not to squirm at his forwardness. Maverick nudged between us. Reggie lowered his hands and stepped back.

He suddenly seemed anxious to return to his notes, so I wished him well and walked outside. The cool air felt good and cleared my head. Maverick and I hopped in CJ's truck and rolled down the street with every intention of finding a gas station, but I was surprised to find us pulling into the parking lot at the county park. Well, maybe not that surprised.

A flicker of uncertainty crossed my mind. Would my curiosity take me too far one day? Maverick licked my cheek and panted enthusiastically. I dropped from the truck, but before I slammed the door, I heard a woman's enraged voice. I left the door slightly ajar, and we followed the shrieking to a small clearing at the end of a service road.

The small woman with the ratty fur coat had finally cornered Willy Zasko and seemed unwilling to release him from her grip. She backed him into one of the cars and wrestled with him, grasping at an elbow, the lapel of his jacket, any part she could latch onto, as he attempted to shake her off.

She clutched the fabric and screamed. "You'll never get away with it. I know your darkest secrets. You had that battle-axe all wrapped up. I want what's coming to me, and don't you forget it."

He peeled back her fingers, uncurling them one by one, yanked free, and shoved her away. She brought up her fists and pounded his back. When he spun around to face her, his arm flew up.

As Willy loomed over her, Maverick barked and streaked down the slight incline. I chased my dog, calling his name. Willy looked up. When he caught sight of me, his arm dropped to his side. He narrowed his eyes. His gaze stopped me in my tracks, and I stutter-stepped. I fought to regain the balance I lost with the abrupt change in momentum. Maverick returned to my side, tail wagging, delighted by all the action. The woman turned her attention our way, and Willy took that moment to dash to his car. Gravel spit and pinged on the wheel wells as he roared away.

The woman grunted in disgust. She pulled the two sides of her coat together and followed Willy before I could make sense of anything.

Back in the truck, Maverick rested his head on my leg and blinked as I asked no one, "Who was that woman? What did she want? Why were she and Willy out here at the park?"

I shook away the rest of my questions. I had kids to attend to and a task to complete. I started the truck, cruised back to town, and found a gas station. The button needed to release the gas cap stayed hidden until a scrawny kid filling his beater at the next pump opened my driver's door and flipped the switch. Warm under the collar and probably red-faced, I thanked him and filled not one but two tanks. I think I ground the gears only once or twice the entire trip due to the idiot who pulled out in front of us as

I eased to the curb at the inn.

Ryker. He and his pals honked and laughed, burning rubber on their way to wherever.

My seething abated when my phone pinged, and multiple text messages rolled in at once. Jane asked when I'd be joining them, and I had to deliberate on my answer. Dad's selfie sported a pouting face and a crying emoji; I returned one laughing.

But the third text made me cringe. Gray bags sagged under Pete's unusually dull brown eyes. Dark curls hung over his forehead. Half the collar of his light blue shirt stuck up and the other half buried itself under his wrinkled white coat. And a grinning ZaZa appeared in the photo, standing next to him in the ER, making me wonder who sent the message.

Wish you were here.

The tips of her scarlet-painted, perfectly manicured nails peeked out from the end of a gauze bandage, the kind used to wrap a sprain or strain—real or imagined? My nose turned up.

ZaZa and I had a complicated past. Charles had no idea she had secretly harbored the notion he was the one and only for her until he fell in love with me. After graduating from our mathematical cryptanalyst program, I never heard from her, even after his murder. Then she applied to teach mathematics at Columbia High School. Who resigns a job with a security agency in Paris to teach high school math in west-central Minnesota? Unless she had an ulterior motive.

I sighed and repeated, "I have faith in Pete. I have faith in Pete." It took three tries to capture Maverick's eager face next to mine in the photo I returned with the identical message.

Wish you were HERE.

I waited for an answer, scouring the past photos in Pete's thread, and noticed dust, in the shape of hands, on my shoulders in my selfie. I brushed it off and moved on to Jane, responding with a thumb's up emoji, an LOL, and the photo of ZaZa. If anyone could wrench me out of these itty-bitty doldrums, it would be Jane.

Seconds later, my phone buzzed. I shouldn't have read the screen.

TWENTY

The "Leave it," cue in our dog training jargon meant to ignore whatever unexpected, unhealthy, or unsafe item a dog might try to pick up or eat. I'm sure it meant something entirely different when addressed to me in a text from an unidentified sender. Maybe I'd received the message in error and as I couldn't decide on just one thing to leave, I ignored it and sought one of my phone favorites.

Jane answered on the second ring. "Hey, girlfriend? What was that pic all about?"

"You know ZaZa." Sometimes I wished I didn't. "I'm on my way. Where should we meet?"

"I'll text you." She ended the call. Her immediate follow-up text message included her location complete with a selfie highlighting the success of their short shopping foray with heaps of bags and four beaming faces. Galen looked pale; his eyes glazed.

Looks like you need help. I'll bring CJ's truck.

Absolutely. You can transport these bags and free up our arms for more. BTW Kimber Leigh's calling tonight. Don't let me forget.

What time?

IDK but I need to pay attention to my phone, so I don't miss it. Just ignore Mlle. Sassypants!

A most unladylike guffaw escaped my lips, and I looked around to make sure no one heard me before continuing the exchange.

I can do that — good name though! I'll be there in a few.

I pulled up next to Galen. Large and small bags in white, pink, hunter-green, blue, and black hung from his shoulders, arms, and hands. He arranged the purchases in the back seat with an exasperated exhalation.

Jane mounted the running board and mimed rolling down the window. "Carlee found just the right outfit to wear to meet her grandparents tomorrow. But she's definitely slowing down. Would you take her back with you? Patricia is looking for a special gift and we don't have too many shops left. Let's meet back at the bed and breakfast in an hour. It would be nice to have a quiet evening for a change." She gave us permission to take the packages to the inn, allowing us to skip out on the final sixty minutes of odious spending.

Galen climbed in the rear and Carlee crawled into the passenger seat. She let her head drop against the headrest as she blew out a long breath. "Whew."

I turned to wave but Kindra, Patricia, and Jane had disappeared before we pulled away.

The gears ground, and Galen laughed. "Drive much?"

"Very funny. Did you buy anything?"

He stopped chuckling. "No, but Carlee made me try on all kinds of shirts and pants. It was awful."

Carlee forced a hoot. "Haha."

"I feel your pain, Galen." It was my turn to laugh.

We parked at the bottom of the hill, and when the driver's door screeched open, I heard muffled dog barks. CJ wanted to work on his special story of Danica, and I didn't want them to interrupt his reminiscing, so I hurriedly snared about a third of the bags. Carlee grabbed one, and Galen scooped up the rest. We toted them through the front door and into the foyer, catching Ryker and his sidekicks tiptoeing down the steps carrying their luggage.

I let my bags slip to the rug, scrolled through a list, and hit redial. Sheriff Zasko answered with a surly, "What can I do for you now, Katie?"

"Why do we have to remain at the inn if Chesterfield and his cronies are free to leave?"

"What?" I heard a chair squeak and imagined his face suffused in red.

"Would you like a word?" Ryker and his buddies overheard my question and halted on the steps. I turned the speaker on and held my phone toward them.

The sheriff hollered, "I'm not finished with you. You knuckleheads better not be thinking about skipping town before checking with me or so help me I will send the state's best agents to pick you up in front of your parents, your employers, your classmates, teachers, and anyone else and throw you in the slammer so fast ..." Sheriff Zasko continued with his colorful tirade.

Ryker's eyes grew small and daggerlike before gesturing to his friends. They turned around and scrambled back the way they'd come.

"Thank you, Sheriff."

"Need me to come up there and make my request in person?" he yelled.

"No. I think they received your message loud and clear."

The sheriff hung up as Galen eyed the space they'd vacated. "I don't trust those guys," he grumbled.

"You and me both. And if they hadn't been sneaking out, I would've thought they'd been allowed to leave and never called the sheriff. I wonder why. I thought they were here for the week."

Unless they had something to do with Edith's death.

There was no love lost between Ryker and Edith, but what history could they have had? They hadn't acted like they'd met before. Or had they?

By the time we doled out the packages to the appropriate rooms, the dogs expressed a need to get outside, Galen's stomach growled, and Carlee yawned. I hooked the dog pack over my shoulder and so I wouldn't be held responsible for an exhausted shopper or a starving jock collapsing on my watch, I sent Carlee to rest, and Galen and I detoured to the kitchen to locate enough calories to positively adjust his blood sugar. He pocketed an apple, a banana, and unwrapped a protein bar. I nabbed another kolache, and after scanning the many-paged instruction manual, determined which buttons to push on the NASA-influenced control panel of the nuclear beverage machine to make two cups of hot cocoa.

I interrupted the steady stream of steaming chocolate with a heaping tablespoon of miniature marshmallows and handed the first mug to Galen. "Can't have you fading away."

He chuckled and popped the last bite of protein bar

into his mouth. "Good thinking."

I dug in our dog pack, tossed Galen a fabric frisbee, and pointed to the exit.

Galen wiped away the last few crumbs. "I'll take this job any day rather than intrude on that final shopping sprint," he said, playing keep-away from Renegade.

We accompanied the dogs out the rear door, around the side of the house, and stopped abruptly when we heard irate voices directly above us. The tails of sheer, white lacy curtains fluttered in and out of the narrow opening beneath the window sash.

"You're in charge. Edith's no longer here. Surely Nicki can help out, especially since you're planning to offer dinner on top of breakfast fixings. You can't expect me to do it all myself."

Galen threw the frisbee, and Maverick successfully retrieved it.

"If you can't do it, Lauren, I'll get someone who can." The edge to Reggie's words made me cringe.

Galen tossed the toy again. Renegade fetched it and dropped it at his feet.

"I know what goes on around here," Lauren responded icily. "You'd do well to reflect on what I can contribute."

Galen and I stepped quietly away from the conversation toward the playful pups but couldn't fail to hear Lauren's cutting remarks.

"We'll provide a tasty supper, and Nicki will assist," Lauren said with unexpected authority. "She can still remain in the background if you'd like. How many can we expect?"

Papers shuffled and Reggie said, "The four guys here for the beer festival—"

"Ugh. When are they leaving?" I could almost see Lauren shudder.

"They're paid up until Friday, at more than double the regular rate, I might add. They seemed desperate to be here and—"

"So you milked it for all you could. Is that why Edith allowed them to stay?"

"Among other things. The family is here until Friday as well. They are expecting two more adults tomorrow, so plan for fifteen."

We edged down the hill, but the sound continued to travel, and Lauren said, "It's short notice so tonight we'll have chili, tomorrow, a soup. After that, we'll see what there's time for. And Reggie, I expect to be well compensated."

"We just opened. Realize, I have a long way to go before I break even."

"I'd consider a small share in the business. That would provide me with more incentive to do my job well."

Footsteps clomped out the front door. The dogs stood still, and a rumble started deep down in Maverick's throat. He bolted, followed by Renegade, and we chased them around the corner of the inn.

Ryker and his friends traipsed down the cement steps, monitoring the movement of my intuitive canines. Ryker held up empty hands, but his glare could have singed my nose. I entwined my fingers in Renegade's collar as she barked, flopping back and forth behind her friend. Maverick stood at attention and eyed the group.

A Range Rover slid to a halt behind Ryker's car. The door opened, and Willy slithered from the front seat. Ryker sneered but ended the staring contest with a "Hey, Will-yum." He and his three friends climbed into their red car and roared away from the curb.

The library window came down with a thud and Galen turned to me with knitted brows. I probably reflected similar questions on my face, but only until I laughed and pointed at the white marshmallow froth on Galen's upper lip.

He licked what he could reach and wiped off the rest with the back of his hand. "Better?"

Before I could finish nodding, the back door banged, and I flinched.

TWENTY-ONE

Lauren marched to the carriage house at the edge of the property. Minutes later a garage door growled open, and a blue sports car thundered down the drive.

Galen jerked his head. "Whoa. There are some big bucks in that car."

I looked up at him. "Why?"

"That's a newer Mustang. I didn't catch the model but—"

"But it's not a cheap set of wheels."

I vowed to pay better attention to car makes and models.

Galen's eyebrows shot up at the same time we heard a horn honk from the street below. Renegade and Maverick had already descended the slope, ready for their meet-and-greet. The girls bounced from Jane's SUV and raced the dogs, toting a minimum number of packages, crisscrossing, and zigzagging across the patchy yard.

Jane pressed her key fob and the locks chirped. She beamed.

"Your trip was successful?"

"Kindra and Patricia bought a leather valise for their mother. It was on sale at seventy-five percent off. I found the most adorable light blue sweater for Carlee. It's so soft and it will make her even more huggable. How is she?" Movement caught her eye, and she looked up.

Carlee trudged onto the porch, and she waved. Her face had paled even more, but she tacked on a huge smile. The girls dashed to her side, squealing with delight, and dragged her inside.

"I found the funniest T-shirt for Drew, and ta-da," said Jane. She handed me a gold-foil bag.

I squinted and bit back a smile. "For me? Why? It's not my birthday."

"Because I can." Generous-to-a-fault Jane never held back when it came to spending money. She learned from a pro. Her dad owned Sapphire Skies, an aviation company that catered to the flying needs of those who could afford to go anywhere at any time. "Go ahead. Open it," she urged. Her shoulders rose to her ears. She folded her hands together and fluttered her fingertips in front of her lips.

"You really didn't have to." I carefully peeled aside the crinkly gold tissue paper to reveal a small rectangular wooden box. I lifted it from the bag and examined the five stock photos held in place by ornate frames on the cuboid. I turned the block over in my hands and searched for the latch to open each frame. "A hexahedron."

"A what? Katie, you're scaring me." She gave me an incredulous look and laughed. "It's a puzzle box." She squealed, giddy, as we meandered up the hill. "You have to solve the clues on the bottom to figure out how to open it to get the old pictures out and new ones back in. This was the last one in the shop, and because they lost the instructions, I got it for a song."

"You don't know how to open it either?"

"Where's the fun in that?"

Jane held the heavy front door, and I stepped through, continuing to study the three-dimensional enigma. I was so lost examining the top, bottom, and sides I nearly dismissed a text ding on my phone.

Thinking of you. I hope you're having fun but not as much fun as we would have had in Sonoma.

Not a chance. Jane took the kids shopping today.

I chuckled at the laughing and crying emoji Pete used in answer, followed by a heart. I replied in kind and sighed.

Jane peered over my shoulder. "Say hi to Pete," she sang before hauling shopping bags up the stairs.

Jane says hi.

Hi Jane. Back to work. Don't do anything I wouldn't do.

I hope you're bored.

As long as I was in the throes of texting, I sent one to Dad.

How are the slopes?

When he didn't respond, I figured they had good skiing conditions after all, or they'd found something equally riveting to do. The fireplace sounds of snapping and popping caught my ear. I meandered into the living room and sent a text to Ida.

How's your cousin?

She responded immediately.

Doing well. We're catching up and talking over family history. There's so much I never knew or have forgotten!

In my mind, I echoed her sentiment.

When will you be returning to Columbia?

My cousin might not need me as long as she first thought. She has a FRIEND coming.

Male?

Yup. You know, my cousin says I'm finally acting my age. I'm not sure if that means I'm acting more mature or less. Have I changed much since you moved in?

Nope. I think you're always charming.

I'll probably be back by the end of this week or early next. How are Carlee and CJ?

As well as can be expected. Carlee's grandparents are coming tomorrow for the memorial. Fingers crossed.

Even though we'd been busy, I missed my everyday connection with Dad and Ida, and I couldn't wait to hear all the stories during our first dinner at home. She made the best everything. I flopped into an upholstered chair, tucked my phone away, and focused on the puzzle box.

Jane popped her head in and said, "I'll get us a snack from the kitchen." I was pretty sure Jane left the room while I concentrated on the box, studying the faces.

The numbered patterns of squiggles and lines on the bottom panel suggested an order with which to begin. The first instruction arrow gave a direction, so I skimmed my finger along the edges of the box and across the surface, pressing lightly. A corner brace moved. I slid it up and away, but it required another step. I rotated the edge piece one hundred eighty degrees and two very short shims retracted, freeing the glass. After learning the trick to open the first frame, the rest followed in short order.

I returned the pieces to their original positions, re-creating the box, and placed it on the mantel. I couldn't wait to substitute my own images, and I had loads with which to fill it. Sunlight warmed the fragrant yellow blossoms of the flowers in the front window. By the time Jane reentered the living room with a tray carrying a plate of giant chocolate cookies and glasses of milk, I'd deadheaded the flowers and accumulated a pile of wilted blooms. "Moved on from the puzzle already? Don't give up. You'll get it."

I simply smiled.

Jane interrupted my reverie. "Do you think we should answer the door?"

I became aware of the hammering which should have elicited a response from Reggie or Lauren or the mysterious Nicki, but no one appeared.

"I suppose it's either us or the door will fall off its hinges."

We approached the door together. Jane furrowed her brow when the pounding sounded even more frenetic and challenging. She shrugged and pulled on the knob.

A familiar little woman barreled in, shoving between us. She pulled the two sides of the shabby dark fur coat together and it nearly swallowed her whole. "I demand to know where Willy Zasko is hiding out." Her beady eyes shot daggers as she glared back and forth between Jane and me.

Jane shrugged.

"What good are you then? You should be fired."

"We don't work here. We're guests."

The woman turned up her nose. "Then I'll just wait here for him." She observed the grandfather clock. "That can't be correct." She hiked her sleeve past her wrist to check the time on her watch and grumbled. "I need privacy." She darted into the dining room and crashed the doors together.

Jane's face squinched as though smelling something putrid. "Ugh. What a revolting woman."

As we retreated to the living room, I whispered, "That's the woman I spotted yelling at Willy Zasko at the restaurant Saturday evening. I saw them again ..." I faltered, but I'd already said too much. "Today when I drove out to the park."

Jane tilted her head. "Katie, what were you thinking? You went there by yourself?"

"Not exactly. Maverick rode shotgun."

"Very funny. And you saw that odious woman out there? And Zasko too?" Thank goodness a buzz from her phone distracted her. A call from Drew would be most welcome now, but by the huge brown eyes and tight frown on her face, it had to be someone else.

"Who is it?"

"It's her." Jane sounded panicked. "It's the photographer, Kimber Leigh."

"Go ahead. Answer it."

She punched accept and stammered, "H-h-ello?"

Clipped harsh sounds emanated from Jane's phone. She nodded her head. I rolled my two fingers in front of my lips, urging her to talk; no one would hear a head bob. The tension on her face eased a tiny bit and she began her one-syllable replies. I headed for the archway, but she cinched my arm, nails biting into my elbow. I patted her hand and her pleading look relaxed. At the same time, I began to hear sounds repeating, stuttering just out of sync. Her panicked look returned as I stepped toward the doorway. I put up my hand; my five fingered signal for wait shifted to one finger for hold on. I mouthed, "Be right back."

TWENTY-TWO

I put my ear to the dining room door. Like ripping off a band aid, I yanked it open, revealing the crabby little woman crouched behind the table. She raised a fist and narrowed her eyes but continued carping at the phone on the table and scribbling notes. An unmistakable voice responded. Jane turned when she heard her reverberating self. She pulled her phone from her ear and stared across the foyer.

Kimber Leigh continued to yell into the speaker. "Well? What have you decided? I don't have all day."

Jane took tentative steps across the foyer, cocking her head as realization set in. The chime on the grandfather clock echoed. "You're Kimber Leigh?"

The woman glared at us. "I'm on a private call."

"With me." Jane held up her phone. "You're not at all what I was expecting."

Kimber Leigh registered understanding and pointedly disconnected. "What of it? You're not what I was expecting either." She folded her hands atop her notebook. "I'll have to check my openings, and I'll give you three possible dates for this wedding."

Jane shook her head. "How do I know you're really Kimber Leigh?"

"You contacted me. Who else would I be?" The woman crossed her arms over her chest.

Jane fiddled with her phone. "The photo of Kimber Leigh on the website is definitely not you."

"I am most certainly Kimber Leigh."

Jane turned the screen. "This isn't you, so how do I know any of the photos are real. I imagine the entire website is a hoax." Jane shook her head. "You're a fraud."

Kimber Leigh slammed her hands down on the table. Jane and I jumped. "Find someone else to take your lousy wedding photos then."

Jane raised her chin. "I'll just do that."

"You won't find someone nearly as talented as I am. Look at my reviews."

"They can be faked too."

"And don't ask for a refund." Kimber Leigh sneered, exposing crooked, yellow teeth.

"I wouldn't dream of it." A sardonic smile crept across Jane's lips, and her eyes twinkled. She raised her phone and snapped a photo of the sourpuss who glared at her. "The internet is a tremendous tool. I want to make certain my review is out there with all the rest. You won't take anyone else for this rollercoaster ride."

Kimber Leigh stammered. "You can't do that."

"Oh, but I can. Here's a bit of our exchange." She played back a portion of their conversation and batted her lovely, long eyelashes, but her dark brown eyes burned with fire.

Kimber Leigh shrank in the chair. "You'll get your refund, but it'll take a while for me to scrape together the funds."

Before Jane could respond, the door from the kitchen crashed into the wall behind Kimber Leigh, and Reggie barged in with a fresh pitcher of berry-studded water. "I thought I heard voices. What can I get you ladies?" The smile on his face fell as he looked from Kimber Leigh to Jane and back to Kimber Leigh. "Kimberly, what are you doing here? What's going on?"

Kimberly?

"Where's Willy?" Some of her bravado returned. "I need to speak to him immediately."

"I don't know where he is." Reggie set the pitcher on the sideboard. "And I don't take orders from you."

"You'd better find him and tell him I require his presence. When and where are they reading the will?"

Reggie's face flushed, and his jaw turned white. "That's none of your concern."

"You're wrong there. Re. Gin. Ald. Edith and Willy were partners, and I never signed the divorce papers. Me and Willy? We're still hitched. He's an attorney. He understands these things, and now it seems he's afraid to talk to me."

With their attention diverted, Jane and I inched our way toward the exit. The closer we got the faster we moved.

Something in Reggie's voice changed. "I'll be sure to give Willy your message, Kimberly. Meanwhile, may I interest you in a glass of ice-cold berry water?" For some reason, his placating tone grated on my nerves. I turned and bolted. Jane scampered next to me.

Jane huffed as we rushed upstairs. "How could I have been taken in? Look at these lovely photos." She shoved her phone screen at me. Even though the photos bobbed up and down, I could see the wide range of stunning colors and use of light. "I was duped. Do you suppose her reviews are all phony too? I wouldn't put it past her to have written them all herself. I wonder if she took *any* of the photos. Next time I'll get a verbal recommendation from someone with experience, someone I know and trust."

We slowed on the landing, and as long as she was discussing the wedding, I asked, "Have you decided where you want to get married?"

She stopped, inhaled, and exhaled. "In Columbia."

I wrapped her in a tight hug, and as we rocked back and forth, we nearly toppled. I clasped the banister. "One decision made, and I think it's the right one."

She pouted. "I really thought I'd found our photographer."

Before we finished our trek to the second floor, we met the girls trouncing down.

"We're going to the library. Wanna play a game? It doesn't have to be Clue this time," said Kindra, signing some of her words for Patricia.

"That sounds like a fabulous plan." Jane's mood rose whenever she talked with our students. "Anyone else joining us?"

"Carlee fell asleep. Dr. Bluestone is still working on his message, but Galen will be down in a few minutes," said Kindra. "Ms. Wilk, Nicki stopped by again, but you were busy. We could hear that awful, cranky woman." She tilted her head and raised her eyebrows. "Anyway, Nicki gave us a clue for the puzzle."

"She left you the code?" I knew the kids hadn't imagined this Nicki person, but I didn't appreciate the unsanctioned interactions. "Is she still around?"

"I don't think so." Patricia smiled gently. "She's really nice. I can't wait for you to meet her." I read the word 'hint' at the top of the strip of paper she handed me. Giráshi.

Our footsteps boomed in the empty foyer as we trucked down to the library. No sounds emanated from the dining room. We made our way into the library through the stacks to the large conference table in the back. Patricia opened the cupboard and retrieved a deck of cards—a game requiring unusual answers to silly questions and cooperative scoring. Patricia won the first round before Galen joined us. He won the second and went to bother Carlee.

Kindra had shuffled the deck and dealt around the table again when Lauren peeked into the room, "Chili and cornbread will be available in the dining room in fifteen minutes if you're interested."

"Thanks," said Jane.

Kindra gathered and repackaged the cards. She positioned them on the shelf and closed the cupboard.

"Carlee would like to get some fresh air." Galen stretched. "Is it okay if we take a short walk?"

Kindra hooted. Patricia made kissy noises with her lips, and Galen blushed.

"I'm almost out of gas. Katie and I are going to run to the station." said Jane. "You have ten minutes."

He took Carlee's hand. They grabbed coats and headed out the front door. Jane and I followed, stumbled down the hill, laughing, and scrambled into her car. She cranked the engine, steered her Edge toward town, and we returned in seven minutes, catching Galen and Carlee sauntering back up the walkway.

Jane slammed her door and shouted, "Three minutes and ticking."

Not that either of us had a competitive bone in our body, but we raced up the hill, and tried to squeeze through the door at the same time. Between gasps and chortles, I heard Maverick and Renegade barking, big, low, loud, angry snarling and baying. Our tittering stopped. We continued our rush to the second floor and stopped dead in our tracks.

TWENTY-THREE

Chesterfield and his cronies crowded the door of the girls' room, taking up way too much space. Although Kindra's words were disinterested and exacting, the pitch in her voice sounded tense. "Please leave."

"Hey, sweetie, your chaperones left you all by your lonesome. We just thought we'd protect you from any unsolicited advances."

Patricia clearly said, "Buzz off."

"Hey guys, if you'd excuse us, it sounds like they want me all to themselves." Ryker's unctuous voice made me shudder.

Jane gave me another look, this one furious and outraged. We marched up behind the dolts. One of the tailenders turned around, looked down at Jane and me, and sniggered. He nudged the cretin next to him and lifted his chin, motioning our way. The sneering terminated when I opened our bedroom door and released Maverick and Renegade. Jane's phone was poised, hopefully ready to punch in the number for Sheriff Zasko.

"Out of my way." I elbowed into the room, purposely connecting with ribs, arms, hands, and whatever else was within reach at each step, ready with clenched fists if anyone should attempt to stop me. "If you don't understand English, do you speak idiot? The girls said, 'please leave,' and 'buzz off.' In case you're wondering, that means get lost, depart, split, vamoose, scram. Need more definitions?"

Maverick scooted between the forest of legs and sat in front of Kindra. She knelt and ran her hand from his head to his tail. Ryker raised his hands in surrender. "Didn't mean anything. Just being friendly." He turned back to Kindra. "Must have misread your signals." He slurred his words and his eyes raked over her frame.

Patricia lunged at him, and if I hadn't had to hold her back, I would have charged him myself. Ryker scoffed, and Maverick rose to four paws, the hair on his back standing at attention.

I smiled sweetly. "Jane, how soon before the sheriff arrives?" A low, gratifying rumble accompanied my question. Maverick seemed to sense my irritation and his growl grew louder, further intensifying my intention to remove the morons from sight.

"Sheriff Zasko certainly won't get here before the dogs take care of these ignoramuses. Maverick and Renegade are awfully difficult to control once they know their protective services are in demand," Jane cooed. Maverick yapped. Renegade echoed the sentiment.

"C'mon Ryker," one of his pals urged. "Let's get out of here."

Ryker fumed and stalked to the stairs, his pals continually sneaking peeks to determine the whereabouts of the dogs, or maybe Jane and me, and prodding him forward. When Ryker halted on the landing, Maverick barked and sped after him. Ryker's friends hooked his arm and quickly resumed their ascent.

"Maverick," I said as loudly and as unambiguously as possible. He stopped at the bottom of the steps but remained on alert. "Sit." He sat. "Stay. Good boy."

I took Kindra's ice-cold hands in mine. "Are you okay?"

"I'm fine. We knew you'd be back soon, but what vermin they are."

"Who's vermin?" Galen asked, popping his head in the door.

"Those jerks from upstairs," Patricia said.

She signed something, and Kindra laughed. "Brainless. I agree." Patricia and Kindra finally slid to the floor when they were satisfied we'd properly learned the sign and let out a slow breath.

"Galen, did you bring Carlee back with you?"

Carlee rubbernecked from behind him. "Right here, Ms. Wilk."

"Do you know where your dad might be?"

"We met him on our way back here. He wanted to clear his mind and heart." She glanced up at the ceiling and back at me, smiled, and said, "I think he's ready for tomorrow." She sighed. "I hope I am too."

Galen rubbed a large circle on his nonexistent belly. "I'm starved." That released the strain in the room.

"Lauren has chili and cornbread for our dining

pleasure." I tapped my thigh and Maverick returned to his place next to me. I scratched the spot between his ears, and he leaned in for more. "Let's eat early in case the jerks from upstairs also want supper."

Carlee stepped through the doorway, stifled a yawn, and flopped onto her bed. "I'm not really hungry. I think I'm going to take a breather. I want to be fresh for tomorrow but promise you'll come get me before you do anything fun."

Galen scrutinized her face. "Are you sure you're okay?"

"I'm fine. But I'm really tired."

She convinced him she wouldn't change her mind and he backed out of the room. We closed the door and jiggled the knob, checking the lock.

Maverick and Renegade settled on the floor in the middle of the hall. I conjured two dog treats. While they snacked, I took another gander at the coded message left for the kids before tucking it behind a baggie filled with one of my pet's favorite mini delicacies.

Confident the locks and protective dogs would deter any wandering, lecherous, vengeful men, we headed to the dining room. We clattered down the stairs as Lauren opened the front door and admitted CJ. He hung his jacket and joined us, giving Renegade extra loving.

"Where's Carlee?" CJ's eyes wandered up the stairs.

"She looked a little tired and wanted to take some time for herself," Jane said. She looped her arm in his and guided him to the dining room.

CJ nodded. He understood needing time to oneself.

The supper fixings Lauren set on the sideboard teased our olfactory senses. We filled our bowls and the bread plates before settling into the chairs and digging in. The chili had a little kick, and Lauren had elevated the cornbread by baking it in a Bundt pan and loading it with fat corn kernels and cheddar cheese. Condensation dripped down the sides of a pitcher of ice-cold water augmented with floating lime slices. She'd lined a platter with chocolate-covered coconut macaroons to satisfy any sweet tooth.

Lauren appeared at the conclusion of the meal with Davy riding on her hip. "Anyone for more?"

Galen, the food barometer, sat back in his chair. "I'm stuffed. Thanks. But can I put together a small sampling of your great supper and take it to Carlee?"

"I can do that." She returned minutes later with a tray. "When she's finished, she can—"

"I can return it to the kitchen." He placed a folded linen napkin over his forearm and nabbed the tray. Lifting it to his shoulder, he straightened and trooped from the room, looking like the *maître d'* from a three-star Michelin restaurant.

Lauren turned to us. "If you need anything, call on the house phone and I'll get your message. Reggie has a date tonight."

Jane said, "Where will you be?"

"Davy and I have one of the apartments in the carriage house." She laughed, curtsied with exaggeration, then vanished into the kitchen.

"Do you have any last-minute tasks for us, CJ?"

"I think I am prepared. I spoke to Kahula, and they are spending the night in St. Cloud. She is most anxious to meet her granddaughter." He rotated a tall glass in his hands. "It is time for Carlee to meet them as well."

It was coming together—the service, the family, the meeting, the remembrance, but unfortunately, not all the answers CJ had been looking for.

A tiny giggle escaped from Jane's side of the table. Her shoulders twitched, and her fingers flew across her phone. One corner of her mouth inched its way up into a smile. It had to be Drew. I felt a twinge of jealousy and pulled out my phone, checking for texts.

"Say hi to Drew for me and—" My thoughts exploded into a million tiny pieces as loud footsteps pounded down the stairs.

"Dr. Bluestone!" Galen's voice filled the foyer. "Dr. Bluestone," he yelled again. "Ms. Wilk!"

Kindra jumped from her chair. Patricia followed, frowning. I raced to the doorway and looked back to see CJ shove away from the table and drag himself upright. Jane had stashed her phone and taken a stand next to him, ready to act as support. He hopped the first few feet to get his bad leg moving under him and hobbled into the foyer.

TWENTY-FOUR

The muscles in Galen's arms strained against his shirt sleeves as he cradled Carlee to his chest. "She won't answer. She won't wake up." His huge eyes looked black in his ashen face. "I don't know what's wrong with her."

Patricia quickly fit the pieces of what she saw together and tapped Kindra's arm, signing forcefully. At first Kindra shrugged her off. When Patricia persisted, Kindra concentrated on the finger spelling, nodded, and said, "I'll call 911."

"Tell them we're bringing her in." Jane snagged jackets from the entry and headed for the door. "I'm driving," she said in a tone no one in their right mind would dispute.

CJ reached for his daughter, and Galen hugged her tighter. "Go. I've got her, sir." CJ briefly rested his hand on her arm, pivoted, and shuffled after Jane.

Adding the number of bodies and coming up a few spaces short in either vehicle, I palmed the keys I'd yet to return to CJ and said, "We'll follow in the truck."

I secured the dogs in our room, grabbed my bag, and raced down the stairs where Lauren stood, hands on hips. "What's all the commotion?"

"We've got to go," I said. Kindra bolted for the door. I tugged at Patricia's sleeve, tearing her attention away from Lauren.

My insides burned and I felt the tips of my ears turn red. "We're taking one of my girls to the hospital." I glared at Lauren and choked out the words. "She won't wake up."

Lauren gasped, and her hand covered her heart. I yanked open the front door and we dashed to the truck. A small receding voice called out from behind us, "Be careful."

The truck fired to life, and I shifted into gear, but my hands circled the steering wheel and came together at the bottom, numbing in a tight clutch. I had no idea which direction to take to the hospital.

Patricia increased the volume on her phone. She threw a questioning glance at Kindra who nodded, and the voice began dictating turns. I signed thank you and hit the gas. As we followed directions down Main Street toward the beautiful church, words of prayer tumbled over and over on my lips, and my eyes flicked toward heaven.

Our GPS dictated an unexpected turn. The truck squealed into the roundabout to the first exit, and I leaned heavily on Patricia, squishing her against Kindra as if we were on a Tilt-a-Whirl carnival ride. Scores of lights from our destination cast chilling shadows on the athletic field behind the Catholic school and illuminated the adjacent parking lots packed with vehicles. The girls jumped out at the ER doors, and I went in search of an empty space.

I drove onto a side street, stopped, engaged the parking brake, and ran two blocks to the hospital, jacket fluttering, heart pumping, arms swinging.

CJ just found his daughter. He can't lose her.

The doors whooshed open in front of me, and I came face to face with a glowering security guard. His right hand rested on his belt, threateningly, and I came to a screeching halt.

"What's the emergency?" he asked with a smirk.

Seriously.

Fighting words filled my brain but arguing wouldn't get me where I needed to go. I commanded the muscles in my face to unknot. "We just brought in an unconscious teenager."

He slowly glanced around the waiting room. "Ssshhhure." He looked at me, by myself, and raised an eyebrow. "Why don't you come back tomorrow when you're not imagining things. Everything will look better in the morning."

"You don't understand. I need to find my friends."

A voice behind me said, "I'll vouch for her, Bill."

Bill screwed up his face and peered over my shoulder. "If you say so, Rianna." He gave a snort, hitched the utility belt, and pushed through a set of double doors.

I turned to thank my champion. The woman in scrubs waved a hand. "Sorry about that. Bill's a retired truancy officer and not very trusting. He puts on a uniform, and he thinks he's got the last word. You're looking for Dr. Bluestone, I presume." Her blue eyes twinkled, and one side of her mouth curled in a tiny smile. "I'll take you to them."

I followed her, my heart thumping, anxious to connect with CJ and Jane, but she spoke in a calm voice and took measured steps. "We've hooked his daughter up to IV fluids. She is terribly dehydrated. I don't think she told anyone, but she hadn't been feeling the best and it caught up with her. She's undergoing tests but she is lucid, and we're fairly sure it's food poisoning. She should be fine."

Using such a calm demeanor, I almost missed what Rianna said.

"Should be? Food poisoning?" I squeaked. "How did that happen?"

"Actually, I was hoping you could tell me. Knowing this is the second bout in as many weeks, there has to be something at the White Star Inn. We may have to send in an investigator. Food is served on a regular basis at that establishment, and the kitchen must meet strict health codes. Any thoughts?"

I salivated, thinking of the continental breakfasts, snacks, cold meats and cheese boards, *Vomacka*, the chili supper, and the smattering of sweets we all tasted. Then my mouth dried up and I found it difficult to swallow. "Everything served at the inn was served on the buffet and shared." I even remembered Galen finishing Carlee's dinner at the restaurant Saturday night and the kids dividing a large pizza at the café on Sunday.

"Could someone have intentionally targeted her?"

"No." I shook my head, drawing in my chin. I couldn't conceive of such wickedness. "I know you can't confirm or deny, but if Lauren's son Davy had the other bout of food poisoning, and he ate something at the inn ..." I nibbled my bottom lip while I considered possible foodstuffs that could be altered or doctored or spoiled. "We all had the same food unless ... Maybe it's the candies." Her left eyebrow rose almost to her hairline. "It could be anything, I suppose, but when the housekeeper finished her daily cleaning, she left a candy on our pillows. Carlee's favorite were the watermelon taffies. Maybe some of them are contaminated."

Rianna searched my face, nodded, and reached for the handle on the door.

In the waiting room, Jane sat on an orange couch, fixated on her phone. Kindra's furrowed brow and intense set of her jaw reflected in the window overlooking the glimmering lights of the nearby houses. A sullen Galen leaned against the far wall, arms crossed tightly over his torso, face down, searching his shoes. In my peripheral vision, I saw Patricia hurtling toward me and prepared for the tackle. She wrapped her arms around me, tears streaming down her cheeks.

"I've got to get back," said Rianna. "We're a little short staffed, but if you need anything, you know where you can find me."

"Thank you," I said and steered Patricia to the nearest seat.

No one spoke. Waiting would be difficult, so I fished my debit card out of my billfold and ran it through the vending machine. Six bottles of water noisily dropped through the chute.

"Drink," I said in my best teacher voice as I delivered one to each. All we needed was someone else to suffer from dehydration.

The quiet minutes dragged on, until the door opened, sounding like an explosion. We all turned and took a step in that direction.

TWENTY-FIVE

I'd never seen stoic CJ with red-rimmed eyes, or a face streaked white with tension. Galen rushed him, breathing heavily. CJ reached out and placed his hand on Galen's shoulder before he collapsed. "She will be alright. She needs her rest and a night of fluids and will be released tomorrow."

"May I see her, sir?"

CJ shook his head imperceptibly and seemed to think again. "For a moment." He returned the way he'd come at a steady pace, towing an overeager teen behind him.

Kindra dropped into a chair. Patricia sat next to her and rapidly signed her questions. Kindra answered with deliberateness and a gentle reassuring smile. She grabbed both of Patricia's hands and held them together. "She'll be fine," she said carefully and pulled her into a hug.

Jane joined me and looped her arm through mine.

"Rianna said it was probably food poisoning."

Jane looked at the floor and her eyes crawled back and forth over the same memories I had, searching for something that would have made Carlee ill and no one else. She looked up and her eyes opened wide. "The taffy? She's the only one who wanted the watermelon ones."

"Maybe." I shrugged and wondered again about that Nicki person who made up the rooms, or Lauren who restocked provisions in the dining room, or Edith handing out goodies the first night we'd arrived. "I don't know if we can find accommodations anywhere else in town but we're not eating at the inn again."

Kindra and Patricia sagged into chairs opposite Jane and me. "We'll head back as soon as Galen returns," I said gently.

Catching the defiance burning in Kindra's eyes and her flaring nostrils, I said, "We can't do anything for Carlee here. Her dad will stay with her, but ..." I leaned forward and whispered. "Maybe we can figure out what made her sick."

"And we want to make sure everything runs smoothly for the memorial," Jane added. "We can take that off their plate, and we can be available to greet the grands."

Patricia said, "Great idea." Although thirteen months younger than Kindra, she paid rapt attention to what went on around her and understood with more maturity than most adults possessed. She finished off her bottle of water and deposited it in the recycle bin. Kindra followed her lead and we pretended to patiently wait for an update from CJ and Galen.

When the door opened, I jumped to attention. Galen's cheeks had a touch of color though I could still see deep into his enormous eyes, filled with the residual fear of what might have happened. His hands swung freely at his side and one corner of his lip curled up.

CJ followed, wearing a tight smile. He leaned heavily on his cane, rubbing his thumb over the dog sculpted into gray-and-black resin at the top. "I am staying the night. Expect a call in the morning. Kahula knows about Carlee, and they will most likely appear earlier than expected. Rianna has a breakfast reservation for all of us here in the cafeteria at eight. Get rest." The truck keys dangled from my fingers. He held out an open palm, and I dropped them in. He reached out, squeezed Galen's shoulder, nodded, and disappeared through the doors again.

"She said I was a dork." Galen beamed as we followed the red exit lights into the night. "She told me to be prepared to lose my arm-wrestling title."

Jane herded the kids, letting them move at a snail's pace. The locks on her Edge chirped and we climbed inside. Before she turned the key, we all took a huge cleansing breath.

I texted Pete the scant information we had about Carlee and received an immediate response.

Call you as soon as I have a free moment.

The silent ride provided time to pray. With only a thin sliver of moon to get in the way, we gazed at the glittering sky, mesmerized. Jane jammed the Edge into park at the bottom of the hill in front of the inn and one by one we climbed from the vehicle. She pointed out the Big Dipper, the Little Dipper, Orion, Canis Major, Cassiopeia, and Sirius, which led to a chat about astronomy and astrology.

My phone buzzed. I answered and stepped away, careful not to break into sobs. "Hi, Pete. CJ is staying with Carlee at the hospital tonight. Apparently, she'd not been feeling well and hadn't told anyone. She was dehydrated, but they have it under control."

Jane and the kids started up the hill.

"And they think it was food poisoning? Do you need me there?"

I almost jumped all over that with a huge yes, then remembered how tired he looked the last time I saw him— the red rims and dark circles under his eyes, his mussed hair, the sagging wrinkled scrubs—and squelched my selfish answer.

"CJ said she'll be released tomorrow. I think we're okay. But I'll tell him. He'll probably want to talk to you." I had a fleeting image of a Frenchwoman hanging on his every word and almost changed my answer.

"He's calling now. Gotta go."

"Miss you," I said to empty air, and my eyes wandered halfway up the hill where the kids and Jane congregated in a small bunch. The inn sat in complete darkness, and I scurried after them.

"Someone's up there on the porch," Galen hissed, pointing at the front of the manor. We trudged up the hill, and Patricia was the first to shine her light on the sheriff's tense face.

He raised his hand in greeting. "I heard about the food poisoning and thought I should get over here as fast as I could. You never know what someone might do with the evidence. No one answered. I figured you were all at the hospital, and I thought I'd wait, but I guess I snoozed a bit. I didn't mean to frighten you."

"Your timing is impeccable." I thought for a moment before guessing correctly. "Rianna told you?" He nodded. "She's your wife." He nodded again. "You married up. *She's* delightful."

"I'd like to search the kitchen and dining room," said Sheriff Zasko. Galen bounded up the stairs. He fitted his key in the lock and opened the door at the same time the sheriff said, "Wait."

With the door open, I could hear the exasperated barking more easily. I hopped onto the porch and raced in front of Galen so I could find out what had happened to my dog.

I heard another, "Wait," but couldn't stop myself. I ran my hand up and down the wall next to the door hoping to brush against the switch but found nothing. The window at the landing let in just enough light for me to see where the stairs began and illuminate the plastic rectangle of the foyer control panel. I took long strides across the wooden floor and flicked the switches. Nothing happened. The lights weren't merely turned off.

"The power's out," I shouted over my shoulder. I flipped on my phone light and mounted the steps two at a time, calling to the dogs, "I'm coming, Mav. Easy, Renegade." I dug in my pocket and extracted the room key before sailing down the hall. Nails scraped against the door, and this time I didn't care. I turned the key in the lock and released the barrage of wagging tails and prancing paws. Dropping to my knees put me at just the right height for nuzzling and the tickling tongue-lashing I'd earned, and I giggled.

After a loud pop, the hall light flickered to life, and I wriggled to standing. I ducked inside and grabbed the leashes. "C'mon you two. We've got people waiting."

The dogs, eager for more petting and maybe a treat or two, slalomed down the stairs like seasoned skiers, reminding me I needed to check in with Dad.

By the time I joined them, Jane corralled the exhausted kids and led them to the steps. "Sheriff Zasko turned the power on, but we all need to get some rest."

"Breakfast at eight. Goodnight," I said and waved at the slow-moving troop. "I'll be up soon."

A short trip outdoors would be in order. I snared the collars on the moving targets, clipped on the leashes, and started for the entry, but Maverick and Renegade had other ideas. They yipped and I couldn't get them to move. No matter how much I bribed, cajoled, coaxed, and pulled they stayed glued to a spot in front of the living room doors.

I slid the doors apart. "Hello." No one answered. "See. Nothing." I hit the switch on the wall and pursed my lips.

Drat. Right again, clever canines. The room had been upended.

Maverick and Renegade bustled inside and dragged me through the chaos. The room was warm, and I unbuttoned my jacket. Instead of the usual roaring fire, however, tiny remains of orange and red embers crackled and dropped through the fireplace grate. A poker handle clattered to the hearth, and I jumped. Feather light ashes drifted into the air. I grabbed the ring at the end of the tool and hung it on the hook, brushing aside dark fur on the ground lest it ignite. Gathering scattered and torn papers littering the floor, I noted the words, "Marital Settlement Agreement" emblazoned across the top. As I shuffled them together, a black, plastic circle slid into my palm. I aligned the pages with the corner of the registration counter, planning to use what I thought might be a lens cap as a paperweight. The dogs wriggled anxiously, so I pocketed the plastic disk as my foot kicked a familiar wooden box. I stooped to pick it up. Jane's gift to me had finely detailed blue edges. This similar box sported dark green corners. Always one for a puzzle solution, I followed the strange clues on the bottom as I had with Jane's gift and smiled as the front face slid to the side.

Folded papers exploded from the packed interior. I hastily retrieved them and stuffed them back inside the rectangle, shimmying them back and forth between a stack of envelopes. I secured the lid and took a few steps to the sculpted mantelpiece. Positioning the box at a precise forty-five-degree angle to the back wall, I hoped to draw on my nearly non-existent artistic gene and make it appear as an embellishment. Stepping back to appreciate its placement, something crunched beneath my foot. Shards of bright-pink stick-on fingernail adhered to my shoe. I plucked off the pieces and placed them next to the box. That's when I detected a deep gouge in the otherwise unmarked finish of the frieze. My thumb brushed away tiny new paint chips and teeny gritty splinters and noticed a second chip chiseled from the surrounding marble apron.

Maverick yipped. I turned and slipped in liquid pooled on the floor near an end table on which lay an empty glass turned on its side. The smoky odor of Scotch wafted in the air. A mountainous sandwich of meats, cheeses, and Lauren's signature banana peppers perched precariously on a plate.

Following the dogs' stares, I asked, "Are you hungry? Let's get a snack."

Maverick sat. Renegade sat. They wouldn't budge so I surveyed the rest of the room.

Two pots from among the sea of lilies had tipped over, spilling dirt and white dots of vermiculite on the table. I tidied the mess, stood the flowers upright, and kicked over a purple and white gallon jug of an herbicide. I righted the jug and exposed three pieces of wrapped taffy. I tentatively picked up the candy to transfer to Sheriff Zasko, turned, and gasped.

A balding pate glistened through sparse strands of steel gray and rested against the overstuffed chair in the bay window.

"Good evening," I said. I took tentative steps, afraid of frightening the sleeping man. "I don't mean to bother you, but the power's running again." I rounded the chair and reached out to wake the man, but my hand stopped in midair.

Sheriff Zasko called from the hallway. "I found the circuit breaker. Everything should be fine now."

I blinked and hurried to the dogs. Burying my face in Maverick's neck, I mumbled, "Not by a long shot."

TWENTY-SIX

I gripped the dogs' collars and sank to the floor. "Sheriff." I cleared my gravelly throat and wiped a tear from my eye. "Sheriff," I said louder.

"What is it now?" He sounded tired and a bit annoyed as he marched through the open doors, brushing cobwebs from his chin and hands, scowling. "They need to clean that basement." I'm not sure what he saw in my face, but he asked with uncharacteristic gentleness, "What is it, Katie?"

I swallowed what felt like a dust ball the size of a watermelon and couldn't spit out the words. My teeth chattered, and my finger trembled as I pointed. His eyes did a thorough sweep of the room, coming to rest on the shape seated in the alcove.

Sheriff Zasko advanced around the chair to confront

the victim. His features fell. He removed his hat. "Oh, Willy."

He slapped his hat back on his head and took a deep breath. He retrieved his phone and pushed its buttons. "This is Zasko. I'm going to need a crime scene unit at the White Star Inn." He listened and, fuming, punched out each word in his answer. "Yes, I'd call a body with a gunshot wound a suspicious death." He huffed and pocketed his phone.

He took two steps to stand next to me and said, "Katie, we need to get you out of here." He lent a hand, and I staggered to my feet. I shook my head, trying to erase the image of a dark-red divot in the man's forehead.

"I'll get the kids and Jane. We'll throw everything in our luggage and—"

"I'm sorry to tell you, we got a call from the Chamber of Commerce. They wanted local law enforcement to be aware that all the rooms in town are booked for the beer festival, so we'd be prepared. It's imperative you and your party remain here."

"What did you say?" My voice rose. "We can't—"

"We'll rope off this area from prying eyes, and I'll station an officer in the foyer as well." He barked disgustedly. "Willy's likely been here the entire time I sat on the porch." The sadness in his eyes colored them very dark. "You wouldn't happen to remember the time you left and if you saw anyone?

"The hospital will have Carlee's admission time. The kids and I followed soon after I told Lauren we were taking Carlee to the emergency room. Rianna might be able to pinpoint the time." I waited for a response. "Sheriff?"

His thoughts were miles away. He answered, glancing

at the ceiling. "Hmmm? Lauren. She still lives out back in the carriage house, correct?"

"I think that's right."

He rubbed the back of his neck.

I gripped the dogs' leashes and drew them close. They gazed at me with something akin to understanding. I cleared my throat. "I didn't see Mr. Zasko right away and didn't realize it might be a crime scene, so I started to clean up."

The sheriff scrubbed his face with both hands, groaning, trying to wipe away his obvious frustration. His hands stopped on his chin. "You compromised a second crime scene?" He inhaled dramatically. "What did you touch?"

I took a gulp of air, cataloging a long list of possible transgressions. "I put the divorce papers in a neat pile on the counter and the puzzle box on the mantel."

His brow crawled to his hairline. "The what? Whose divorce papers? Never mind. I'll see for myself."

I held out my hand, exposing the wrapped candy. He scrunched his face in distaste until I said, "Carlee's favorite are the watermelon flavored taffies. She ate the green, pink, and white ones. I don't think anyone else did."

He exhaled and said, "Fingerprints." I placed the taffies on the registration desk, and he ushered me out the door to the bellow of sirens. "You need to inform Ms. Mackey and Dr. Bluestone. We'll take fingerprints from everyone in the morning."

I started to protest.

"We need them to identify who's been in this room. Even to exclude someone." He jerked his head toward the stairs.

"But—"

He shook his head, and like the ominous finger-pointing specter of the Ghost of Christmas Yet to Come, he stood unspeaking, directing me to the stairs. I trudged to the landing like a doomed woman on her way to the gallows. I turned and called down, "Sheriff, I think you should check out the puzzle box on the mantel."

He looked at me hard and long and jabbed his finger upstairs as the sirens ceased.

My hands felt gritty. I smeared fine yellow dust onto my jacket front and finished making my way to the second floor. Jane answered my knock on the door of the girls' room with a hearty, "Come in."

Renegade bounded onto the bed and licked Patricia's face, causing her to giggle. She gently stroked the dog and said, "What's going on with all the pulsing lights outside the windows?"

I couldn't very well say nothing. "There was another death."

All four sucked in air. In answer to who, what, and where, I replied, "Mr. Zasko passed away in the living room, and the sheriff would like us to remain at the inn because there's really no place else for us to go. The sheriff will post someone downstairs. Are you okay with that?"

Galen threw up his hands. "Like we have a choice."

They searched each other for understanding and slowly nodded a consensus.

"This is surreal," said Galen, shaking his head from side to side. "How did he die?" My silence was understood too well. "He was murdered?"

I noted the dread on the sisters' faces.

"Could we have some canine company tonight?"

Renegade nestled next to Patricia.

Kindra pleaded, "Please." I nodded and she heaved a contented sigh. "It's late. I'll call mom again tomorrow. She won't be too happy, but at least we didn't find this one. What else can we do?"

"Stay out of the way." Jane's suggestion came with an accusatory glance at me, as if I didn't understand the words.

Although Jane was absolutely correct, I had to ask anyway, "If any of you saw or heard anything that put your guard up, made you pause, or just bothered you, please tell Ms. Mackey or me. It might not be anything, or it may be important. We just don't know."

Jane said, "Girls, will you be all right?"

Patricia hugged Renegade. "She's an incredible guard dog. We'll be fine."

"Galen?" Jane gave him time to think and decide if he would be okay solo.

"I'll be fine too. Are you going to call Dr. Bluestone?"

"That's next," I said, not relishing adding more for him to stress about.

By the time we left the room, Renegade had stationed herself between the beds and the door. No one would get by her.

CJ didn't answer. I left a message.

Maverick plopped on his watch spot in the hallway outside our room and gave no indication he would move. Jane's nightly conversation with Drew required a bit of finessing. I donned sweats and pulled the linen off the bed and into the hall to join my dog. The floor wouldn't be any less comfortable than worrying about the kids with my eyes open wide, lying awake in the bed, listening to every little sound in the creaky old house. I checked the late, or rather early hour on my phone, and didn't set an alarm. Maverick would wake me in a few hours.

Jane finished murmuring her unending litany of sweet nothings into her mouthpiece and stuck her head out the door.

"Did he read you the riot act?" I asked.

"Scarier. He didn't say a word." She rolled her eyes. "Come on back in. You don't need to stay out here."

"I won't sleep well anyway," I said. Jane frowned. "You don't have to join me, Jane. I've got Maverick to give me a heads up if anyone creeps around on the second floor, and I can keep an eye on Galen as well."

"Sheriff Zasko assigned an officer to stay downstairs, right?"

"But I feel responsible for the kids and you. I'll feel better if I don't leave you all unattended."

She dropped to the floor and pulled her knees up with one hand while petting Maverick with the other. "You're my best friend, Katie." Her fingers drummed his collar. "But even though I'm exhausted, I don't think I'm going to sleep on this floor."

"I wouldn't dream of it. Go to bed, Jane."

"Yell if you need anything." My head dropped forward, and my shoulders shook with nervous laughter. "Katie, promise me you'll call me if you need me," she said and stood, all hint of hilarity gone.

I sucked in a breath, chewing on the insides of my cheeks to sound solemn. "Yes, Mother, dearest."

She hustled into our room and closed the door.

I rolled myself in the sheets and blankets like a fabric burrito and snuggled up to Maverick. I closed my eyes and a slide show of Pete flashed by on the inside of my eyelids. On high alert when he was in call mode, a text would wake him if he'd been given any chance to rest, so I let my dreams take over, and I fell into a deep sleep until the keen of the lone flute roused me. The music maker was becoming more proficient.

I unwrapped the bedding and crawled nearer the bathroom door to hear the somber notes more clearly. Maverick found his way under my fingers. While I scratched his neck, I tried to picture who would take the time to learn to play the unusual instrument.

The mournful musings brought thoughts of Edith, Willy, and Carlee to mind, jumbled with a need to talk to the most important people in my life—Pete, Dad, and Ida. However, none of them would appreciate receiving a text before rising. My thoughts shifted to an unwelcome torrent of reflections concerning Ellen and my mother. Anger flared, but the thought of Charles and my promise to him as he lay dying cooled my temper. I would live a good life.

The flashing lights receded and the noise from downstairs finally abated. Although I found it impossible to get comfortable, exhaustion took its toll. All the energy drained from my body, and I drifted off again until my head fell back and hit the doorjamb. I jerked awake. The music had been replaced by strange words spoken so softly, I reached up, cracked open the door, and strained to forge a message out of the low sounds.

It sounded like, "If I can't … then no one can."

The peculiar music never returned.

TWENTY-SEVEN

One sweep of his warm wet tongue over my cheek brought me into focus. Maverick sauntered across the hall to the girl's room. Renegade yipped in answer to my furry friend's scrape on the wood. Kindra opened the door, yawned, and stretched, and I pinned my lips together to keep from following her lead. Renegade slithered out through the narrow gap.

"It's still dark-thirty. Go back to sleep," I whispered. "I'll get you up in time for breakfast."

Her eyes slammed shut even before the door closed, and I waited for the clunk of the lock before I took the dogs to the kitchen to have breakfast.

Deputy Gray sat on the chair in front of the living room and sulked, not anxious for civilian interaction yet. I threw up my hand in greeting as my whispered promise of kibble lured the dogs through the foyer.

I filled their food and water dishes, chatting idly to keep my mind from fixating on recent events. It seemed our housekeeping fairy adhered to the postal service creed: Neither snow nor rain nor heat nor gloom of night stays these couriers from the swift completion of their appointed rounds. Succumbing to the aroma of the fresh, warm buttery-rich pastries piled on the lazy Susan, I stared at the sweet roll in my hand, weighing the likelihood of its being another source of food poisoning and justified each nibble of the poppy seed kolache as merely a taste test. A cup of hot tea awakened me enough to notice the unexpected rain lashing the large windows.

Water dripped from a yellow slicker hanging in the back hall. I slipped it over my sweats and leashed the pups for a short foray into the yard. It wasn't quick enough for me to avoid the splatters of rain pasting my hair to my forehead and weighing down my pants legs. The dogs romped through puddles and splashed muddy water onto my face. Ya gotta love 'em.

We returned inside, and after shaking and showering me with more sprinkles, the wet dogs settled on the carpet near the oven, still radiating heat from early hours baking.

Following the long list of extreme instructions, I pushed the buttons to brew a caffeine concoction and texted Pete.

Good morning.

Good morning, Sunshine.

You're chipper.

My last patient was admitted at one and I slept the rest of the night. How are you doing really?

Should I tell him? I typed the first few words.

We had another death.

My finger hovered with indecision. He'd find out anyway, so I pressed send. And when my phone buzzed at the same time the water finished dripping, I answered the call.

"Tell me you're all fine. What happened?"

After he heard the condensed version, he said, "When will you be back?"

"As soon as the sheriff gives us the go ahead."

"Wait…" I heard phone noise and he said, "I've got to go. Katie, be careful. I'll call again the first chance I get. And Katie?"

"Hmm."

"I miss you."

The sullen officer sitting guard straightened when I balanced the fancy coffee and a sample of fruit-filled sweet breads on a silver tray.

"I hope you like coffee and rolls, Deputy. These came from the astounding continental breakfast fixings in the kitchen, taste tested by yours truly."

He stood and almost smiled. "Indeed, I do. Thank you." He plucked the cup from my hand and snagged the plate with the rolls. He took a huge bite. He must trust the food.

"How was your night?" I asked.

"This place was as quiet as a tomb." His eyes grew round. "I didn't mean it like that."

I shook my head. "No worries. It's been a strange couple of days. Is there any news? Was the sheriff able to speak to Lauren?"

Gray took another big bite, chewed with deliberation, and swallowed. "Sheriff Zasko will make an appearance by nine. You'll have to ask him."

Stymied by the officer, I returned the tray and retrieved the dogs for our trek upstairs. My blue-edged wooden box sat on the table tucked into the corner under the shadow of the grandfather clock. I thought I'd left it on the nightstand in our room, but, with everything going on, I must have moved it. Gray sipped his coffee and peered out the window over the tree limbs in the yard taking craggy shape in the emerging daylight. I cocked my head and wondered if Sheriff Zasko had already uncovered the contents from the green-edged box or if he needed help reading the clues to open the carving. I tucked my decorative puzzle hexahedron in my sweatshirt pouch to free up my hands and continued upstairs. My students would have fun trying to open it.

With hours to use up before our breakfast reservation, I plopped onto my pile of linen and wondered who could have killed Edith and Willy, and whether there might be two murderers. Edith had an edge to her. Ryker and team hadn't appreciated her disagreeable non-welcome but stayed at the inn regardless. A successful businesswoman might have ruffled a few feathers or aroused a bit of jealousy along the way and perpetuated the petty comments made by the catty women in the salon. If substantial, her assets might have played a role in her demise.

Her attorney, Willy Zasko, would no longer be around to help sort out who benefitted most from her death—her nephew, Reggie, her loyal manager, Lauren, the elusive Nicki, gold digger Irinia, Willy himself, or someone else.

And who would profit from Willy's death? His ex-wife, Kimber Leigh, needed financial assistance. Irinia didn't have a kind word for him, nor did her gossipy friends at the hair and nail salon. He and Reggie appeared to have a common purpose, but perhaps that was all for show. And it even seemed that Willy was acquainted with Ryker Chesterfield.

I buffed the top and raised the box to eye level so I could refer to the clues on the bottom. The squiggles were easier to understand the second time, and I slid the front edge of the box out of the way, unprepared for the onslaught of papers that erupted when released from the interior.

My box should've been empty. It wasn't my gift from Jane but an identical box.

I held the burgeoning pages, turned the stack, and read the title on the topmost one: Last Will and Testament of Edith Farthington. Bewildered, I squinted and reread the words, then searched the rest of the stockpile. Some of the other pages had jumbled combinations of letters I would've loved to decipher, but I slid the pages back into the rectangular space and turned it over in my hand. It looked like the same box. Where had the contents come from? I hoped Sheriff Zasko had opened the green cuboid and read the documents. When the sheriff returned at nine, I'd turn this one over to him. Meanwhile, not knowing where the box came from and whom to trust, I needed a place to keep it safe.

I ran various locations through my head. The empty hall provided no place to hide anything. Nicki and Lauren methodically cleaned and straightened the exposed areas in our rooms, dusting and vacuuming every corner. They'd find the box. My luggage had enough empty room, but I wondered if that would put anyone in danger. Ryker and associates as well as Reggie had easy access to every place on the first and third floors. I cringed, thinking of the sticky cobwebs from the basement Sheriff Zasko brushed off his face and knew I wouldn't go there.

I turned the box end over end in my hands, stepped into the pristine bathroom, and set it on the windowsill. After showering, I removed my toothbrush from its plastic case and squeezed toothpaste onto the bristles. As I brushed, I studied the vent near the ceiling.

I exchanged my toothbrush for the box and dug a file from my toiletry bag. I climbed onto the sink, praying my weight wouldn't tear it from the wall. Standing balanced, I fit the file into the grooves on the screwhead. At first, it held fast, but with the correct leverage, I was able to get one and then the other loose, and the screws dropped into my outstretched palm. I reached the bottom edge of the grating and flicked it out. The box slid inside, and I refitted the cover, tapping the screw in place with my forefinger. It would be safe temporarily.

My heart skipped a few beats and I nearly fell off the sink when someone pounded on the door.

"Katie? Are you in there?" Jane sounded exactly like Ida. "What are you doing?"

I carefully scrubbed my hands before opening the door. "And a good morning to you," I said, trying hard not to check the vent and draw her attention that direction.

"My turn," she said, slipped inside, and slammed the door.

My blue-edged box hadn't moved from the bedside tabletop. I eyed it suspiciously. When I finished changing for the day, I sighed thinking about Pete and I sent out a brief missive to Dad, and Ida. Ida responded immediately with a very short text.

Again? You aren't getting involved, are you? Nothing good ever comes of it. Don't start looking for trouble.

Dad's longer text said about the same thing and concluded with,

Be careful, Darlin'. Want me to come get you?

No, we need to stick around for a bit, but thanks, Dad.

I resolved not to get involved, no sleuthing, and crossed the hall to knock on the girls' door. Unprepared for the throat clearing I heard behind me, I whirled around.

Sunlight glinted off Galen's slicked back hair. He sat on the bottom step to the third floor. "I texted. They're almost ready." He smiled without the usual glimmer of playfulness. "Dr. Bluestone said he's having trouble keeping up with Carlee. He'll meet us for breakfast and then he's sure she'll be released. How do you think she got food poisoning, Ms. Wilk?"

"It's strange. We all ate our meals together."

"But she ate all those stupid watermelon taffies." He'd recognized the possibility too. "I hate fake watermelon flavoring, so I even gave her mine." He struggled to keep his cool, but he steamed with anger. "Do you think that's it?"

"I gave the ones I found to Sheriff Zasko, but I don't know. Have you seen any other taffy since we got back?" I hadn't, but I'd been otherwise engaged.

"No. I haven't seen any more and don't want to."

My phone dinged a few seconds later and I smiled at Pete's attempt to humor me.

CJ's texting to keep me in the loop. Right now, he needs you even more than I do. Take care. The week is almost up, and I can't wait. I'll call tonight.

Twenty-five minutes ahead of schedule, we checked out with Deputy Gray. He authorized leaving the dogs behind with him. They slumped to the floor with heads on their paws, blinking dejected brown eyes, accusing us of having fun without them.

Jane wheeled across town and parked near the hospital entry. Exiting her Edge, I sensed eyes on me. I scanned the near-empty lot and the Catholic school playground across the street but saw no one. I even searched the windows on our side of the hospital and still nothing.

The doors whooshed aside and Rianna met us, her cheerful face lighting up the entry. "Good morning. I'm so pleased you're here." She led the way, and my stomach rumbled at the safe, mouthwatering smells wafting from the cafeteria. CJ stood at the end of a table, waiting, Mr. Eveready, with a brilliant smile on his slightly less ashen face.

Rianna used her badge and paid for our selections. The eggs, bacon, cereal, fruit, yogurt, juice, coffee, toast, pancakes, and waffles we scarfed down could have fed a small army but helped us get ready for the day.

CJ headed for Carlee's room. We bussed our dishes, and Galen said, "Ms. Wilk, I'm going to help Dr. Bluestone get Carlee back. Okay? We should be along shortly." He leaned a little closer and whispered, "And I'd rather not be the first to meet the grandparents, in case they come before Carlee and her dad get back, if you know what I mean."

"Absolutely."

"Everything will be okay, won't it?"

I answered with all the positivity I could muster. "Yes, sir."

I certainly hoped it was so.

TWENTY-EIGHT

Lauren met us in the foyer. "I'm putting away all the fixings unless you want something to eat." She juggled a loaded tray from hip to hip.

"No, thank you. We had breakfast at the hospital."

"You and everyone else." She rolled her eyes, and I wondered what she meant. "It'd be considerate of you to tell me. I don't like wasting resources or time. And so you know, the food poisoning wasn't on me. I taste tested everything I served."

"We needed to check on our friends, but where did you hear about the food poisoning? How?" I sputtered.

"It's all over town." She pinched her lips together and said through gritted teeth. "I would never put my son at risk." She harrumphed and spun on her heels.

Deputy Gray stretched out on a folding chair in front of the yellow crime scene barrier. He tipped an imaginary hat and shook his head to indicate the sheriff hadn't arrived yet.

Jane and I searched for a quiet place to sit and talk, pausing before entering the parlor where we found Reggie and Irinia, sitting thigh-to-thigh on the oversized velveteen couch. They looked up. For a moment, she beamed. A stream of thoughts seemed to cross her mind and she hung her head. A frown slid into place, replacing the inappropriate grin as she continued to listen to him. When she tucked her black hair behind her ear, she wiggled her ring finger and flashed a glittering gem on her beautifully manicured left hand.

"Excuse us," Jane said, backing out and drawing the handle with her.

"Come in," said Reggie, popping up, and marching toward us. "We're finished here."

Irinia's mouth fell open, and she did a double take. It didn't appear she'd finished, but she sighed and rose with purpose, slowly smoothing the wrinkles on her vivid blue dress and shaking back her sleek hair.

"Are congratulations in order?" I asked.

Reggie's puzzled look morphed into embarrassment when Irinia said, "You're very astute. Sadly, our untimely engagement comes on the coattails of Edith's passing, but it's official."

He mumbled affirmatives and ushered her from the room. The door closed with a snick.

"That's a lot to take in," said Jane. "What do you think?"

Before I could answer, Galen's voice boomed from the foyer. "We're back."

We left the parlor and chuckled at Gray's futile attempt

to calm the dogs, culminating with nails clacking and scraping across the tile, bounding and barking, until they heard a shrill whistle and immediately settled.

The tap of the cane preceded CJ's entrance. He stood in the doorway, crossed his arms, and fixed love-filled eyes on his daughter. Kindra and Patricia appeared on the landing. Carlee's smile lit the room. She walked across the foyer with her arm looped through Galen's and waved at us with her other hand. "I've got to get ready for my grandparents' visit," she said and disappeared upstairs.

"She looks great." Jane threaded her arm through CJ's.

"She does." He beamed.

Sheriff Zasko knocked on the door behind CJ and Jane. They turned and stepped to the side. "Good morning, folks. We'd like to take fingerprints from everyone. Procedure, you know." He removed his hat. "Dr. Bluestone, do you have a minute?"

He escorted CJ to the dining room and closed the door. Jane looked to Deputy Gray for some kind of answer as he unpackaged what he needed to fulfill his duty. He pursed his lips and shrugged.

After Gray took my fingerprints, I dashed upstairs to the bathroom, removed the vent, and panicked for a second when I had to root around for the box because it had slipped farther into the air duct. I cradled the box in my arm and returned to the foyer. Jane tilted her head quizzically but within a few seconds, the door slid to the side and CJ emerged, sans smile. He raised his chin, gritted his teeth, and lowered his shoulders. He exhaled slowly. "I am relieved Carlee is better, but it was not food poisoning. It was deliberate. They found the taffy favored by Carlee and Edith, and most likely Davy too, doctored with an herbicide.

Zasko remained seated at the table, turning pages in a small notebook, and scribbling. I approached him with trepidation. "Sheriff?"

"Katie, I'm very busy. Be quick."

I placed the box on the table in front of him. "When you opened it—"

"Not another one. The confetti blew all over. I didn't find it particularly funny." He frowned.

"Confetti?" I squinted, as if it could help me understand. "Don't you think the last will and testament is important?"

"What are you talking about?" He tossed his pen and leaned back in the chair. "Tiny bits of paper do not a will make."

I picked up the box and examined each of the sides. Once again following the encoded instructions on the bottom, I slid the front face to one side. I peeled off the topmost page—the last will and testament of Edith Farthington—and flattened it out in front of the sheriff.

His eyes opened wide, and he raised one eyebrow. He extracted and donned nitryl gloves and gave me a look, as if I'd disappointed him again by tainting the evidence. He perused the paper and dropped his head in his hand. He picked up the box. "Where did you find this?"

"On the table next to the grandfather clock in the foyer."

Neatness calmed my nerves. I nabbed the pen and lined it up parallel to the edge of the table.

Sheriff Zasko cast a baffled look at me. "Although it looks much the same, this isn't the box from the living room." He grunted. "Our technician is not very patient. She used brute force to open the box and there must have been a self-destruct mechanism."

"You never saw anything but confetti?"

"We did not."

"What about all the envelopes?"

"I'd like you to write down what you remember about the contents. However, this ..." He tapped the document. "Have you read it?" I shook my head, insulted by his insinuation, and a little angry at myself for missing the opportunity. He diligently removed the rest of the contents piece by piece and scowled, studying the papers, envelopes, and finally dumped a key on the table in front of him.

While the sheriff picked over the items, I wriggled to scan the words 'William Zasko,' and 'Reginald Farthington' on the cover page of the will but when Sheriff Zasko looked up, he narrowed his eyes, curled the corner of the will over his fist. and said, "You are free to go." He lowered his gaze. "And thank you," he added.

Dismissed. Again.

I chuffed, and as I headed to the door, tossed a comment over my shoulder, "Jane bought me a puzzle box yesterday when she was downtown."

The sheriff stood quickly. His chair squawked and scraped and tipped dangerously close to crashing to the floor. He seized the top rail to keep it from toppling and said with forced pleasantness. "Please go get Ms. Mackey."

Deputy Gray halted in his task of removing the yellow tape from the living room door and scratched his chin as I bolted up the stairs. I collected my gift, at the last minute remembering the other pieces of taffy I'd tossed on the shelf in the closet and grabbed Jane.

We hustled into the dining room to cool the simmering sheriff. Standing in front of him like recalcitrant children in line for a scolding, Jane exhaled loudly and dropped into a seat, waiting not too patiently. Sheriff Zasko had sorted the papers. One, a pile of envelopes yellowed with age banded together with a piece of yarn, and the other, random handwritten pages. From where I stood, words on the loose pages he'd organized on the table screamed *read me.*

He caught me craning my neck, attempting to unravel the string of characters in front of him, and luckily for me, Lauren appeared with a pitcher of ice water crammed with lemon slices. In her discontented haste to avoid contact, she sloshed water onto the sideboard and groaned. Using the corner of her apron to wipe the spill, she glanced at the boxes on the table. "Nicki does great work, doesn't she? She's sold them all over town."

Jane, the sheriff, and I stared at her.

"Wha-at?" Lauren said. Her fists moved to her hips.

"I need to talk to Nicki," said the sheriff.

Lauren shrugged. "I haven't seen her yet today. You should check with Reggie."

"Where's Reggie?"

"Around here someplace."

"Do you know Nicki's address?"

"Of course."

We waited. The sheriff said, "May I have it?"

Lauren rolled her eyes and smirked. "Here, just like everybody else."

Here?

"She has a room in the inn?"

"Duh. Third floor, end of the hall, through the sitting room."

We made a beeline to the stairs. Sheriff Zasko pointed at Jane and me. "Stay." He mobilized Deputy Gray who tossed the roll of yellow tape to the floor and raced after him. Jane and I exchanged glances, and we trudged into the living room.

"Where did you find him, Willy I mean?" she asked, scrutinizing the space.

"In the pink chair which is no longer here."

"Look at all the dust. Other than that, it doesn't look much different, does it? How do you think they know which fingerprints they need?"

I shook my head. The remnants of the sandwich and spilled contents of the glass had been tidied. My shoe scraped across the floor. I lifted my foot and found a single splinter of pink stuck to the bottom. As I leaned against the fireplace to dislodge the sliver, my hand brushed the marble and stopped on the new indentations marring the smooth finish. I dropped to my knees and discovered another cleft in the previously pristine slab. After checking the stone for residual heat, I slid the debris into a pocket. Wondering what could have defaced the frieze, I stuck my head inside the fireplace and peered up the flue.

I reached up and the tips of my fingers grazed a hard object blocking the narrow space, but my arm was too short. Knowing I'd already used up my free passes from Sheriff Zasko for possibly contaminating evidence, I searched for something to lend an assist and nabbed the poker. I shoved it up the chimney and extended my arm. I jabbed and hooked an object.

"Little lady, what do you think you're doing?" Sheriff Zasko thundered from behind me.

The words 'little lady' roiled in my gut. Not wanting to say something I might regret, I pushed hard and poked deeper. Soot billowed onto my face and drifted into my eyes and throat. I coughed, spewing ashes.

"Katie!" the sheriff blasted from behind me.

I blinked rapidly to clear the smokey powder blurring my vision while continuing my quest. I'd read *The Problem of Thor Bridge*, and it looked like someone had tried to mimic the juicy plot of Sir Arthur Conan Doyle's story. I snagged something and yanked.

"Wilk!" Sheriff Zasko bellowed.

A stretchy cable jerked back but I hung on and turned to face him, dragging my trophy by the trigger guard.

TWENTY-NINE

Sheriff Zasko recognized the weapon, momentarily massaged his temples, and shouted for Gray.

The deputy dashed into the living room and came to a halt next to the sheriff, staring at my face and hands. He removed item after item from his rear pocket, like a law enforcement Mary Poppins, extricating an evidence bag, marker, gloves, tape, notepad, the stub of a pencil, and his phone. Gray approached slowly as if I were strapped to an unstable bomb.

After he snapped a dozen photos from every angle, my leg muscles trembled and began to cramp. I said through gritted teeth as I held fast to the retractable cable, "I hope one is Christmas-card worthy."

Gray winced and his ears turned red. The phone

disappeared into his pocket. He released the bungee cord, and it snapped back into the hinterlands. With gloved hands, he took possession of the firearm, and bagged and tagged the gun.

"It wasn't murder. It was suicide," I declared. My legs gave out and I slid the rest of the way to the floor.

Without a word, Sheriff Zasko whirled, and as he stomped from the room, I thought I heard him mumble, "Not possible."

"What did I say now?" My eyes misted.

"The sheriff and Willy Zasko were often on opposite sides of the law, but the sheriff appreciated the fiery streak of righteousness in another Zasko." He completed reorganizing his pocket and asked, "How did you know?"

I gestured to the scrapes and ran my finger in the groove on the marble. "These weren't here before. After Willy shot himself, the gun attached to the elastic whipped back into the chimney and smashed against the stone, leaving this trail."

Gray lowered his head. "Willy and the sheriff fought like brothers, and this is going to tear him apart. It'll be difficult for him to accept Willy committing murder or suicide. He might not say thank you, but this should conclude the investigation."

"Do you believe Willy committed suicide?"

He deliberated for a moment. "Very likely. One …" He held up his forefinger. "There's a most disagreeable Kimberly, who is not his ex-wife according to the unsigned dissolution papers and has always maintained he owed her. Two …" He held up another finger and continued counting. "He spent four years investing the almighty dollar in his law associate, Irinia Holocek, and she recently accepted a lucrative job with another firm."

I felt my eyes bug out.

"Three, he'd recently reported receiving anonymous threatening phone calls. Four, his research assistant filed a lawsuit for breach of contract. And five, there is the untimely death of his longtime friend and business partner, Edith Farthington. And if he killed her, the future could've definitely looked bleak."

"What business did Willy have with Edith?"

"Aside from being her attorney, Willy invested in many of Edith's properties, and she had quite a number of holdings."

"Did he invest in this inn? As an attorney, he must have kept himself protected in case of her death," I said more to myself. "Were they romantically involved?"

Gray frowned and tentatively shook his head. He stepped to the door as another question surfaced, and I asked, "Assuming he committed suicide, why would he make it look like murder?"

"Some insurance policies don't pay out in case of suicide. Or maybe he didn't want to lose face. Or maybe he wanted to frame someone else." Gray shrugged on his way out. "If you think of anything, the sheriff will be in the dining room."

Jane and I were left contemplating possible answers in the macabre room. She cleared her throat, grinned, and pointed at my face. "May I?" she asked pointing her camera at me.

I rolled my eyes, posed, then went in search of a mirror.

The grimy image staring back at me from the glass in the foyer also belonged in the story of Mary Poppins. The ash only smeared as I vigorously rubbed at my cheeks and forehead, finally capitulating to its superior ability to adhere to my face.

As Jane studied her phone screen intensely, she knocked into the flower table in the window alcove, and I caught the teetering lamp before it crashed to the ground. "Drew texted back F-u-l-i-g-i-n-o-u-s?" she read. "What do you think it means? Sometimes he drives me nuts." I peered over her shoulder and pursed my lips, reading Drew's smart-alecky response as if he'd heard every word.

It means sooty.

When we met Drew, he acted so full of himself, wielding his multi-syllabic word of the week, I put him in the disturbed pile, but he'd been using just one of his many undercover personae. He started the school year as a communications teacher with the gallant intention to break up a drug ring infiltrating our school. Now I accepted my best friend's fiancé, foibles and all.

"We should check on the kids," said Jane, raising an eyebrow and pocketing her phone.

Gray came out of the library, arms filled with another decorative box and a stack of file folders. He lowered his eyes, avoiding any interchange, and tramped past us. A second uniformed officer, carrying a similar load, followed him.

I sighed. "What was I thinking?"

"You were thinking about the tragic loss of life, whether done at the hands of another or self-inflicted. Let's find CJ." We linked arms, and she guided me across the foyer, past the open door of the dining room. I peeked at Gray and Zasko huddled over the table, jabbing at various stacks of papers, organizing their data, and recording their findings in the notebooks in front of them. We found everyone in the parlor—the dogs, CJ, the girls, and Galen lightly patting Carlee's back.

"What's wrong?" I knelt in front of her and searched her ashen face. "Are you feeling okay?"

Carlee nodded and it sounded like she wanted to answer but couldn't. She examined my face, threw back her head, and let out a hearty laugh. "Oh, Ms. Wilk. Only you."

If she could've seen beneath the soot, she'd have probably seen bright red.

"We have to delay the memorial for a few hours," Galen said. "Carlee's grandparents had a flat tire. They'll arrive by two, and Father Svoboda agreed to begin the service at three-thirty."

I smiled. Carlee smiled back and said, "I was prepared to finally meet them, and now I'm nervous all over again."

"It'll be great. You'll see."

"As long as they meet *you* first, Carlee," said Galen.

Lauren knocked on the door jam. "It's a little early, but I have some—" She blinked her eyes and gawked. "What happened to you?"

"She stuck her nose where it doesn't belong," said Jane. "Again."

Lauren continued as if Jane's utterings were commonplace. "The sheriff has given me the go ahead to serve food. Snacks are available in the kitchen today. And the supper Reggie added to the inn's nightly offering, served after happy hour, will be *Zelňačka,* **a sauerkraut soup.**"

The air in the room stilled, and I glanced at the stricken faces around me. "Don't go to any trouble on our account. I don't think we'll be needing anything tonight but thank you, Lauren. We have so many things going on today, and the times are fluctuating, we can take care of our own dinner."

Her lips flattened and she squinted. "Are you thinking of skipping breakfast again tomorrow?" she asked testily. "Not eating the food we provide doesn't change the room rates."

"That is understood," CJ said. "May we let you know this evening after our memorial? Hopefully the rest of our party will have arrived safely."

Her face softened. "You've prepaid for the week, haven't you?"

"Yes, we have." Lauren's eyes opened after hearing CJ's peaceful tone. "How is Davy?" And he knew just what to say.

Her eyes lit up. "My angel is doing great. Thanks for asking." She glared at me for a moment as if waiting for me to learn a few things from CJ before she headed to the kitchen.

Patricia and Kindra scooted together and lined up the pieces on a chessboard. Jane's busy fingers flew over the keys on her phone. Galen's reassuring murmurings tugged at the corners of Carlee's mouth. CJ raised his chin, clasped his knees, and closed his eyes. Even sitting, he struck a stately pose.

I retreated upstairs, washed off as much grime as I could and changed out of my clothes when I remembered the coded message left for the kids and retrieved it. I read the words, and it seemed as though I'd seen words like them before. Through my phone, I accessed a number of dictionaries and finally found Giráshi. It meant 'to love.' The online translator spouted *tears*, *ice*, and *sand* for the first words in the message. I slowly cracked the code for the rest, and interpretation in hand, rose and quietly left the room.

I knocked once on the doorframe. Sheriff Zasko

frowned, but Gray said, "What can we do for you, Katie?"

"I think I might have figured out how to decipher the messages on the other pages in the box." I plowed right through their gauntlet of disbelief. The sheriff gritted his teeth. He squinted and dropped his head into his hands as feelings oscillated over his face. I set my decoded copy on the table.

Gray cleared his throat.

"Using the Hidatsa language dictionary and Code Talker decryption techniques, I decoded a familiar phrase. 'Tis better to have loved and lost than never to have loved at all.'"

Sheriff Zasko barked, "What's Hidatsa?"

Gray skimmed his phone, grabbed the pages and his stubby pencil, and began his own translations. "We'll get right on it. Thanks."

I backed out of the room and into a solid body.

"Sorry," I said, squirming under the hands on my shoulders, holding me in place. I turned into Reggie and slithered out of his grasp.

He snorted. "No problem. I'm heading in there myself." He saluted, walked into the dining room carting another file, and closed the doors.

I returned to the parlor and while I watched Kindra beat Patricia in a serious game of chess, Jane put a hand on my collar. Some of my tension leeched out through her touch, that is until she switched to adjusting the cut of my shirt. Ever the fashionista, she tried her best to help me overhaul my casual wardrobe and rehabilitate my careless dress. The hands on the clock moved like molasses.

When Reggie rapped on the doorjamb, CJ opened his eyes. He excused himself and walked out of earshot.

Reggie handed him a plastic sleeve of fluorescent green spheres.

"What's that about?" Galen wondered aloud.

After shaking hands, Reggie left through the front door, pulling it closed behind him.

If I didn't know better, I'd say CJ was trying very hard to look carefree and he wasn't very good at it. He spilled the contents of the tube into his hand and juggled the tennis balls in the air. Drawn by the unexpected and amazing skill, like butterflies flitting to vibrant blossoms, the kids rose quickly and joined him in the foyer. "It is time to take the dogs out to play. Carlee, you need color. Your grandparents will arrive shortly, and we want you to look your very best. We also want Renegade and Maverick to impress them so we must try to wear them out."

We headed toward the front but were detoured by CJ pointing to the kitchen door and the rear exit. "There is more privacy in back."

The nearest neighbor was more than a block away. Jane turned my way and scrunched her eyebrows into a question. I had no comeback, and we followed the pack into the yard.

The doggie yips and the kids' squeals of delight mixed with hearty guffaws reminded me of a birthday party. Dogs careening all over the yard to fetch the tennis balls elevated the mood and ate up some of the wait time until one toss crossed to the side yard.

Carlee chased Maverick. CJ, who rarely raised his voice, slammed the joyful mood to the ground with a loud, "Stop." Either Carlee didn't hear him, or as many teenagers are wont, she ignored him.

CJ stumbled forward and dropped his cane. He called

again and tripped, tumbling to the ground. Galen rushed to help, but CJ clawed at the sod and whispered, "Stop her."

Galen and I rounded the side of the house and rushed head long into the pandemonium. Ryker and his cronies had exited the car they'd parked behind a cruiser with bright flashing lights, shouting questions at Reggie. "What's happening now? Don't you think it's time we get a refund? This is not the vacay we were promised. We should have stayed where we were."

On the porch, Lauren rocked a sobbing Davy. "It'll be fine, Davy-boy. You'll see."

Maverick bounded to and fro along the path in front of Carlee, teasing, but she ignored him and stood transfixed, watching the sheriff march a handcuffed dark-haired woman toward the rear door of his vehicle. Mesmerized, Carlee trailed them to the bottom of the hill.

"Nicki, after all she did for you, how could you?" Reggie snarled before he turned and saw the crowd filling his yard. He waved his hands, insisting we disperse. "Go back."

Striding from the house, Irinia emulated the handcuffed woman's walk, holding her head up, and throwing back her shoulders. She even wore a similar blue plaid wool jacket. With her demeanor and dark hair coloring, they could be sisters. "It's about time," she said.

The sheriff turned to me and called, "Thanks for your help, Ms. Wilk. Your code decryption helped us prove Willy's murder was made to look like suicide. The retractable cable was a ruse."

Overwhelmed and probably not fully recovered, Carlee fell to her knees, and Galen beat me to her side. "What are you doing to Nicki?" she said.

CJ had limped from the back yard, leaning heavily on his cane. Seeing his daughter's crumpled form, he cried out, and I could hear the anguish in his voice. "Carlee."

The woman Carlee called Nicki had turned her head when she'd heard her name. Recognition dawned in her eyes, and they looked so much like Carlee's. She stepped away from the car, but Sheriff Zasko thwarted her forward momentum with his hold on the cuffs at her wrist. I watched as her resolve disintegrated. Her shoulders drooped. A husky voice unused to making sounds croaked, "Chantan."

THIRTY

CJ dropped to Carlee's side and took her hand. His eyes followed her gaze to the woman she called Nicki. He froze in place. The world stopped for the two of them.

"No," CJ whispered as the sheriff ducked her head and tucked her into the vehicle. Carlee curled up and sobbed in CJ's arms. Questions filled his face as he turned his tormented eyes to me. "Katie, what did you do?"

The lights pulsed and the siren blared. All eyes watched Sheriff Zasko speed away with his charge.

Reggie marched to CJ and stood over him. Steaming, his voice erupted. "Why do you think I told you to keep the kids in the back yard? They didn't need to see this."

Galen lifted Carlee from the ground. CJ ignored the outstretched hand and slowly raised himself. He towered over Reggie and narrowed his eyes. "You knew who she was."

Reggie recoiled and said, "Of course, but I never thought she'd killed them." He stomped to the rear of the house.

CJ turned and moved silently up the hill. Carlee watched him, and then called out, "Dad?"

His shoulders slumped for a moment, then he threw back his head, plodded onto the porch and in through the front door.

Deputy Gray stepped next to me, jostling the carton in his arms. "It's a good thing Edith kept everything so well organized. The key from that box fit the cabinet in the library and her records are meticulous. That woman ..." He nodded to the space vacated by the cruiser. "She had the strongest reasons to want Edith dead. And the sheriff was right. Willy didn't commit suicide. Love and money, two of the oldest and strongest motives on the books."

"What do you mean? Who is she?" I asked, not really wanting to verify what I thought I already knew.

"Her name is Danica Bluestone. You didn't know?" My head moved slowly side to side. "The language dictionary aided in translating some of the pages of a journal, and we were able to decrypt more of the encoded messages. She's been here for—"

"Seventeen years."

He repositioned the box. "Danica worked for the Farthingtons all that time. According to the notes we found, at first she appreciated Edith's support and assistance, but recently, she was feeling more and more like an indentured servant with no way out. She was taking a shot at emancipation and expressed her frustration to Willy Zasko, but it wasn't going well. The sheriff believes she finally blew. The journals would have taken a long time to decode without your help."

"But I didn't do anything." What else could go wrong?

A battered black truck ground to a halt behind Ryker's car. I recognized the tall, gaunt balding man, wearing thick wire rimmed glasses and a glower, as he exited and slammed the door. I'd had a fleeting glimpse of him once before when CJ and I searched for Carlee. *Could it have been five months already since their reunion?* His long black trench coat whipped behind him, reminding me of an undertaker laboring against the wind. His face darkened as he took in the tattered remains of our group, telegraphing the message that this was the last place he wanted to be. Carlee's grandfather opened the passenger door and lifted his hand to a petite woman, helping her to slide gracefully to the ground.

Her silver eyes flashed up the hill, and with her gentle smile, Davy's wailing became whimpers. Ryker and his entourage stopped their noisy pestering and beat a hasty retreat inside. A mercurial white streak in her long black plait reflected the sun. The braid fell over her shoulder as she cocked her head in response to the excited, yipping dogs. They sat and dropped flat to the ground. Another dog whisperer, I thought.

Irinia failed in her attempt to make herself invisible and avoid the woman's examination; with her dark hair and vivid blue coat, Irinia could have been a relative. The woman panned the yard and when her warm eyes found Carlee, she lifted her arms. Recognizing the resemblance, Carlee rushed to her, keening, "Grandmother."

Galen stepped next to me. "What happened, Ms. Wilk?"

"The woman Sheriff Zasko arrested …"

"He arrested Nicki," he said. "I don't get it. She's the one who chiseled the wood carvings of Maverick and Renegade. She's been so nice to us."

"I think Carlee has just met her grandmother." I spoke painstakingly. "Carlee is going to need your support. I believe Nicki is CJ's wife …" Galen sucked in a breath. "… and Carlee's mother."

Galen jerked back. "How can that be? She's dead."

"I think she's been here the whole time, but I have no idea why or how."

"What do we do now?"

I didn't have a clue. But for CJ to find his wife after seventeen years just to have her torn from him again was too cruel. What proof could the sheriff have found? And how had I contributed to the investigation? Why would Danica have killed either Edith Farthington or Willy Zasko?

I heard rumblings of dissatisfaction and turned toward the grouching voice emanating from a sour faced Kimber Leigh, tramping on the sidewalk.

"What are you gawking at?" she snarled at the older gentleman. "Where's Reginald?" No one answered. "He'd better not be ignoring me, or he'll be sorry. This could be all mine." She fanned her arm to encompass the hill and continued down the sidewalk.

The older man's façade never altered. He glared at her as if he could wish her away with enough intent. When that didn't succeed, he hiked up to me. "Do you know where Chantan John Bluestone is?"

The front door banged open, and CJ returned with a pack over his shoulder, his felt hat on his head, his keys dangling from his hand, and determination cemented on his face. He strode purposefully down the hill, pausing only to whistle. Renegade bounded to his side.

"Dad?" Carlee sniffed.

He raised his head and continued to his truck. "Stay with your grandparents, Carlee."

"Chantan?" the woman said softly. She reached out her free hand.

He stopped again. Without turning his head, he said, "Kahula, I failed her."

Her brow creased. She maintained her calming touch on Carlee and said, "Tell me."

He turned his haunted eyes to Carlee. "I am sorry."

The older man marched across the yard, growling, "Sorry? That's all you have to say? How dare you … you took her from us. I've been wanting to do this for years." He swung his arm with everything he had. His fist landed in CJ's huge palm.

I could barely discern the intake of breath as CJ forced the man's hand down to his side. He stood as still as a statue and fixed his gaze straight ahead. Renegade glanced back and forth, confused by CJ's stoicism and Kahula's perplexity, and anxious to take on the new adversary writhing to free his hand from CJ's iron grip.

"Paul, please." Kahula looked from her husband to CJ. "What is it? You must tell us."

CJ's eyes glittered. With a determined look on his face, he released his grip, continued on the path to his truck. The door screeched, and Renegade hopped inside. The truck roared to life and hurtled toward town.

"My dear, what just happened?" Kahula asked.

Carlee shook her head. "I don't know." Kahula drew her closer and held her tight.

"If what we've discovered in the journals is true, if it checks out, you'll hear nothing but praise from the sheriff." Deputy Gray panned the sky, observing the dark clouds swirling together again. "You'd best get inside. A spring storm can be a doozy."

"May I see the pages?" I asked.

"I don't know. That sensitive evidence is still part of our active investigation. Maybe if you come to the station and talk to the sheriff, you might be allowed a peek. But don't get your hopes up."

The sky opened up and we scurried inside to escape the pellets of icy rain.

I wish I'd never asked what else could go wrong.

THIRTY-ONE

Paul, Kahula, Carlee, and Galen huddled in the corner beside the grandfather clock. Galen kept his eyes on Carlee. "Sheriff Zasko arrested Nicki, but her real name is Danica Bluestone."

Kahula raised her chin. Paul shook his head. Carlee gasped. "My mom?" She pressed her tear-streaked face into Galen's chest and her shoulders heaved. Kahula gazed at me with a worried expression as she led them into the parlor.

Patricia and Kindra dropped onto the steps leading upstairs. They signed their entire conversation and I understood none of it. Lauren snugged Davy onto her hip and whispered something to Jane who nodded. Lauren tiptoed to the kitchen.

On the other end of the foyer, Ryker cracked a can of beer, and the hiss circled the room uninterrupted. He swallowed long and hard. "Ahh. That's better."

"Jane," I whispered. "I think CJ followed the sheriff. I've got to find him and see what I can do."

She fished her keys out of her pocket before I finished my request and dangled them from her pinkie. "We'll hold down the home front." Maverick sat at her right side. "See. Even your pup understands the need for emergency behavior."

I looked into his bottomless, calming brown eyes and scratched behind his ear. "Take care of them," I whispered.

Jane leaned close. "I'll make sure Patricia and Kindra talk to their mom. We'll be responsible for Carlee and Galen, and Maverick will keep the slime at bay." Her eyes trailed the four sleazy men retreating to the dining room.

"Thanks. I don't know how yet, but I have to help." I grabbed my coat and pack and darted out the door.

My GPS instructions took me to the police station instead of the sheriff's department. While I contemplated where to head next, I caught sight of CJ's truck parked next to a cruiser similar to the one Sheriff Zasko had used when arresting Danica. I parked Jane's Edge and slid from the driver's seat. My phone pinged.

Again with the **Leave** it. Someone's creativity was sorely lacking. I didn't have a clue what I should leave so I dismissed the message for study later.

The commercial building did not have an approachable feeling with its shallow brick steps and heavy industrial glass doors. I took three quick breaths, marched up to the entry, and pressed the security buzzer. Upon admittance to a sterile entryway, I pressed another intercom button and asked to see Sheriff Zasko.

"Hold on," came the disembodied voice. Seconds later, a signal droned, and I yanked open the access. I followed the one-way path to Deputy Gray, waiting in the hall, arms crossed, lips forming a grim line.

"You didn't think I'd come, did you?"

"I was hoping you wouldn't." He dropped his arms to his sides. "Follow me," he said, resignedly.

We joined Sheriff Zasko, CJ, and two police officers in a small conference room. The palpable discord in the room ignited when Gray conducted me in.

"Grand Central Station," harped an exasperated gray-haired man in a crisp blue uniform. "Who're you letting in now?" He threw a pen across the table. "You can't just go bringing in all these civilians."

"Officer," Sheriff Zasko paced and said, "One of the goals of our sheriff's department is transparency. We'll figure it out. This is Katie Wilk. She unraveled the convoluted mess in the notes among Edith Farthington's papers."

Perfect timing for my opening. "Sheriff, may I look at the pages again?"

Sheriff Zasko said, "No," at the same time the woman in blue said, "Great idea. Maybe then we can determine where our money would be best spent. My house, my rules." The staring contest ended in a loss for Sheriff Zasko; he looked away and nodded, begrudgingly.

"Rebecca Connelly," the mahogany-haired woman with bright eyes said. She reached out her hand. "Sorry we have to meet under such grave circumstances.

"Chief, I don't think—" the other officer began, and he stilled under her glare—a formidable opponent.

"You never do, Ed." She turned her nutbrown eyes

to me. "If it hadn't been for your astute observation, the words would have remained gibberish, the translation never would have happened, and the murderer would have gone undetected." Unchallenged by anyone in the room, she continued. "You absolutely can look at everything. Maybe you'll stumble upon something else, and we'll be able to answer the question, 'why murder?' more expeditiously. Gray, bring the cartons in here, please. We can examine the contents. Together."

CJ radiated intensity, and I couldn't look his way; I was certain I'd contributed to his heartache. I didn't know what I could do to make it right, but I had to try.

Gray and Ed returned, carting cardboard boxes with Farthington/Zasko written in wide black marker on the open flaps.

"According to Edith's notes, seventeen years ago Danica landed in the hospital parking lot—comatose, bloody, and septic. She contracted a severe infection, and almost died."

CJ inhaled sharply but stayed rooted in place. Gray positioned the box on the table, observing CJ out of the corner of his eye.

Ed dumped the contents of one carton. Four exquisitely carved puzzle boxes tumbled onto the table, and he stacked them next to a leather case rolled around some tools and tied with a narrow leather strip. He opened his palm toward the boxes. "Have at it," he said dismissively.

I leaned forward and ached to solve the puzzles, open the cuboids, and satisfy my curiosity by examining the contents.

Gray coughed. He removed the lid on the second carton, retrieved a tall stack of folders, and continued his story. "The notes indicate the unidentified patient had given birth, but no one could find any trace of the baby she called for in her delirium. The IV antibiotics eventually saved her life, but with one headshake from the doctor, Danica thought her baby was gone. She withdrew into herself and almost succumbed to her injuries. When she finally was well enough physically, the staff tried their best to help her through the trauma of losing a child. She remained heavily sedated and although her physical health returned, her voice did not. Her doctor couldn't determine if she understood questions posed to her, if she'd lost her ability to grasp what had happened because it had become too complicated, if she had limited understanding of what was going on, or if she'd chosen to forget."

"May we see her?" My tinny voice didn't reach far.

"I'm afraid not. She's under arrest for the murders of Edith Farthington and Willy Zasko."

CJ rose swiftly and stormed from the room. The throbbing in my head, amplified by the silence left in his wake, nearly drowned out the scolding officer.

"Told you," Ed blustered and shoved away from the table. He stomped after CJ.

"What possible motive could she have? Is there any clue among the notes you uncovered?"

A loud commotion took Zasko and Connelly from their seats and out the door. Gray turned his head away, tapping the paper on the table. I spun the open file and read notes about providing the tragic but beautiful young woman with a home and a job. Over time, it seemed Danica had accepted her fate, living with and working for Edith. I reached to turn the page for more, and the door clicked open. Gray's fingers drew the file onto his stack and closed the cover.

"Where is she?" Kahula glided into the small space and said quietly but with the weight of a mother in terrible pain. "I haven't seen my child in seventeen years. You will bring her to me."

Connelly guided her to the table. Kahula stood stiffly behind the black plastic chair next to mine. Connelly nodded at Gray. He left the room.

"I'm Chief of Police Rebecca Connelly, and you are?" Connelly said and tilted her head.

"My name is Kahula, and I will see Danica Bluestone now." She raised her chin and crossed her hands in front of her.

"Kahula, please sit." Connelly pulled out the chair.

Kahula's eyes lit from within. For a moment, all combustible material was at risk. She exuded incredible power. She perched next to me and patted my hand under the table but kept her intimidating glare on the chief. The clock ticked twenty-seven seconds, and the door opened again.

A tall, beautiful woman with straight black hair, strong cheekbones, and icy gray eyes entered. Danica's expectant look faded when she saw Kahula and me. She seemed to be expecting someone else—perhaps CJ. Her head sagged to her chest, and she lumbered forward, the dangling chains of the handcuffs clinking at her wrists. She trudged two steps into the room, and Kahula rose. Her fierce defiant glower silenced any comment. She opened her arms, just as she had for Carlee. Danica stepped into her mother's embrace and melted.

Kahula's palms caressed her daughter's face; her fingertips scrutinized Danica's long-lost chin, hair, and followed the line of her nose and lips. "My girl."

Kahula traced the tears coursing down Danica's cheeks. "I'm sorry." The young woman squawked the two words.

"Have a seat," Chief Connelly said. "Please."

Kahula settled Danica in an empty chair and took the adjacent chair for herself, entwining the fingers of their hands. She regained her composure and said, "This is Katie Wilk." She cocked her head toward me. "You've met Sheriff Zasko and Chief Connelly."

Zasko made a small noise promptly shushed by Kahula's raised forefinger. "Danica, what has brought us to this?"

Danica lowered her head, closed her eyes, and delivered her words on the edge of her breath.

"I thought my life was over." Her voice gruff from disuse didn't match her lovely face. "No husband, no place to go."

Kahula tensed but said, "And?"

"No child—"

"Your child is alive."

Danica looked up with resolve, and her penetrating silvery blue eyes met mine. I saw Carlee staring back at me, strong, single-minded, and full of love. "I felt a connection though I thought I'd lost my mind. I frightened myself with hope. She's the young one called Carlee?"

I nodded. A calm façade replaced the sadness in her demeanor and before I could wonder what we would do next, Zasko pulled a pair of glasses from his pocket and Mirandized her. He perused a long list of printed questions and opened with, "Why did you kill Edith Farthington?"

"I didn't kill her," she barked.

"The facts say otherwise."

"Then the facts are wrong."

"Tell me when you last saw her."

Kahula nodded and Danica answered, "Friday evening."

The sheriff removed his glasses and said, "Is this the same Friday evening Reggie proposed marriage and Edith told him he wouldn't be marrying you unless it was over her dead body?"

THIRTY-TWO

Blindsided, I blurted. "What? But Reggie's engaged to Irinia Holocek."

"Reginald Farthington's proposal was a standing offer I always refused."

If Kahula had been shocked, she didn't show it. "She requests an attorney," she said.

"Ms. Bluestone?" Zasko said. Danica searched her mother's impassive face and nodded an affirmation. "Then we're done here. Gray, take her back to the cell. If you can't afford an attorney—"

"We'll hire one," Kahula said.

Danica stood and helped Kahula to her feet. She gripped her daughter's hands. "We love you. We'll get you out of here."

Danica stepped through the door unassisted, head held high, purpose in her step, her mother's daughter, followed closely by the parade of Connelly, Zasko, and Gray. Before Gray pulled the door closed, he caught my eye and glanced at the contents of the carton spread across the table. I took it to mean, 'It's all yours.'

The door clicked and Kahula slumped back into her chair, the weight of the visit taking its toll. "It's up to you." She composed herself and closed her eyes; she could honestly say she didn't see anything.

I dug beneath dated spiral notebooks containing yearly summaries of business dealings going back decades and extracted a manilla folder. None of the enclosed pages would be allowed to leave the room but I'd been asked to help, sort of. I quickly fished out my phone and snapped as many shots as I could as I rifled through the dossier. The inventory included a handful of official documents— multiple copies of various wills for Edith Farthington arranged from the most recent to earliest, power of attorney assigned to William Zasko, legal forms, property transfers, reports, and bills. The sticky notes attached at the top identified the owner.

A second much skimpier file held Zasko's will, marriage certificate, incomplete divorce papers, police reports, and personal contracts.

The third folder bulged with the chronicle of Edith's life, the bigger events—significant correspondence, diplomas, a current ledger, up-to-date contracts, and a large copy of a family tree. I slid aside the monstrous paper and uncovered the short stack of unopened stamped envelopes held together with fraying red yarn. Each was addressed to Lieutenant Chantan John Bluestone, and either the postmarks had faded, or the envelopes had never been mailed. I cleared my throat, and Kahula opened one eye. I lifted the pack so she could read the addressee. Her eyes went wide. She squeezed them closed again.

I combed through the papers in the file. Gray had penciled the English translation from the Hidatsa dictionary on four encrypted pages. I snapped a photo of those as well as the yet undeciphered pages. When I peeled back the last piece of evidence, I did a double take, and my heart sank. I'd hoped for more. What could I possibly find that would be any different or any more helpful than what the Sheriff's Department had uncovered?

I closed the folders and stacked them neatly. My chair scraped the floor as I heaved myself forward, bracing my forearms against the table, and began swiping through the array of pictures on my phone. Zooming in on Edith's signatures, they all appeared the same—no forgeries, but what did I know? The figures in the ledger seemed to generate a steady income.

I skimmed Gray's decryption. *I am ready to take on the world, but Edith doesn't believe I have the capacity able to navigate the world on my own. I have to get away and succeed or fail on my own terms.*

Searching among the photos, I found a legal document dated sixteen years prior, naming Edith Farthington caretaker for an enfeebled female, recently awakened from a coma, impaired after an extended hospital stay, unable to communicate, in need of assistance making financial and health decisions, and identified as D. Curious, I consulted my phone for specific details regarding conservatorship.

The chair whined as I sat back and thumbed through the scant logs. Danica had suffered too many great losses for a young woman to handle and withdrew from the world. Although Edith made most decisions on Danica's behalf, Danica recorded her first entry on Carlee's second birthday in flowery, loopy, blue script. It only seemed encoded because no one knew the language of her birth. Perhaps she'd found a place to belong, an oasis where Edith's assistance proved invaluable, helping her navigate her new world. I couldn't wait to translate the latest annals because she seemed perfectly capable of making decisions and running her own life now.

Kahula tapped the table to get my attention. She'd unrolled a woodcarving tool kit and pointed to an empty slot. Her eyes were wide and shining as she re-tied the leather strip in place and slid the bundle across the table.

In one translated piece, I read about Edith's desire to have a family and she created one with Danica and Reggie. The Danica we'd met could've been trapped for many years, and not just financially but emotionally as well. She had a number of reasons to want Edith out of the way.

I squinted to make sense of some of the police reports among Willy's papers. If he fought to keep Danica in Edith's guardianship, I supposed she would've had reason to want him dead too.

When the doorknob twisted, I chucked my phone in my pack, afraid the contents might add fuel to their already roaring fire. Gray and Connelly found me seated quietly next to Kahula. Gray pursed his lips and raised an eyebrow.

"May we leave now?" said Kahula.

"Yes," said Chief Connelly, "But please make sure your party remains at the inn. We may have more questions."

Kahula walked out of the conference room with a spring in her step, her chin thrust forward, and a look that could make a grown man cower. The entire station watched as she marched, full of assurance, through the department.

"Paul could not open himself up to believe Danica might be alive. He will have to see for himself. He dropped me off. I expect to ride back with you."

I almost laughed. She was clearly used to giving orders. As we neared Jane's Edge, I noted the empty space where CJ's truck had been parked. Where could he have gone? What would he do next?

Kahula took my arm and climbed into the passenger seat. Only after I started the vehicle did she exhale the emotions she'd held in check. Her rigid backbone collapsed, and she deflated like a hot air balloon upon landing. I reached out but she said with a bowed head, "Go."

Our crew jumped from the porch of the inn when we pulled in front. Carlee flew down the hill, stopping abruptly when her hands slapped the forest green hood. Kahula's door opened with a grinding, and she slid to the ground.

Between gasps, Carlee said, "Is it her? Is it my mother?"

Like a telescope, Kahula zoomed in on Carlee. "Yes."

"How is she? Where is she? Can I see her?" The words somersaulted over one another.

"She's fine, and no, you may not see her at this moment."

"What are you doing to get her out? What can I do?"

"We're working on it."

"Not hard enough," Carlee nearly screeched.

Maverick stuck his nose between her fingers. She glanced down and scratched his ears. Flanked by her supportive friends, Carlee brushed aside her tears. "I'm sorry. I shouldn't yell at you. I know you're doing what you can." She sniffed. "Where's my dad?"

THIRTY-THREE

Kahula took Carlee's idle hand in both of hers and looked to me for an answer.

"We don't know, but we're going to find him."

Maverick stood and wagged his tail. He cocked his head and woofed just enough of an answer to raise one corner of Carlee's mouth in a half-smile. "I believe you," she said.

"We'll mind the store, won't we kids?" Jane and Kahula herded our brood back to the inn. Jane called over her shoulder, "You've got this, girlfriend."

Did I? What did I need to do next?

Maverick jumped through the driver's seat and took up residence as a passenger, tongue lolling, anxious for our next adventure. I climbed in after him but was more circumspect. Where would CJ go?

I read the time on the dash. If we hadn't found Danica, we'd be holding her memorial in about twenty minutes. Either way, a consult with Father Svoboda was in order. CJ might have cancelled the service, or he might have sought solace, but St. Wenceslaus Catholic Church would be my next stop.

Maverick panted, and his head ricocheted back and forth, scanning the main street through town. We pulled in next to the parish house, hopped out, and jogged the short distance along the sidewalk. A rotund smiling woman answered the bell, dragging the heavy door aside.

"Good afternoon, girlie. What can we do for you?" She dried her hands on the apron tied and straining around her waist and dusted flour from the tip of her turned up nose.

"Is Father Svoboda in? I'd like to have a word with him."

"Matter of fact, he is. Follow me, please." She swiped at the loose strands of tight gray curls around her face.

I glanced at Maverick. "Let me just put him back in the car—"

"Bring him with you," she said expansively, her arms circling and directing like a cowboy driving his cattle. "I love dogs." She funneled us down the hall and into a large office as she rubbed his ears. "Aren't you a handsome devil."

The massive desk dwarfed Father Svoboda. He rested his chin on his fist and concentrated on the assortment of papers in front of him. The housekeeper said, "Father, someone to see you." He continued to be engrossed, peering through the lenses sliding down his nose. She cleared her throat and said a bit louder, with a familiar touch of a reprimand in her tone, "Father Svoboda."

"Hmmm?" He tore his gaze from his work and my presence gave him a start.

"Ms. Wilk." He nodded to his housekeeper. "The Lord works in mysterious ways. Your friend already told me about the change in plans—"

"You saw him. Do you know where he is now?"

"Why, no. I'm sorry. I was preparing my vestments when he found me in church. He said he's located his wife. Alive. Such good news."

My attempt at a poker face failed.

"Dr. Bluestone was difficult to read. You, on the other hand, Ms. Wilk, are advertising a vivid undercurrent of adversity. May I help?"

"Father, we did find Danica, but she's under arrest." He cocked his head, waiting for more. "For murder. We could use every prayer in your arsenal and a good lawyer. Did Dr. Bluestone give any hint where he might go next?"

Father unfolded his lanky body and grunted. "Some days are tougher than others." He pursed his lips and stood slowly. "You might try the cemetery. When we initially spoke, he asked about a burial plot, and I told him there is comfort among the repose of our dearly departed ancestors. It is a peaceful place."

"Where do I find the cemetery?"

He picked up a pen and hastily drafted an answer.

I grabbed his crude sketch. The words "Go with God" floated behind us as Maverick and I bolted. We drove the few blocks north. I understood seeking consolation might have sent CJ to view Danica's final resting place, but why go there when he knew she was alive?

Maverick's barking began one block south of our

destination, communicating his uncanny ability to find a friend. We drove beneath the metal arch above the entry and followed the paved path to the domed chapel near the center of the large expanse. An angel mounted atop the green-tinged patina blew a soundless horn. CJ sat on the steps in front of the double doors under the Archangel Gabriel, staring. With his elbows on his knees, he dangled his hat from his hands, threading the brim through his fingers. Renegade sat next to him, her eyes fixed on her partner's face, watching. Our approach didn't trigger recognition from either of them.

We exited the Edge soberly although I could feel Maverick's excitement about to bubble over. "CJ?"

His eyes clamped shut like a heavy overhead door. I almost wished the ground would open and swallow me whole, but that would have been the easy way out. I sat next to him and ran my hand down Renegade's back. Maverick circled behind and dropped his chin on CJ's shoulder. CJ breathed deeply and laid his head against my dog for a moment before he said, "She's been here the entire time."

"She has."

"She left her daughter and husband behind."

"You don't know the circumstances."

He flattened his tone. "There are no acceptable circumstances. She was here."

"But Monica left her for dead when she took Carlee."

The wind whistled in the tops of the trees and a few dry shriveled leaves skittered in front of us. Renegade jerked, curbing her desire to give chase. I gave her a tiny shove, releasing her from her watchdog status, and she romped on the lane in front of us, playing keep-away with Mother Nature's tiny tan toys.

"She did not contact us. She did not contact me." His voice was thick and raspy, and he struggled to breathe. He broadcast a drive I'd felt—the need to make all things right in the world and not understanding how to best channel the energy.

"CJ." I took his hand, tethering him to this place. "Danica almost died." He attempted to pull away and I tightened my grip. "You may not believe me, but Sheriff Zasko and Chief Connelly have a stack of letters addressed to you. Edith told her there was no child and we both know that was not true. Monica Parks had her. No one understood Carlee had been taken but was alive. And Danica thought she'd lost you too. She had nothing. You never answered her letters."

With a flash of anger, he yanked his hand from mine and glared at me. "I never received letters."

"That wasn't because she didn't try. Don't you see? One tragedy upon another, one tiny mistake compounded. How long were you hospitalized after you were wounded?" I let that sink in. "Neither of you knew what had happened, and …" Perspiration collected at the small of my back. I resisted the urge to let my temper fly; it would only make everything worse. I wanted to shake him. "If it hadn't been for your wonderful, sparkling, intelligent daughter, where would you be now?

"Danica was put under Edith's conservatorship. When she awoke from her coma, she either could not or would not communicate. Her doctor believed the substantial loss of blood deprived her brain of much needed oxygen. Throughout her long recovery she lacked the capacity to make decisions on her own. The first sample of Danica's writing I found in the carton of evidence was dated on

Carlee's second birthday. What if Edith withheld the letters, never mailing them? Maybe she did it to protect Danica. Maybe she had selfish motives, but after time, even your forwarding address would've been outdated. When Danica was able to do things on her own, it would've been too late. She'd found a place to live here."

"She had her parents."

"You told me the last thing Paul would ever give her was his consent to marry you. If you had been in her shoes, what would you have done? She thought she lost you. She never knew she had a daughter, and you *do* know what that feels like. You can make this right."

His nostrils flared. His respiration increased.

"What information did you provide the sheriff?"

THIRTY-FOUR

I swallowed hard. "I directed the deputy to an online Hidatsa dictionary, and he was able to translate some of her notes. I hadn't realized Nicki was Danica. None of us did." I hung my head. "I'm sorry. What can I do?"

"We have to fix this. For Carlee. For Kahula." I almost didn't hear his next words. "For me."

"I saw Danica at the station." His mouth opened but no words came out. "Kahula has more clout." He almost smiled. "Danica is beautiful, smart, and perfectly capable. If she didn't do it—" CJ bristled, but I held up my hand. "If she didn't do it, we have to determine the real guilty party from the evidence at our disposal. The sheriff believes he has her dead to rights and may prematurely close the books on the murders. They invited me to take a look at the cartons they removed from the inn because my involvement helped seal the deal in the first place." CJ stiffened. "When we figure out who killed Willy, I think we'll also identify Edith's killer. They've got to be connected."

"Danica could not kill anyone."

I'd heard often enough that anyone is capable of murder given the right set of circumstances but now was not the time to bring that up. "I took photos of much of what the sheriff has in his possession."

CJ nodded. "Show me."

I reached into my bag to retrieve my phone when a loud, low voice boomed from somewhere behind me. "No dogs allowed. Can't you read the signs?"

I wheeled around. A tall man with broad shoulders and a shock of white curly hair barreled down on us. His stiff, stained canvas jacket rustled as he marked deliberate steps with a black cane.

"No dogs. Get them out of here." He halted and waved the end of the staff.

CJ stood and drew himself to his full height, leaning forward lightly on his own cane. "It is my fault. I went off to mourn the loss of my wife and did not inform anyone." He looked down at his shoes. I'd never heard a false word pass his lips before and I couldn't look at him for fear I'd give him away. Although, technically, he'd spoken the truth. "Renegade is our dog." Renegade sat at CJ's side and tipped her head, displaying a melancholy expression. The man didn't need to know that was her natural state. Her head tilt, as always, was like kryptonite to a dog lover. "They are training to be search-and-rescue canines and …" He nodded at Maverick who held a serene, intelligent stance.

"He found me. We are sorry. We will leave now."

"Search-and-rescue, huh? I owe them kind of dogs. One of them found my grandson when he was lost in the woods last spring, and I ain't gonna get in your way. Sorry I bothered you, but next time you should take the dogs to visit the cemetery on the west side. They ain't so particular."

"Thank you. We will leave shortly."

"Sorry for your loss." The man waved a hand as he walked back the way he'd come. We plodded to the Edge. I placed my phone in CJ's outstretched hand.

We sat quietly in the SUV, and he scrolled through the stream of photos. I took in the view—the statuary, trees, monuments, markers, chapel, and the peace and calm Father Svoboda said would be here whether or not we grieved a loved one. When Maverick licked my ear, I shook myself back into the moment. We would find proof Danica did not kill Willy or Edith—if it existed.

I watched as CJ paused to reflect on each of Danica's notes. His jaw tensed at Officer Gray's translations, but he didn't need the dictionary to register the accuracy of the words. He touched the screen, caressing the printed lines as he continued reading out loud. On what would have been Carlee's tenth birthday, Danica had written she couldn't even think of another man. She had rejected an admirer who hadn't wanted to take no for an answer, and she'd been a bit afraid.

"Did she identify the pursuer?"

CJ shook his head.

Over time, the succinct entries grew more focused. Danica indicated a desire to go to school or learn a trade, and she questioned Edith's rejection of her ideas. Edith repeatedly expressed concern about her unfitness and incompetence. Even so, Danica discovered a love of music. Edith's approach to nurturing that natural talent was to purchase musical instruments and self-instruction books. Instead of providing an avenue for outside education, opening doors, widening horizons, she isolated her in every possible way.

"She had no income but what was provided by Edith, no place to go, no one but Edith or Reggie to rely on. Edith utilized Danica's skill as housekeeper, but the staff was very small—probably Lauren, Reggie, and Danica. It sounds like she felt duty bound to stay, with no way to break out of the cycle."

I turned the key in the ignition, but before I shifted gears I said, "I'm taking you back to the inn. You've got to be with Carlee. She was anxious about where you might've gone, and you can't allow her to worry about both parents. She may not look it, but she's fragile."

He didn't speak. We were both lost as to what we should do next. In the drive that seemed to take forever, I cataloged the people we'd met and tried to decide how they might fit into the lives and deaths of Willy Zasko and Edith Farthington. I worked my way from the insiders out.

My fingers itched to check the photo I'd taken of Edith's will. I was certain I saw William Zasko listed on page one. He might have secured assets or control of some or all of her holdings. In the arguments I'd witnessed, Kimber Leigh acted as if Willy had something to gain from Edith's death and she, in turn, expected a windfall. Would Willy have come through and shared or would she still have been left out in the cold? She might have had cause to see both Edith and Willy out of the picture. I had to remind myself not to allow my dislike and distrust of phony photographer Kimber Leigh to color my feelings toward her, but her utter offensiveness sent her to the top of my list.

As Edith's nephew, Reggie had the most to lose and much to gain when she died. Edith hadn't spoken of having any other family. Though Reggie indicated provisions only for the White Star Inn, he might benefit from the division of her other assets. However, I couldn't conjure up a reason for him to want Willy dead.

Lauren might have had a reason to dislike Edith weeks ago, but she'd been effusive in her praise of Edith for providing resources to care for Davy during his recent illness. I wondered if Lauren would receive anything from the estate. Of course, then I wondered about the size of the estate.

Irinia Holocek. Her personality grated on my nerves too, and she hadn't had much nice to say about Edith before or after we knew of the death. With Edith out of the way, it seemed Irinia had a freeway to Reggie's heart. Or maybe his check book, I thought.

It looked bad for Danica. If a record of the circumstances surrounding her stay with Edith existed, it might provide valuable insight, explaining the bond that enabled Edith to get her to stay and motivations for her to leave. An account of Danica's servitude, voluntary or not, must be somewhere—how long Edith had been guardian, what skills Danica had lost or kept hidden, when those abilities resurfaced, and how she came to terms with her future at the inn? Reggie had been around during that time, working for Edith. Maybe he'd better comprehend the workings of their interdependence.

My itchy fingers no longer merely expressed my

eagerness but had become a real thing. I scratched the top two joints on my right hand and noticed a few red bumps. I had no idea what I'd gotten on my hands but briskly rubbed them and hoped the irritation would disappear.

I mulled over the last few hours, hoping I'd find some of the answers I needed among the photos from the cartons of evidence. If not …

"Katie?" CJ's concerned voice broke in. "What do I tell Carlee?"

THIRTY-FIVE

Y ou tell Carlee the truth," I said to CJ as I pulled up to the inn.

I parked Jane's Edge, and the kids poured out into the yard, following Carlee down the hill like a short row of ducklings. She marched to the passenger window and mimed rolling it down. CJ complied.

"Don't you ever do that to me again." Carlee's overwrought voice trembled. "Do you understand? I can only deal with so much at one time. I love you, and we will get through this, but don't make me do it alone."

Carlee teetered, and she might've buckled, but she lifted her chin, and the resemblance to her mother and grandmother was astounding. Strength poured out of her, and CJ capitulated to her resolute words.

She crossed her arms across her chest and raised one eyebrow. "And where did you leave our truck?"

CJ lowered his eyes. My face felt hot—I, too, had forgotten about the truck.

CJ mumbled his answer. "I had a productive conversation with Rianna at the hospital and parked it in the west lot. Then I took a walk." He looked up. "Perhaps Ms. Wilk and I can—"

"Absolutely not." CJ was lucky her jabbing finger didn't stab him in the chest. "I'm not letting you out of my sight." She took a huge breath, and her knees finally gave out. CJ flew from the vehicle and squatted at her side. "I'm fine," she said, trying to wave him away. She breathed heavily and wriggled to standing. Renegade planted herself on Carlee's other side, nose under her fingers. "I just have a few tipsy moments. Galen?" He appeared next to CJ. "Would you ride with Ms. Wilk to the hospital and pick up Dad's truck? That way I can keep my eyes on him."

Galen trooped to the Edge and slid onto the passenger seat, pulled the door closed, and bobbed his head, indicating he was ready for the quick trip. He gripped the grab bar above his head and swung his dangling elbow back and forth.

We rolled away from the curb, and a minute or two into the drive, he cleared his throat. He continued looking through the windshield as he said, "She's so bull-headed and won't slow down, but she'll be recovering for a while. I'm frustrated and I have no idea what to do to help her."

"You be there for her. That's all she needs. She'll tell you what else she wants." I watched him out of the corner of my eye. "You're still troubled."

He seemed to deliberate and chose his words carefully. "I liked Nicki. I can't imagine her as a killer, but I'm not sure I'm a good judge of character."

"You go with your gut."

"My gut tells me Nicki didn't murder anyone, but my head tells me Carlee's mom has good reason to be rid of Mrs. Farthington and Mr. Zasko. She worked hard at the inn and was locked into her job because of her finances, or lack of, and her deep fear of the unknown. Do you think Mrs. Farthington knew about Dr. Bluestone?"

I thought back to our check-in when CJ told the story about why we were here. "She might have realized the connection when Dr. Bluestone provided the circumstances of our visit." Galen looked like he had something else to say. "What more is bothering you?"

"I don't like those guys from the third floor. When they sit and ogle Carlee—" He inhaled. "And Patricia and Kindra, it's way out of line, and I'd like to put them in a wrestling hold—flat on their backs, begging for mercy. You'd think after you and Ms. Mackey talked to them, they'd leave them alone, but they're still making all kinds of suggestive remarks. I don't ever want the girls to be alone because those stinking scumbags are despicable."

"They certainly don't instill confidence. I'm going to do some checking—"

He turned to look at me. "You mean investigating, right?"

I had to tamp down the eagerness in his voice. "Maybe a bit. Nothing in depth. I need to know more about the people we've met. I also want to check all the boxes so Danica is not railroaded into an unfair guilty accusation."

CJ's truck stood at the farthest end of the lot. I pulled up behind it and Galen said, "I can help, Ms. Wilk. Let me take the truck back and meet you—"

"Not now, but I promise I'll let you know when you

can assist. Meanwhile, until we're allowed to leave the area, you'll have your work cut out for you. Carlee needs you for support, and Dr. Bluestone will need you to run interference."

He grumbled. "You call if you need anything." He stepped to the ground and said, "Meet you back at the inn?" I nodded and he closed the door, giving a two-fingered salute.

I pulled forward to allow Galen a wide berth to turn around, and my phone pinged with a text from Jane.

Are we at the ruling out stage of investigation? If so, Kimber Leigh held a live session with details about how her business account had been hacked with an apology to anyone affected.

How did you find that out?

I watched last night's replay. She performed her crazy, lying act for the entire time we were in the hospital. As Drew would say, her prevarication was propitious. She couldn't have killed Willy.

Darn.

No one will take my negative review seriously, even though we both know she's a charlatan. I wanted her to be guilty.

Me too.

But she might not be the one. TTFN

Galen honked. I slid my phone into my jacket pocket and followed him. He drove to the parking lot where CJ picked up the award winning Juicy Lucys and texted a question mark. I hesitated for only a second before texting back.

Perfect. You order. Get extras. I'll pay.

He answered with a thumbs-up, and we joined the line in the drive-thru.

I'll text Dr. Bluestone and Carlee, so they'll know to expect us.

Understandably, they wouldn't give Galen the order without the money in hand, so I was rewarded with the aroma of cheesy burgers and sizzling hot French fries and salivated as we completed our trek.

Galen and I toted the white lunch bags and multiple drink holders up the hill and into the dining area where our party sat around the table, patiently waiting for the delivery. Paul looked aggrieved, scowling at CJ. Kahula rested her hand on Carlee's arm. Patricia and Kindra tapped their phones, wearing smiles of contentment. Noting our provisions from an off-property kitchen, Lauren stood against the back wall next to the sideboard, frowning, until offered two of the extra meals.

"Davy's favorite." She held up the bags in triumph. "I don't suppose you'll be wanting breakfast tomorrow?" she said resignedly, accepting the unpleasant inevitable.

Surprisingly, half our party responded with a yes and half with a no. We were fairly certain the sheriff had collected all the taffy and there weren't any other offending foodstuffs, but we still hadn't determined how the candy had been tainted.

"Then I'll provide pastries and beverages."

Lauren fled the dining area.

Jane scrunched up her nose and whispered, "I don't think she's capable of murder, but I suppose she has to stay on the list of suspects with Kimber Leigh, until we can prove the alibis."

I was so caught up considering the possible suspects, I almost missed the fabulous flavor bursting from my burger. I chewed and a thought struck me.

THIRTY-SIX

Lauren lived in the carriage house and spent her duty nights there as well. If she hadn't been summoned by one of the guests, she would've had ample opportunity to slip from the inn, but she needed someone to look after Davy. That would be my next question.

"Excuse me. I'll be right back." I pushed away from the table and entered the kitchen.

Lauren bustled from the oven to her workstation to the stove and back. Possibly distracted with so much going on, I decided now would be the time to make my inquiry.

"Lauren, do you have any … Ah … lemons? I was thinking about making some fresh lemonade." She looked at me as if I were sprouting a second head.

"The lemons are in the produce drawer of the fridge

along the right side."

A knife whacked the butcher block cutting board and sent me into a tizzy. I jerked back from a vision of the recent murders, and Lauren tilted her head in a question. She proceeded to cleave a bundle of fresh herbs into tiny slivers and added them to the boiling pot on the stove. Trying to normalize my actions, I pulled the silver handle on the fridge and the glacial air collided with the aromatic vapors wafting from the steaming stew. My eyes closed and as I inhaled the savory fragrance, I forgot why I'd opened the door until I saw the bright peels, and decided four lemons ought to be enough to tackle my bogus endeavor.

"It's a lot of work for only one glass. If you wait a bit, I'll get out the juicer and help you make a pitcher of my best lemonade." Lauren brushed the small bits of greenery clinging to her fingers into the pot, set her utensils aside, rinsed the heavy blade, and dried her hands. She hauled the cumbersome juicer from the pantry and thumped it onto the counter next to the full bag of lemons and a plastic tub of what looked like sugar.

I tried not to shudder when she picked up the knife again. She looked me over, and rather than teach me the fine art of turning on the juicing machine, she handed me the knife, handle first. "Halves, please."

"Where's Davy now?" I asked with a nonchalance I didn't feel.

"He's with his uncle. Since Davy's hospitalization, my brother doubts anyone else can take care of him better than we can. Davy and I are very lucky."

"Do you have other family around?" Lauren froze and stared at me. "I'm sorry. That's none of my business."

We squeezed the lemons and added sugar and water.

Trying to redeem myself, I said, "That must be very

difficult. You're lucky your brother is able to take care of Davy. Does he live with you?"

"He's staying for the time being. *His* mother isn't happy with his life choices either. She makes me crazy. But his job lets him work from anywhere."

My head filled with questions, but I needed to tread lightly if I wanted her to continue talking to me. "What does he do?"

"Research."

And with a particular tone of voice and that declaration, she closed off my questions.

Lauren gritted her teeth as she poured the finished concoction into two clear glasses filled with ice, a curl of lemon peel, and a mint leaf garnish. She took a big breath. "Try it," she said with a knowing smile.

"Cheers." We clinked glasses, and I looked deep into the light-yellow liquid, spotting tiny bits of pulp and conjuring antidotes in case of poison. Lauren waited for me to take a sip before she shook her head and raised her own glass. I needn't have feared her foodstuffs. "Ambrosial." I smacked my semi-puckering lips. "Do I have to share?"

Lauren chortled and took a long look at me. "You don't fake well. You had no idea how to make lemonade. What is it you're really after, Katie?"

I set the tumbler on the center island and decided I rather liked Lauren. I was tempted to trust her, just not too far. "I don't think Nicki killed Edith and Willy. Do you?"

She sighed. "No, I don't. But someone killed them. I had the utmost regard for Mrs. Farthington. Although I know she wouldn't have made Davy sick on purpose, and she did everything she could to help him get well, she was a difficult person to work for, especially for Nicki. I think

Nicki felt she owed Edith for taking her in, but she was so sad sometimes. I never understood why she stayed after she started making her own money."

I perked up. "What did Nicki do for money?" Did I want to know the answer?

"She sold her carvings, especially the boxes, to the gift store downtown, and they always asked her to make more. She had top-notch skills and had been commissioned to create a few special pieces. It's funny. Edith must've been very proud. She bought a lot of Danica's puzzle boxes." She took a long drink from her glass.

"What about Willy Zasko?"

"I couldn't have cared less about Willy. He'd show up as another mouth to feed, another guest to clean up after. Our interactions consisted of refilling his plate or drink, or providing an extra towel, and then he'd complain about the temperature of the food or not enough of one ingredient or another in his glass." Lauren shuddered. "I never thought about it, but it seems Nicki tried to be absent when Willy was present."

Maybe Willy had made the unwanted advances Nicki had written about.

"Willy stayed here?"

"Never here. We haven't been open long enough, but he often stayed at one of the other properties. Before White Star Inn opened, I'd say he'd mooch off Mrs. Farthington once or twice a month, staying late after their business meeting to discuss her holdings. He acted like she was his only client."

"How many properties did Edith own?"

"She worked hard and did well. She owned a few empty lots, another bed and breakfast, a few rental units, an apartment complex, and partnered up in other ventures. A management company took care of the ones we didn't, but I think she sold off the apartment building and the B and B before she and Reggie opened the inn." Her brow furrowed.

"What are you thinking?"

"Willy Zasko owned the management company."

"Who will take care of the properties now?"

"I guess since Reggie is her nephew and they were together on this project, it makes sense that he might understand the way her business works." She swiped the countertop.

"How long have you worked for Edith?"

"I started working for her when I was a senior in high school." She looked down. "She even kept me on after having Davy."

Her brow furrowed and she chewed her bottom lip. "Irinia Holocek began working for Mrs. Farthington at the same time. She worked until she joined Willy's firm, and, as an associate, she knew everything that went on in that office. She might know what happens to the properties now. I know Mrs. Farthington had a will." Lauren blew out a quick puff of air. "She made a new one every couple of months and I was the witness for many of the ..." She looked down and it seemed like she was reading the covers of the cookbooks lined up on the lower shelf looking for the elusive word.

"Repetitions?" Math crept into my head. "Iterations? Revisions?"

One corner of Lauren's mouth crinkled, and she nodded. "Revisions. It seemed like she added and deleted or changed something almost every other month. I never knew what was in them, I just witnessed and signed the papers." She sighed and opened the oven door. "I'm going to miss the old broad. I sure hope Reggie has the wherewithal to keep up her high standards. I like this job."

"Do you think Reggie is in line to inherit everything?"

"I can't imagine who else would."

I remembered the words Galen and I had overheard her saying to Reggie. She knew things. Even with all Lauren's help and insight, I couldn't rule her out as a suspect.

Lauren turned back to the stove, and I lifted the pitcher of nectar, but we both jumped when the door banged open.

THIRTY-SEVEN

J eepers, Jane. I thought something bad happened."

"I was wondering what took you so long." Jane pouted as she dabbed at the sticky beverage sloshed over my hands and shirt. "Sorry."

"No harm done. Thankfully, there is still enough lemonade, which I helped make with my own two hands—" Lauren snorted, and I smiled. "For everyone to get a taste."

Jane grabbed the goblets Lauren offered and held the door for me. CJ sat at one end of the table with Renegade's head in his lap. A sullen Paul and a proud Kahula sat at the opposite end.

"The kids escaped. Wish I could," said Paul, glaring at CJ.

Jane poured the lemonade and duly impressed me

by topping off the beverages with Lauren's decorative garnishes. I delivered the beverages and we sipped and sat in silence until Carlee rushed in, her friends close on her heels.

"Dad, how do you do this?" She handed him another decorative puzzle box. He turned it over to read the clues on the bottom. I heard a gasp, and the box was snatched from his hands.

"Where did you get this?" Paul demanded.

Paul could not have been prepared for the depth of Carlee's spunk. She seized it back and said, "Ask nicely, and I might tell you."

"Carlee," CJ said softly. "This is your grandfather."

"I have no time for niceties. If he can't show some civility, I ask that he leave me alone."

Paul's mouth formed a big oh, and Kahula began to chortle. "She is the spitting image of her mother, is she not, *grandfather*."

Paul slowly raised his chin and said, "I made these when Dan … my daughter was young. May I see it?" He held out a hand. "Please?"

Carlee sought confirmation from CJ who nodded solemnly, but only once. Paul examined the bottom face and deftly pushed and pulled and slid the exquisitely carved pieces in the correct order for the box to safely open.

"It is her. She's here," Paul whispered, astonishment surging from every pore. "When I made these, she perfected the art of sanding the glides." He pressed his palms to his eyes to staunch the flow of tears.

Carlee put her hand on her grandfather's shoulder. "Let's see what's inside." Carlee retrieved the box and set it on the table, carefully emptying the contents.

"Where did you find that?" Lauren had entered the

dining area and studied the objects organized on the table.

Galen shifted uncomfortably, turning a bit pink. "One was left in the girls' room on a shelf in the closet." He handed over another box.

"You're not in any trouble," I said.

"The blue one was in our room, so Galen searched the suite and found the red one," said Kindra. "We thought it important to pick up that one too."

"I'm glad you did. There has to be a reason we have them."

Paul expertly opened the second box. Patricia selected pieces of similarly colored torn and stained paper amid the contents. Jane and Kindra fitted the sections together like a jigsaw, and we gaped at the pages.

A century of names grew in branches of a convoluted family tree. It began in the late eighteen hundreds and stopped about forty years ago. Jane ran her finger through the paternal line. I followed the maternal path and jolted to a stop, tapping my finger on the surname. Chesterfield was too much of a coincidence.

Jane wrinkled her nose. "I think these pieces came from a trash can." She pointed. "This looks like a coffee stain and over here …" She moved to the far left side. "It smells like sauerkraut."

"Do you think the boxes are from Nicki, I mean my mom?" asked Carlee.

Kindra said, "Who else?"

"Why would she divide the scraps between the containers?"

"More likely she did it so at least one of us would discover part of an answer," I said. I retrieved my phone and rapidly swiped through the photos I'd taken at the police station. I remembered a similarly hand-drawn trunk growing many branches bearing oval leaves with names written inside. When I realized I hadn't taken a photo of that piece of evidence, I groaned in frustration.

I snapped a photo of our completed jigsaw as Kahula said, "Look at this." She held up a piece of variegated wood, whittled into a squared-off hook.

"That's a key," Paul said. Kahula dropped it in Paul's outstretched hand. He examined it closely. "The narrow end slides between the floorboards until it catches. You turn the key, and it pushes a wooden latch out of a groove, so you can remove a section of your wall or box or whatever. When she was young, Danica and I fitted one in the floor of her bedroom for her to store her treasures." He turned steely blue eyes to CJ. "That's how we found out about you."

Paul rotated his head around a room covered in beautiful paneling. "This old house is full of places to build a hidey-hole."

"Wouldn't it be smartest to hide whatever in her room?" Carlee's bright silver-blue eyes glittered with hope.

Lauren rattled a ring of keys. "I can access her space, but I won't take the kids up. You never know what we might find, and I won't intrude on her privacy any more than we need to."

With a truce in the works, CJ and Paul followed Lauren up the stairs, giving each other a wide berth.

Jane and Kahula herded the kids into the library, hinting at a game to take their minds off the contents of Danica's possible cache.

I grabbed my jacket and the leashes and escorted the dogs outside for one final excursion for the night, but I wasn't prepared for their barking and pulling, and neither was Kimber Leigh.

"Please hang on to them," she cried, sneaking from the shadow of the trees. "I'm not doing anything wrong."

"Sit, Maverick. Sit, Renegade," I requested in a friendly voice. "Quiet."

I think I was as surprised as she when they settled at my feet. Under my breath, I said, "Just be ready for anything."

I crossed my arms in front of me. "Why are you skulking around at this hour?"

She bristled. "I am watching out for my investment."

"You invested in the White Star Inn too?"

"No. But I'm sure Willy did, and I want to protect my inheritance."

"Even if he did invest, how do you know it will come to you? Do you know what's written in his will? There are all kinds of ways to make gifts or deny someone a bequest."

She shook her head of salt-and-pepper waves. "We were still married."

"That won't matter if he named another beneficiary." I waited as she mulled over my words.

"I'd contest it." She scrunched her face. "I deserve whatever belonged to Willy." She took a menacing step toward me. "I need it."

Sometimes my mouth worked faster than my brain. "Did you kill him?"

"Absolutely not." She snarled through gritted teeth. Maverick read the tension in the air and stood. He roused Renegade with a touch, and Kimber Leigh paled. She turned and slipped back into the trees.

"Thanks, guys." I dug in my pocket for my ever-ready baggie of tiny training treats, but before I could get them out, the dogs caused a stir again, dragging me around to the front of the inn. "Kimber Leigh? You have to stop sneaking around," I called, hoping I could rein in the dogs again. "They don't like that."

A door slammed and Irinia Holocek emerged from the car at the bottom of the hill. She wore a long camel hair coat, leather gloves, and tall brown boots. She'd pulled back her hair and formally made up her face, dressed for a night on the town, but probably not this one. She peered down her nose at Maverick and Renegade and barely acknowledged me as she tromped to the front door. She tried the knob, but it wouldn't budge. She banged on the door. "Reggie? It's me." She rapped a few more times and called to me, "Is Reggie here?"

"I don't know. I haven't seen him."

She crossed her arms and chewed on a hot pink thumbnail. The door opened. "It's about time," she said. The house swallowed her whole.

"She sure is friendly." The dogs totally missed my sarcasm. We'd started around to the back yard when the front door reopened.

Reggie held Irinia by the elbow and wrestled her toward her car. "I told you I'd call."

"You don't love me."

"Of course, I love you, but there's too much going on here, and you need to stay away."

"What else can I do to make you forget her?" She wrenched her arm out of his grasp and stalked a few steps away, halting halfway down the hill. The heat of her glare singed me. "I dyed my hair to match hers. I gave up my job. I bought a new wardrobe. I tore up the family …"

"What? What else did you do, Irinia?" He hiked toward

her. As Reggie slowly inhaled, one pup tore the leash from my hand. Renegade made a beeline toward Irinia, strap, tongue, and ears flopping in tandem, ready to play. Irinia yelped and twisted on her high heels, crashing into Reggie. He kept his balance, but not his cool.

"Tether that dog," he growled, towing Irinia down the steps.

Maverick and I raced past them. "Sorry," I called. I watched as Reggie urged Irinia into her car.

Maverick and I caught up with Renegade and reentered the house. Paul had unlocked the cache as predicted, and he and CJ arranged the contents of Danica's stash in the parlor.

Jane opened a small box containing a harmonica and pointed to the other containers. "All of these instruments come with instruction books, but does anyone know what they are?" she asked, pointing her phone and adding the photo to an app to put a name to the unusual instruments.

"Danica loved music." CJ picked up each instrument and repeated its name. "Kalimba. Ocarina. Mouthpiece for a bagpipe. Tin Whistle. Didgeridoo. Recorder."

Nestled inside a hard plastic case sat a long wooden flute, but the pile of money under the flute caused a stir.

CJ said, "Katie, please call Sheriff Zasko."

He didn't pick up, and I left a message. "Sheriff, this is Katie Wilk. We found a few more items that might be of interest. Please give me a call."

Paul raised an eyebrow at the message I left.

I chewed on my bottom lip and sighed. "I'm already on his bad side. Maybe he won't pick up."

Sheriff Zasko's text came an hour later. "Very busy. Unless another body, can it wait?"

Nothing we had found wouldn't wait. "Yes."

Jane whipped up two cups of her hot chocolate, using the tantalizing aroma to lure me to the library. I wrapped my hands around the warm cup, sipped, and concentrated on untangling the thoughts fogging my brain.

"You always do that when your mind is elsewhere." The office chair creaked as Jane leaned back to view an entire shelf.

"Do what?" I stifled a yawned and glanced at the books in front of me, neatly arranged by height, shortest on the left.

"You ordered the books by size without regard to titles, author names, cover colors, genres, or age." She knew me well. "What's going on in that head of yours?"

"The money Paul found was a surprise. If Edith had retained guardianship, she'd have been able to access Danica's money in a regular bank account. But the cash was still there so I doubt Edith or anyone else found it. Danica could've used the funds to finance her departure. What if she didn't think Edith would let her go? What if Willy and Edith colluded to keep Danica right where she was? Who else would want Edith dead? Or Willy for that matter?"

"You're sleuthing again." Her voice had a slightly accusatory sing song quality. "But, this time, I'm with you. Danica didn't do it. She couldn't have."

Not true. She certainly could have murdered either or both of them.

"We have to prove she didn't commit the murders," I said. "Otherwise, there will be lingering doubt, people thinking she got off because of a legal loophole or because someone lied. I think the sheriff has made up his mind, and we have to find something to irreversibly change it."

Jane's eyes grew wide. "What do we do?"

"We think. I'll call the sheriff again tomorrow. The pool of suspects in Edith's death is sizeable, but only someone with access to the inn would have had the opportunity to kill Willy—Lauren, Irinia, Reggie, Kimber Leigh, and Ryker."

"Or one of Ryker Chesterfield's cronies."

"True, but I don't see someone who follows Ryker's lead so closely having much gumption to go off on his own. They appear spineless. "

"A little weasley, that's for sure."

"I need to talk to them again, before they're allowed to leave, which probably will be in the near future."

THIRTY-EIGHT

I tossed and turned all night, but we rose early.

"You'd best get started," said Jane "I'm tied up. Kahula would like to visit Danica today and I think she's convinced Paul to come as well. He has embraced the thought Danica is alive but is beside himself—not having done enough to find her or even look for her over the past seventeen years, nor being able to get her out of the trouble she's in now."

"He and CJ, both."

"I may be driving, but Kahula's instincts have been finely honed over the past seventeen years and are quite sharp. I'm doing it all her way."

Jane jerked her head pointedly at the door. "Looks like Ryker and two of his pals are on their way to the kitchen," she whispered. "Good luck."

I didn't have to pretend I liked the kolache I chose for my breakfast pastry, but I did have to feign interest in Ryker's opinions so I could ask him about Danica's arrest. I stood behind him in line, waiting for my chance to use the space-age coffee machine, and asked, "How is your week going?"

He stared at me, coldly. "Why do you want to know?"

"I've heard only good things about the brewery. If we ever get back here without kids in tow, I think I'd like to make a visit."

He nodded. "They are hosting one of the biggest festivals in the state, and they have some of the best beer." He looked me up and down. "They didn't have teachers like you when I was in school."

The abrupt change in topic caught me off guard. I tamped down my ferocious comeback and ignored the lurid comment. "You saw they arrested Nicki—"

"The mute with the origami towels and the candies?"

I nodded. "I wonder why she did it." No response. "We'll probably be allowed to leave soon, but will you be staying to finish out your beer week?"

"I think that's a great question," one of the other young men said, taking a big bite of a cheese Danish. He swiped at the flakes that drifted onto the front of his shirt. "I've been liking the beer tasting. We could stay for a good time. Plus, we prepaid, right Ryker? I don't see your bro returning any of our hard-earned Benjamins."

I couldn't blame Ryker for being wary. I hadn't wanted to be all that friendly before today, and he still unnerved me when I thought about him and my girls, but he pounced on the opportunity to deny any wrongdoing. "We didn't have anything to do with the killings so we're still planning to stay through Friday. What about you?"

I had no idea where the news of the day would take me, nor had I any idea how long CJ, Carlee, Kahula, and Paul planned to stay. We were vested in the outcome whether or not Sheriff Zasko did any more investigating. "I'm not a driver. I just go where the wheels take me."

"Too bad," Ryker said with a too-familiar leer. I tried not to let my distaste color the tone of my voice and deny me a chance to continue our conversation. The way he said 'too bad' made goosebumps crawl up and down my back, but I stayed rooted to my seat at the breakfast bar.

The fourth young man from his party concentrated on his phone so intently, I was surprised he made it through the doorway unscathed. "Hey, Ryker, your phone's been bouncing all over the desk upstairs. That attorney wants to know when you're going to meet …" Ryker coughed, and the young man raised his eyes. His ears lit up like a Christmas tree, and he slid the phone into Ryker's open palm.

The mention of an attorney halted the conversation long enough for me to relish the last nibble of sweet bread, and an idea came to me. I brought up my photos, zoomed in on one, and placed the device on the table, keeping my eyes on Ryker. He tensed. I'd hit a nerve. "We found a family tree with your name on it. Isn't that peculiar?"

He cleared his throat and blanched but couldn't bring himself to look away. "Where'd you find that?"

The quartet of men listened without moving, and I said what might be true. "The sheriff collected it with the rest of Mrs. Farthington's belongings."

He rubbed his chin. "Chesterfield's a name you find all

over the place."

"You're the only Chesterfield I've ever met."

His lips formed an almost sinister grin. He sat back and said, "That's unfortunate." He stood and backed away from the counter. "Time for our brewery tour."

I thought I heard one of his friends hiss as they sauntered out the door, "Ryker. You said no one would ever know."

Know what?

Jane entered the kitchen, looking over her shoulder at the departing foursome. "What did you find out?"

"They're talking to an attorney. I don't know to whom, nor what it means. However, Ryker really didn't like that I had a copy of the family tree, but he didn't send up any red flags. I'm forwarding it to the sheriff. And it can't hurt to ask if the ancestral information is the same as the other tree. The worst thing that can happen is that he doesn't answer."

I sent off the photo, and my phone rang almost immediately.

"Katie, why do you have a photo of this family tree?"

"We found two more of Nicki—Danica's—carved boxes. Each contained torn scraps of paper, and what you have is the picture after we assembled them. Until then, we had no idea what we had."

"You didn't think you should have turned them over immediately?"

"I left two messages." I took a breath and forged ahead. "I think it looks like the family tree you found among Edith's belongings. Could we compare them?"

"I'll send Gray over to collect the boxes and the tree. Anything else?"

I scratched my fingertips on the raised ugly little red bumps and forced myself to ignore the irritation. "We found musical instruments hidden in Danica's floor." I heard fingers drumming. I cleared my throat and said, "And a pile of cash."

His ragged, heavy breathing carried over the phone, and I worried my news might've been detrimental to his health. "Sheriff?"

"We'll be there in fifteen minutes. Sit tight," he said before disconnecting.

Nine minutes later, they pulled up in front.

By the end of our lopsided and uncomfortable conversation, Sheriff Zasko's face burned scarlet, and his reprimand stung. "I warned you not to get involved. This is a serious matter for law enforcement to deal with. You could compromise my investigation."

Gray counted the money. It totaled over seven thousand dollars. To the sheriff, it added fuel to the already incendiary evidence against Danica.

"Sheriff, you translated Danica's first four notes." I glanced up to my right, sifting information, taking my time, making sure I separated the evidence I shared with the sheriff from the contents in the files Gray had allowed me to see. "She was well on her way to independence, and with the cash, her freedom would have been assured. She wouldn't have had to kill anyone."

"Unless one of them threatened to stop her."

"Don't you think if either Edith or Willy would have discovered her resources, they would have confiscated them?"

He hummed and nodded as if he'd just pounded another solid nail in the sturdy coffin surrounding Danica.

"Maybe they did." Sheriff Zasko let that sink in as he collected the cash from the coffee table. He examined each of the instruments and secured them in a plastic tub. As an aside, he said, "Chief Connelly sent along a copy of that family tree. She considered your contribution to her investigation significant and thought you earned the privilege to compare the two, although I don't know what you hope to achieve. Gray," he called.

I pulled up the photo on my phone and pounced on the paper Gray unfurled, noting the inclusion of two additional generations. The name Ryker Chesterfield completed one ancestral line and connected to an unidentified relation born almost two decades earlier. I pointed. The sheriff's face gave nothing away. Gray rerolled the oversized page and slid it into a cardboard tube.

"We should be able to wrap up the particulars of the murders today and you and your party will be allowed to leave tomorrow." The sheriff stared out the window as if concentrating. "Without a doubt, you have assisted in our enquiry." He turned back and caught my eyes. "But you must cease and desist. No more meddling, or I'll be forced to arrest you for obstruction." He and Gray left in a whirlwind.

The temperature in the parlor seemed to drop a chilling ten degrees. The sheriff was right. All I'd done was make things worse for Danica.

I collapsed onto the forest-green loveseat. My head dropped back, and my hands fell to my sides, plucking absentmindedly at the buttons on the tufted upholstery. "I give up," I murmured.

My phone dinged. I hauled myself to sitting and made a mad grab, but my phone tumbled from my fingers and landed upright between the cushions. I fished it out along with dried flakes of food and a small, light-blue, folded square. While reading the text from Dad, I tucked the scrap of paper in my pocket and brushed the tiny crumbs onto my palm.

Ellen completed her first run off the bunny hill today. I gave her the same advice I've always given you. Never give up.

He always knew just what to say. I wouldn't interfere with the sheriff's investigation if I could help it. But I'd never give up.

THIRTY-NINE

Thanks, Dad. I needed that. We might be allowed to leave tomorrow.

I thought hard about family and added to my text before pushing send.

I hope Ellen likes Duluth.

Good food, skiing's okay, but we miss you.

As long as I had my fingers warmed up, I sent a message to Pete.

We should be allowed to leave tomorrow. Can't wait to get home.

I didn't wait for a response and sent the same message to Ida before dropping the flakes in the trash and striding out of the parlor. I heard movement in the kitchen, and determined to tie up a few loose threads, ventured another talk with Lauren.

Her forehead glistened with perspiration. Up to her elbows in a yeasty dough, she blew fine pink wisps of hair away from her face. "You're up and about early, Katie." She gazed at the clock. "Or I'm a little late. What can I do for you?"

"Can I help?" My heart rate picked up. Kitchens seemed to blow up under my ministrations, but I followed her eyes to the countertop. Beads of sweat prickled down my neck and I used two fingers to pull my collar away.

"Would you cut up parchment paper to fit the baking sheets?"

"That I can do." I let out a breath. After a few zips across the jagged teeth, I said nonchalantly, "The sheriff believes he'll have everything wrapped up tomorrow and we'll be allowed to leave."

She stopped kneading and brushed the back of her hand along her cheek, leaving a powdery white streak. "They've settled on Nicki then?" Her face scrunched as she held back the tears pooling in her eyes. "How can they think that?"

"Do you have any idea who else they should look at? Any evidence to give Sheriff Zasko?"

"No." She sniffled. "But it could just as easily have been me. I can't imagine her killing Mrs. Farthington. Nicki and I moved to the inn at the same time, helping to get it ready for the grand opening. Although our suggestions for improvements met with resistance, I don't think Nicki was particularly offended. I wasn't. Mrs. Farthington was a master at making money in the hospitality industry and real estate. With her support, Reggie was trying to make this place a first-class establishment, maybe start his own empire."

"Do you think Danica, I mean, Nicki wanted to leave? Would Edith have kept her here?"

Lauren snickered. "No one could make Nicki do something she didn't want to, but she was accommodating. When her wood shavings showed up everywhere Reggie told her she was making a mess, and rather than quit, Nicki relegated her woodworking to her room. He might have been in love with her at one time. He's been asking to marry her every year I've been with the Farthingtons. She says no and they joke about it and go on as if nothing changed. If she was going to leave, she would've made all the preparations she needed to and succeeded.

"How long have you been here?"

"This is year six."

Maybe Reggie was the persistent man Danica referred to as not wanting to take no for an answer. Was it a running joke between them? Afterall, his engagement to Irinia happened awfully quickly.

"What about Willy Zasko? You said, Nicki avoided him. Do you know why?"

"Nicki was smart and stayed out of the limelight as well as she could. She rarely interacted with our patrons. Instead, she'd get up extremely early to do her job. Mrs. Farthington appreciated her quiet approach. Nicki had warned Mrs. Farthington to be optimistic but skeptical of Willy's intentions, business and personal. Mrs. Farthington never heeded her advice because she respected the way Willy did his job. I guess they made a lot of money working together."

"Did you make a sandwich for Willy Sunday evening or leave the fixings on the sideboard."

She pushed and pulled the dough. "No. Deputy Gray

asked the same question. I put everything away when you left for the hospital. He could have made his own sandwich. He knew his way around my kitchen."

As long as Lauren was willing to talk, I asked about the car we saw her driving.

"That old thing?"

I wished my old car looked like her old car. I'd have to check with Galen again. It looked new to me.

"My brother's a gear head. His newest car is red, and I got a hand me up. I'm not complaining. I didn't have to pay a cent."

"What did you say he does?" I scratched at my fingers. I'd have to find some remedy. They were beginning to burn.

"I didn't, but if you really want to know, he's a forensic accountant and smart as a whip. Our mom wanted him to be a doctor. That's not happening and that's why she's so angry."

She rolled and cut and filled and wrapped the pastries, lining them up on the parchment and covering them with a white flour sack towel. "If you come back in an hour and twenty minutes, you'll have a fresh kolache."

"Thanks. I'll do that." I hadn't gotten any indication Lauren was lying. I believed almost everything she said, but there was something I couldn't pinpoint that made me uncomfortable.

I met Kindra and Patricia on the stairs. Patricia signed and Kindra interpreted. "Ms. Mackey took everyone, except Galen, to the police station, and we're going for a walk. Do you want to come?"

I used one of the few signs I knew. "Yes." I added without signs, "We'll take the dogs too."

I fetched my four-footed friends and knocked on

Galen's door. "It's open."

I stuck my head in. "We're taking the dogs for a walk."

Beams of light streamed in the window like a spotlight on Galen as he hung his head over the desk. "I'll stay here if that's alright with you. I'm studying my lines. We've got a good chance of making it through the first round of the mock trial competition." Our high school team hoped to earn a berth at the state tournament. Galen assumed the identity of Lieutenant Mauritz Hakan Bjornstrom-Steffansson, the role he embraced from our *Titanic* trial, and with a guttural Swedish accent as thick as mud, said, "We go where the winds of fortune take us."

"You okay?"

"Yup, but it's hard watching Carlee. It's ripping her up."

"Carlee has her dad and grandparents and you. I talked to Lauren and I'm checking ..." I stopped before admitting I might continue to look into other possibilities.

Galen picked up on it anyway, slammed the cover of his script, and jumped to attention. "And I'm going to help. Let's get a move on."

When Maverick walked behind, he pulled, so he and Renegade took a spirited lead, not quite running but too fast to be called a stroll. The fourteen-minute promenade took us to the edge of the sleepy downtown. A line of five patrons waited patiently outside the post office. A friendly barber waved a comb and scissors as we passed by. I slowed in front of the photography studio and peered through the cleared windows. Kimber Leigh sat hunched behind the counter. I hoped she'd talk to me.

"Galen, hold these please." I handed off the leashes. "This will just take a minute."

He peered through the window and when his curiosity

was appeased, he said, "We'll get some hot chocolate from the bakery." Renegade jerked her leash, and he added, "And be right back."

A bell dinged when I passed through the doorframe.

"We're not open. Come back later." I cleared my throat, and Kimber Leigh looked up. "It's you. Don't come back later."

"This will only take a minute or two. I have just a few questions. May I come in?"

She leaned back and the fur coat resting on her chairback slid to the floor and left a tangle of dark fur behind. She bent over to retrieve her coat and gestured me farther inside. "Make it snappy. I have things to do."

The animal portraits on the wall caught my eye. "Did you take these?"

She eyed me warily before she admitted, "Yes. No fakes among them. I take better pictures when my subjects don't talk back."

"You do. Why do you sell yourself as a portraitist and wedding photographer?" I lightly ran my fingers over the frame, chuckling at the absurd faces on the pets. "How did you get these odd expressions?"

"I threw treats to food-driven pets, and these are a few of the ones I like." Kimber Leigh closed the ledger in front of her. "Willy called this business my hobby. He said the real money was in weddings. Great lot of good it did me."

"Did you always do what Willy suggested?"

"Obviously not, or we'd still be happily married. I loved him but I'm not sure how much I really liked him."

Patricia and Kindra stepped inside, handing me an extra to-go cup. "Can we bring in the dogs?"

"Sure," Kimber Leigh said. "This place has been going

to the dogs for years."

The tethers were pulled taut, and Galen stumbled in after them. Kimber Leigh reached into a drawer of her desk and before I could object, she'd thrown treats and snapped scads of photos. She previewed her work and said, "Not bad. They're both beautiful specimens." She pulled the memory card and shoved it into her laptop. When she spun the screen, I gasped.

FORTY

My mouth hung open until I could form words. "These are really good." Kimber Leigh had caught Maverick's shiny black coat and mischievous bright brown eyes as he tilted his head. A golden halo encircled Renegade as she bounced playfully but none too saintly, stretching to snatch the treat out of the air.

Kimber Leigh's fingers frolicked across the keys, and she brought up two photos made even better with altered backgrounds. "That'll be twenty-five dollars apiece."

I stammered, "Thank you," as I handed over my card, mesmerized by the photos of the dogs.

"I'll email them."

I typed my email into the address bar. "Jane heard a repeat of your Sunday broadcast and she's expecting you to make good on your promises. We know what you tried to do and she's still posting her review. You chose to wrestle with the wrong bride, but she's already considering tempering her negative comments."

"As you are aware, there were other things going on. I'm sorry about our confrontation," she said earnestly.

Or was she sorry she got caught? Wisps of loose dark fur circled on the ground at her feet and brought back the scene where I'd found Willy.

"Tell her I'll be truthful. She can check. I'll post my own photos and if they're good enough, maybe I'll get some good gigs anyway."

I wouldn't believe anyone who could encapsulate a dog's personality with such precision and candor would stoop to murder. "Kimber Leigh, don't you want Willy's murder case closed so you can go on with your life?"

Her dancing eyebrows fascinated me. "I'm confused. Not. They already have the murderer in custody, and when they read the will this afternoon, I'll know where I stand." I frowned. "You didn't know about the meeting, did you?" she asked. "We gather at the inn at three for the official reading of the will. Both wills actually. Everyone except the killer."

"Danica Bluestone didn't kill Willy or Edith."

"That's her full name? I just knew her as Nicki."

"Why do you think Nicki killed Willy? What could she have had against him?"

"My Willy was after the almighty buck, and Edith was his number one client. They had similar goals. However, Willy never changed our joint account information, and weird emails showed up recently. Nicki had contacted him and was trying to rescind a guardianship but wasn't sure if she was ready or if she could afford it. Willy downplayed the benefits of being out on her own, but he acted strangely on Friday night. He grabbed his briefcase, filled it with some legal documents, and rushed out. I thought he'd decided to help her out after all, but something went awry."

"How—"

"I might have seen him leave."

"Could Willy have killed Edith?"

Kimber Leigh rolled her eyes. Had I uttered those words out loud? "Who gets rid of their meal ticket? He acts … acted the part of a big man but he's too squeamish to kill anyone. He couldn't even put bait on a fishhook let alone remove the fish. No. It wasn't Willy." She secured her camera in the bottom drawer of her desk. "Now, if there's nothing more …"

"Thanks for taking the time to talk to me."

"I hope you like your photos." On to other tasks, she madly typed on her keyboard, so I turned to leave. "Hey," she said. I stopped. "I took down the old website. Tell your friend about our little conversation. I'm sorry, okay?"

The four of us headed back to the inn. Galen walked in front with the dogs and me, and in a very low voice said, "You don't think she's guilty."

"No, I don't." But I couldn't help wondering if Willy would benefit from Edith's death and what Kimber Leigh might inherit from him.

"You don't believe Lauren's a killer either, do you?" I shook my head. "What do you think about everyone else in the case? Do you think there's more than one murderer?"

As much as he wanted to help, I couldn't include my young friend in my investigation so I shrugged but pondered the answers I would have given.

When we'd arrived on Friday evening, Lauren was working at the inn. Reggie was volunteering at the hospital. Willy had visited but probably wouldn't have killed the golden-egg-laying-Edith, unless of course she changed her mind. I still found Ryker disagreeable but couldn't figure out what his motive could've been. Had he known Edith well enough to want her dead? It appeared they'd first met on Friday.

Irinia looked more and more like a viable suspect. When we overheard her at the hair salon on Saturday morning, she indicated she didn't have anything to worry about. Danica rejected Reggie's yearly obligatory proposal, and if Irinia knew it was coming, she had a straight shot to Reggie's heart, no one to get in the way. It sounded like she believed she was already betrothed to Reggie and had Edith's blessing. As Willy's former associate, Irinia might've known many of the particulars of Edith's will. Maybe Reggie had more to gain than he thought.

Danica was dependent on Edith and could've been named an heir, but I wouldn't pursue that line of inquiry; it would give Danica another motive. My head started swimming. What if I was wrong? Who was I to be investigating the deaths tied to the inn? Waves of doubt caught me off guard and caused me to lose my footing. Maverick shot me a quizzical glance when I acted as if my misstep had been caused by my pup.

We could be leaving sometime in the next twenty-four hours. If Danica was guilty, Sheriff Zasko had all the evidence he needed to convict her; I'd given him more than enough with my fumbling help. I couldn't stumble on any more evidence.

But what if she wasn't guilty? What if they had the

wrong person and didn't continue to search for the truth and I'd contributed to them settling on the wrong suspect? Never give up, Dad had said.

We finished our return, walking in silence, each to our own thoughts, until we rounded the corner. Jane's Edge, CJ's truck, and Paul's vehicle took up a long space at the curb behind Ryker's red rust bucket, and the kids raced up the hill to find Carlee.

To avoid another unexpected confrontation with anyone, the dogs and I took a more circuitous route. We entered the rear door and encountered angry voices.

"You did what? What will they think?'

"I don't know. She asked me to sign, and I did. How would I know she'd go and get herself killed? I don't know what it said, but I'm sure it's valid."

I pulled back but the dogs didn't hesitate. Maverick yipped, stood on his hind legs, and drew on the lever. When the handle flapped, announcing his presence, I knocked loudly and said as the door swung wide, "Hello-oo. Anybody here?"

Lauren and her male double turned to look at me. Her face was ashen and his was determined. In the awkward moment, Renegade wiggled wildly and swished her tail, knocking over a fragile glass vase, smashing it to smithereens.

Lauren bent down to help me pick up the glass shards and burst into tears. "Shayne," she sobbed. "What should I do now?"

"Call Sheriff Zasko," he said and excused himself. "Good luck, Sis."

FORTY-ONE

The gray sky of the mid-afternoon worked its way into the rooms of the inn and dampened our spirits. I peeked into the living room.

She'd accepted a new job, but Irinia would finish out working for Zasko by representing the firm at the reading. She stood in front of the fireplace with those mentioned in Edith Farthington's will gathered around her. Reginald lounged in a bulky chair near his beloved lilies in the window nook, one leg crossed lazily over the other, scraping his nails. Lauren Trnka sat bolt upright, rigid, hands on her knees, staring at the mantel. Kimber Leigh was asked to appear because the disposition of Edith's estate could have a bearing on William Zasko's holdings.

Danica was still being held at the jail. Her husband,

Chantan John Bluestone, attended the reading in her stead. He stood erect next to the registration desk, dwarfing everyone else in the room. While he threaded his hat through his hands, his dark penetrating eyes thrust red-hot daggers of distrust at anyone who would meet his gaze.

Sheriff Zasko guarded the door, on site to smooth any ruffled feathers and collect as much information as possible. He closed the door and excluded the rest of us as the minute hand counted down to three. Jane and Kahula pulled the kids into another game in the library, and Paul and I stood next to the ticking grandfather clock.

"I thought she was dead." I strained to hear Paul's words. "I have loathed Chantan. I hated him before they married and blamed him for taking her from us. She loves him yet today and still she has room for her mother, her daughter, and me in her heart. She wouldn't have killed anyone." Fat tears rolled down his craggy cheeks. "What can I do?"

I gripped his hand. Before I could answer, one of Ryker's shadows slid down the banister, hopping off in our direction before he could slam into the newel post, and we leapt out of the way. He whirled around, stared up the steps, and then bent at the waist. "Your Eminence," he said with a flourish of his hand. The other two cronies paraded down the stairs, stepping in unison, buzzing their lips in a royal fanfare fit for trumpeters. His Royal Pain Ryker appeared on the landing, acting as a sovereign surveying his kingdom.

I pulled Paul in front of the library door. The harsh attitude of one attentive grandfather operated well as an ideal deterrent. Ryker glanced at the library entry and then at Paul before jerking his head and leading his minions to the kitchen.

Paul said, "He acts as if he has a stake in the legal proceedings."

The pleasant sound of laughter ringing from the game room stopped abruptly when the door to the living room crashed open. Reggie strode across the floor and out the front door. Irinia raced after him, grumbling, "Don't worry Reg. You know she can't make it go."

Lauren stumbled from the living room, pitching herself in front of the sheriff. "You have to believe me. I never threatened Reggie, but I knew about his poker games. With a reputation that is less than squeaky-clean, you know how difficult it is to do well in this town. But I didn't know about the bequest. Shayne didn't tell me. Maybe he didn't know."

"Sure, Lauren. Even though your brother signed as a witness on Friday?" Kimber Leigh said as she bustled into the room, almost laughing, fanning a handful of papers. "It's a good thing. You do everything around here anyway. Edith finally had the sense to acknowledge your contribution."

"I can't accept. Can't you see? It looks terrible."

"What are you worried about? In a year, if you do a lousy job, Reggie gets it back."

My curious nature got the best of me, and I snatched the pages out of Kimber Leigh's hand. The document was to the point, dutifully signed and notarized on Friday evening. I read through the first two pages. Lauren was correct in the assertion it didn't look good and there could be doubts. There would be an underlying sense of her guilt in Edith's murder. Money in all shapes, sizes, and amounts tended to bring out the worst in people.

"But why?" Stunned, Lauren tripped over her own

feet. "Why would she do this?"

Kimber Leigh snatched the pages back and answered the rhetorical question. "In a roundabout way, Edith is finally paying you back for your years of hard work and service."

"Danica and Reggie were both part of the system for much longer. That can't be the reason." Lauren shook her head.

"The initial idea of the White Star Inn belongs to Reggie, but you were the driving force to get this bed and breakfast open in a timely manner." Lauren twisted her hands together as Sheriff Zasko said. "Reggie liked to be the spokesperson, the face of his budding empire. But not always the very best decision maker. We also know Edith felt responsible for Davy's hospitalization. He'd been with her when he became ill."

Lauren put the back of her hand to her forehead.

"Maybe she had an idea who might have wanted to do her harm," the sheriff continued. "Lauren, according to the most recent copy of her will, your son Davy stands to inherit the bulk of Edith Farthington's estate, at least while you see if you can make a go of it."

"I'm Willy's chief benefactor, and I won't get a thing if the inn does poorly. I trust you to do your best," Kimber Leigh said behind a sardonic smile. "I'm going to miss the old coot."

Relief rippled through me. If Davy received the largest bequest, maybe Danica would be off the hook.

CJ's appearance next to me made me jump. "Where'd you come from" I teased.

He didn't crack a smile.

"What's wrong?"

"Danica also received an inheritance."

"But how would anyone have known?"

"The sheriff has many prior copies of her will. Most of the monetary bequests have stayed the same for the last ten years."

Paul tentatively put an arm around CJ. Together they wandered into the library where the giggles were bubbling again.

Dog yips circled from upstairs. The scritching and scratching at the door to our room ended the minute I let them out. They bounced back and forth, overflowing with excitement. I reeled them in, clipped on the leashes, and we headed out for a long walk.

Although the contents of the will hadn't improved Danica's chance of release, it hadn't removed anyone else from the guilty list either. There were so many disparate pieces to the puzzle, and as we hiked the street to town, I recounted as many as I could remember.

It felt like we'd been here for weeks instead of days, and each day we learned a bit more about the players in the murder game.

Reggie periodically asked for Danica's hand in marriage and good-naturedly accepted her rejections. He was now engaged to Irinia, and she'd been expecting it. Irinia and the busybodies at the salon spouted stories about Willy and Edith even before we knew she'd been killed. The wood shavings found on Edith's body could have come from anywhere but there was as much evidence from Willy's recent project as from Danica's beautiful boxes. Reggie had been marketing his brainchild, White Star Inn, and as a family member might have assumed an inheritance, but Lauren, by virtue of Davy's bequest, would be in charge.

She fretted about being out of her depth, but Kimber Leigh supported the decision.

When I discovered Willy's body, the murder classification morphed to suicide but rapidly reverted to murder. One of the documents littering the floor proved Kimber Leigh's claim as Willy's widow. But our photographic fraud had a dark side. The volatile relationship she had with her almost ex-husband ended when he died. Noting the disagreements I'd witnessed, if she didn't have an iron-clad alibi, she'd have been on the top of my list. Irinia and Willy mixed together like oil and vinegar. Reggie's plants had been overturned. Lauren's prized pickled banana peppers had been dug out of the pantry and used as a condiment on the Dagwood sandwich found next to Willy. And the spilled Scotch tipped the scales another direction. Too many clues.

My fingertips prickled in the cool air. I stuffed my hand into my pocket and brought out more bits and pieces I didn't know what to do with.

Where had the fragment of pink acrylic come from? The last time I'd seen that color Irinia had been pouting and shaking her manicured nails at Reggie. She admitted to dying her hair—maybe to look like Danica, to giving up her job, to tearing something, and maybe she also did away with Edith or Willy.

Dark fur fibers clung to my fingers, and the color matched Kimber Leigh's ratty coat. I turned out my pocket and a scrap of light-blue paper fluttered to the ground.

"Heel, Maverick." He did, allowing me the chance to nab it before it skittered down the street. I unfolded it.

FORTY-TWO

R eg C? stared back at me in red block letters.

I gaped at the items until the dogs decided we'd been gone too long. Before they dragged me down the street, I pushed the pink sliver, the fur, and the note back into my pocket, but the fabric of my jeans chafed my fingertips. The irritating bumps had evolved into tiny stinging blisters.

Our jog back brought us to the inn in time for a large pizza delivery. The air was redolent with onions, garlic, and tomatoes, and my mouth watered.

Even though Danica's family had returned to the police station, obliging the lawyer Paul and Kahula had retained, six large wood-fired pies, in addition to wings and garlic sticks, disappeared in short order. Ryker and his cronies picked up two boxes and retired to the kitchen. The rest of us lit into the food on the sideboard with an appetite that appeased more than just the hunger gods. We ate with gusto and the few scrawny chicken wings that remained wouldn't even top off Galen's late-night snack.

Sweeping up the crumbs, Lauren paled. "I thought there'd be more leftovers. How do I plan for all the contingencies?"

"You can't. We'll just order more pizza when Kahula texts they are returning. Their food will be hot and fresh." Jane bobbed her head.

I followed Jane toward the library. Before we entered, she turned to look at me and stuck her fists on her curvy hips. "Girlfriend, what is wrong with your fingers?" She grabbed my hand. "Angry crimson does nothing for you. You've got to get that looked at." She fished out her keys. "The kids and I are in the middle of a Risk game unlike any other. Go get your hand examined before CJ returns. You can't have him worrying about you too."

I grumbled, grasped her keys, and scratched my fingers again. "I'll keep you posted."

The hospital Urgent Care had a long line of crying kids, harried moms, cranky professionals taking time out of their packed calendars to grace us with their over-accomplished presence by squeezing in an unscheduled appointment, and smiling gray-haired seniors who might have come for the company.

When the texts I sent to Pete and Dad went undelivered, I figured I was in a part of the hospital with bad connectivity, and, although I couldn't see what difference it would make, I used the time to swipe through photos of the documents relating to Edith and Willy. My thumb and forefinger dropped onto the picture of the family tree, and I noticed my phone charge had entered the red zone before I zoomed in on the Chesterfield line.

Rather than surrender to the maddening itch, I concentrated so intently, I missed my name being called and startled when Rianna placed her hand on my shoulder.

"Katie, I can see you now."

She escorted me through the hall of exam bays and smiled warmly. "We've had quite a busy day. No major catastrophes, but the wait time has been unreal. Thanks for being patient."

"When Reggie and Edith volunteered here, what did they do?"

She gestured to a padded chair next to a built-in desk where she brought a computer screen to life and completed my registration. "Tonight, I am wearing my nurse practitioner hat. Let me see, please." She slipped on a pair of purple gloves, drew my hand into hers, and said, "You've scratched the skin raw. Do you have any known allergies?" I shook my head. "Have you touched any strange plants or unusual chemicals?"

I thought about the places I'd been over the past four days and where I might have come in contact with something to make me itch. I suppose I could've had a reaction to a new detergent, but it wouldn't be localized to my fingers. Maybe I couldn't wear fingernail polish. I could have touched a plant while in the park, and I'd been there a number of times. Although I didn't eat the poisoned taffy, maybe I touched another item doctored with whatever made Davy and Carlee ill.

"Not knowingly, but I suppose anything is possible." I remembered standing up the flowers in the living room at the inn. "Maybe it's from handling Reginald Farthington's lilies."

"Let me get you some steroid cream."

Rianna smeared the cream on my splotchy fingers before loosely wrapping them with white gauze. "This will keep the salve from getting all over your clothes." She finished with a swath of tape and leaned back. "There. And to answer your question, Reggie and Edith were volunteers on the overnight general admissions cycle. They signed up for two weeks a year. It's not too taxing. Most of what comes in late are emergencies and are handled in the ER by the staff. The volunteers spend the night and are available to help someone who might be lost or have a question that doesn't need a medical answer."

"Thank you. You've been a big help," I said, flexing my fingers and making my way to the exit. "These feel better already."

As the doors closed behind me, chills ran up my arms, around my shoulders, across my back, and I winced. I had the feeling of being watched for a second time. Compounded by the cold, the falling temperature overpowered my rational thought and fueled my urgent need to ferret out the culprit. I whipped my head in all directions, sure to catch whoever it might be, whether or not it would be wise to do so.

Bright lot lights illuminated the hiding places behind the few remaining cars and widely spaced evergreen bushes, and I found no one. However, even at this distance, I noticed Jane's Edge sagged, leaning heavily to one side, and angrily marched to the source of my frustration.

The closer I stepped, the slower my approach. Two flat tires brought me up short and knocked the wind from my sails. With an outstretched arm, I braced myself against the hood above the front passenger wheel well and stared, making sure I wasn't seeing things. The air had definitely left the tire, which was as flat as a pancake. Shoving away from the vehicle, I took in both tires at one glance. It didn't seem likely I'd fail to notice, ignore, or forget bumping over something that destructive. Had someone let the air out of the tires? Jane would not be happy.

I reached for my phone and repeatedly pressed the screen. It wouldn't light up. It was out of juice.

I backed away from the vehicle and heard a thump and a rustle. It could have been caused by a wind if one had been blowing. Tiny hairs on the back of my neck crawled again. I spun around and this time I caught the angular face of Ryker in the corner window on the second floor of the hospital before the drape swayed as it fell back into place. Nerves on edge and fuming, I immediately trooped back to the entry and expected the doors to whoosh apart. When they didn't, I tapped on the glass to get the attention of the security guard, Bill, who pointedly ignored me and wandered through a set of doors and out of sight. The push bars clacked as I continued to press them while reading the directions for admittance to the hospital after hours, which I'd missed by two minutes, and discovered re-entry required going through the ER.

I plodded around the corner as instructed, and rapid, heavy, insistent footfalls came at me, breaching the still night. Energized by my wild imagination, I turned and fled. Lights glimmered from the churchyard, so I made a beeline across the wide school playground, aiming for the blazing lights at the rectory.

My pounding on the door reverberated around me but didn't bring a response from within. I pounded harder. "Father? Hello? Father Svoboda? Anybody?"

More steps bumped across the ground, and my heart

banged in my chest. I spun toward the sound. "Who's there? What do you want?"

The clomping halted. No one answered.

Feeling exposed by the intense yard light and unable to see beyond the dazzling yellow circle, I took cautious advantage of the moment. I dashed down the sidewalk and across the driveway, seeking sanctuary in the immense church. My footfalls clanged as I raced up a set of metal stairs. I yanked on the door at the top, but it wouldn't open. Neither would the second door I tried. I rounded the corner and rocketed up the concrete steps in front, paused below the vigilant statue of St. Wenceslaus, and shot an urgent prayer heavenward as I grabbed the handles and heaved. Someone had failed to check the left half of the double doors, and the bolt shot out as I pulled it wide enough to slip through. I turned the knob and gently pressed the door back into the frame, hoping the latch would engage.

I crept into a nave cloaked in eerie darkness. The muted colors in the stained-glass windows made the dim faces of the figures indecipherable. The lifelike statues had taken on varying shades of ghostly gray, and I squinted to discern some of the beautiful features Father Svoboda had pointed out. Near the altar at the front, candles in red glass holders flickered, and the dancing shadows writhed and wriggled over the walls and ceiling.

My respiration and heartrate began to decrease. I closed my eyes and concentrated on the family tree from among Edith's belongings. An answer drifted just beyond my thoughts. The image of the Chesterfield line came into focus. The birthdates pulsed. A vision of lilies dropping yellow pollen began to make sense as a door opened, and the building took a quick breath.

I searched for cover. My fingers crawled along the wall, following the sculpted surface of the wood, and I tiptoed, one step at a time, to the choir loft for an overhead view of the church.

Peeking from behind the massive pipe organ, I scanned the vast area below. From the front of the church, on the far side, a hooded shape slowly made its way down the aisle, intermittently bobbing to peer under the pews. I gasped and covered my mouth. The figure stopped abruptly then bolted to the rear.

I felt my way around the loft and bumped into a cupboard. A door creaked open, and I stumbled, tumbling into suffocating fabric which clung to my arms and encased my head. I batted at the lengthy material of what felt like choir robes falling on top of me, and lost my balance, sprawling onto the organ foot pedals. The last thing I remembered before I blacked out was a powerful, rich, bass drone.

FORTY-THREE

Everyone reacts to ice water differently. Athletes might subject their beat-up and inflamed bodies to its healing power. It could quench a driving thirst or numb a painful injury. This ice-cold water revived me, and I reacted by recoiling rapidly and banging my head. I clawed at the fabric I thought had captured me but found myself confined in a scratchy fiber cocoon. Sometime after I'd lost consciousness, someone had trussed me up like a sack of potatoes.

A thump juddered my encasement. I was in a cramped space like the trunk of a car, filling with water. Someone or something shoved the car again, and I slid into the cold, paralyzing liquid. I gasped and coughed.

"Reggie," I called. "I know it's you. The pollen from

your lilies has been everywhere. I wiped it on my pants after we pulled Edith from the culvert."

Another dull, heavy blow resulted in a small roll. I braced myself. More water seeped in and sluiced toward me. I tore at the musty fabric, loosening the tie above my head.

"And it was all over the living room when I found Willy. I didn't know what it was at first, but you always brought it with you. Someone will work it out."

The water inched its way into my space and numbed my toes.

"I'm allergic to your herbicide. I've already been to the hospital. Rianna will figure out that's what was used to tamper with Edith's favorite taffies."

A muffled voice said, "Edith kept giving them away."

No more words came.

I said, "You won't get away with it."

I tried to slither out of the burlap confinement, but I'd lost feeling in my extremities and had no fine motor skills.

"The ancestral chart labels the Chesterfield siblings' birth years, and I found a note in the parlor with part of your name on it." Talking helped me think. I pounded the frame and warmed a teeny bit. "You're Ryker's brother, aren't you?"

A wallop underscored the word, "Half-brother." The car lurched, and the front angled down.

"You're Reginald Chesterfield and no relation to Edith Farthington. She found out." The tie at the top loosened.

"Edith wanted a family in the worst way, just not me."

"Did Willy know?"

The trunk took another pounding. "He discovered my ancestry and after Edith died thought he'd blackmail me, but it won't matter. Irinia ripped up the completed copy of my family tree and threw it away. There's no evidence."

My gut flipped. Danica had found the torn pieces, we'd put them together, and Reggie didn't know Sheriff Zasko had both family trees. I hunted for the emergency trunk release.

"Everyone will think Lauren is the culprit. I left plenty of clues and this car will nail her to the murders," he said.

I hammered against the interior as frigid water soaked my jacket and took away my common sense. "Why did you let them arrest Danica?"

"She should have married me, but if I couldn't have her, I figured no one would." He rammed into the back again. More water leaked into the cavity. "Luckily I had Irinia in reserve."

My lips struggled to form the words. "But now you're pointing a finger at Lauren?"

"That's *if* they find you, but it can't be helped. She took my inheritance, and Danica isn't available to blame this time."

Water poured in. "Did Ryker take your shifts at the hospital?" Thoughts were difficult to hold onto.

"I told you to leave it alone." He grunted. Another pummeling, and the car teetered. I readied myself, curling away from invading liquid and I seesawed back. The slight rocking was intoxicating.

"Reg. Gie?"

The rising arctic water acted like manacles on my chest. My chattering teeth slowed. Every intake of air hurt, and my lungs stopped expanding. I wanted to sleep. It wouldn't be so bad. I could be with Charles. But then I remembered promising him I'd live a good life. The face shifted. In my mind I saw Pete's insistent, shining, chocolate-colored eyes and felt him press his warm lips to mine.

"Reg. In. Ald?"

Blood pulsed more slowly through my neck, and my thoughts drifted, dreaming of Maverick romping through the snow.

My head lolled back and forth as the persistent barking tried to lure me from the soporific arms of Hypnos. I hung on until I wrenched my eyes open, searching for the insistent noisy dog—my insistent, noisy lovable canine companion.

And he yelped close by.

"Maverick." It came out as a croak. My chattering teeth resounded in my ears. "Maverick, here."

I lifted the deadweights I called arms and punched at the ceiling. I directed my inert legs through willpower and kicked out. Sharp pins and needles pierced my nerves as I forced feeling to return to my extremities. The glacial water brushed my neck and I thrust myself forward with every ounce of strength I had remaining. My frozen fingers hooked a tab. I forced them into a claw-like grip and pulled.

The trunk lid popped. The bright moon, doubled by its reflection in the large body of water, lit the night. Maverick had Reggie pinned against a tree trunk. His raised hackles enlarged his shoulders and if I hadn't known better, I'd have thought he was a wolf.

I dragged my chilled-to-the-bone body over the lip of the trunk, dropped into the water, and screamed. I raised my heavy arms and slogged through the slush. The car pitched away from me, and I dropped onto the shore. I lay there as frosty blades of grass cut into my cheek. I closed my eyes, unable to make any part of me move until

Maverick crawled on top of me, laid his head on my neck, and licked my face. I peeled my eyelashes apart and smiled.

Multiple orbs of light bobbed through the trees, calling my name. Renegade reached us first and she emulated my dog, dragging her entire torso over mine. I lugged my arms over the pair of them and waited.

CJ arrived next. With a whistle, the dogs slid off me, and he covered me with his warm coat.

My mouth wouldn't work. I tried several times before he brought his ear close enough to hear. "Reggie."

"The sheriff has him in custody. He tried to sneak past Renegade, but Reginald is afraid of my pup."

"And mine." I tried to laugh but coughed instead.

CJ's brilliant smile outshined the moon. "You did it again. Thank you." He reached out his hand. "Are you able to walk?"

I nodded, and he dragged me to a standing position. He pulled my arm over his shoulder. Walking would take a more concerted effort. I lugged my foot forward and my legs wobbled. Jane appeared on my other side. I could go anywhere with these two.

But I only had to go as far as the road over the culvert where we'd found Edith only days before. Paul sat behind the steering wheel of his battered black truck. Jane marshalled me into the rear and sat next to me, followed closely by our dogs. CJ slid onto the front seat and said, "Hospital."

"No," came out clear as a bell. "We've been there enough." I caught Paul's smile in the rearview mirror, and we headed back to the inn where we were met by four rambunctious, boisterous, happy kids, a drained grandmother, and one beautiful, smiling mom.

"You two." Kahula pointed to Danica and me. "To bed. Now. There will be plenty of time for talking tomorrow."

Danica held out her arm. I took it and she squeezed. We mounted the stairs in grand style, escorted one step at a time by more eyes than I cared to count.

After a hot shower, I dropped onto the tiny bed. Maverick settled in next to me and then next thing I knew, the pink of dawn kissed the edge of the blinds.

FORTY-FOUR

Jane snored softly. I crept down the stairs, and drawn by soft sounds in the early morning, slowly opened the door to the parlor.

Kahula and Paul flanked Danica as they huddled together on the sofa. Half her life had been spent in grief and fear and her fortitude had dissolved. Her shoulders quaked as she sobbed. Reality set in as her entire world flipped.

I felt a presence beside me and when I realized it was CJ, I wrapped my arms around him. When I was hugged out, I stepped to the side and gave him space. Carlee had followed him. She pulled a chain over her head and cradled the blue pendant in her hand. She reached for my bandaged fingers, but grabbed my wrist instead and squeezed.

Kahula squinted into the stream of brightening

daylight. She tipped Danica's chin up to look squarely in her eyes and nodded at our small entourage standing in the doorway. Danica wiped one eye and then the other and raised her chin before rising. Paul held her steady.

She inhaled sharply and stepped toward Carlee who rushed into her embrace with such speed and intensity the two nearly toppled. Danica covered her daughter's hair with kisses. She took Carlee's face in her hands and peered into her eyes. "I have loved you since the moment you were born." Carlee took one of her mother's hands in her own, pulled it flat, and ever so gently tucked the lapis lazuli necklace into Danica's palm, and curled their fingers around it. Danica gasped and brushed at new tears, closing her eyes at the vividly shocking connection.

She lowered Carlee's arm to her side and held it straight and taut, as if it helped keep her upright. She took tentative steps toward CJ and scrutinized his face. "My letters came back. At first, I thought you didn't want me, and then Reggie said you'd probably died. I had nothing left."

CJ started to interrupt, but she cut him off with the wave of her hand.

"I know I had it all wrong, but I thought Edith saved me and I owed her everything. I didn't know you searched for me then, and now. Will you ever forgive me?"

CJ blinked and bowed his head. He forced his stiff words past the set of his jaw. "Only if you pardon me for giving up."

Her voice hitched. "Chantan."

Delicious smells and banging came from the dining room. Kahula rose and led the way. The breakfast spread Lauren laid out filled the table.

"I have my work cut out for me. This isn't the first time the flagship of a White Star line hit an obstacle." Lauren frowned and gawked at her shoes.

We stared in contemplative silence, afraid to break the magic of the moment, and I found my heart beating in rhythm with the grandfather clock.

The doorbell rang and Lauren, Danica, and I turned to answer.

"Danica, you don't work here anymore," I said. "Sit down, relax."

"Yes," said Lauren. "You're a guest now."

Danica smiled demurely and lowered her eyes. "Thank you."

With a gigantic smile, Lauren said, "But I do work here." We chuckled. Danica and I followed her, awash with curiosity. She whipped open the door with a flourish and announced, "Welcome to Trnka Manor. What can I do for you?"

I beamed when I heard the words, then gasped and beamed again.

The concerned looks on the familiar twosome standing on the porch gave me a thrill. I glanced from one handsome man to the other and threw myself into Pete's arms before he knew what hit him.

"Whoa," Drew said and held out his hands to steady us.

I lost myself in Pete's luscious brown eyes. My heart beat so hard and fast I was afraid it would fly out of my chest and the only words I could think of as I began to hyperventilate were, "You're late."

He wrapped his arms around me and held tight until I could breathe normally, and he kissed me. Then he leaned his head away so he could see my face and said, "Now, tell me all the trouble you've gotten into during our spring break."

"First, let me introduce you to Lauren Trnka. Lauren, Dr. Pete Erickson and Agent Drew Kidd." I pulled them inside and closed the door.

Lauren glowed. "How do you do?"

"And Danica Bluestone." I stepped to one side to make the big reveal and noticed the confused look on her face. "What's wrong, Danica?"

"I thought … When I saw you and Chantan this morning … I assumed—"

Maverick burst between Pete and me, vigorously wagging his tail, searching for the scratch only Dr. Erickson could provide. CJ appeared beside her, and with an animated voice said. "You thought what?"

Danica stammered, studying the faces in the room. "Chantan, we've been apart a very long time, and I thought you …" She glanced between CJ and me. "I thought you were together."

He roared with laughter, clutching his side, and his total disbelief put me off for half a hot second, but we are what we are. He wiped his eyes. "Katie will always occupy a spot in my heart because she brought our daughter to me."

Danica bowed her head and said, "I see."

"But, Danica, you have always been and will continue to be the only love of my life."

Tears filled her eyes, and she flew into his powerful arms.

Drew said, "I'm glad that's settled."

"What's all the fuss?" Jane said, yawning and trudging down the steps followed closely by Patricia and Kindra. She ran her fingers through her curly, unkempt hair. "Oh, it's you," she said as if the presence of Pete Erickson and Drew Kidd was totally expected. After a beat, she flew down the steps and threw herself into Drew's waiting arms.

Galen stood on the landing with his hand on his hips. "All's right with the world."

The doorbell rang again, and his face clouded. "Who can that be?"

Lauren arranged her collar and reached for the knob. She raised her chin and pulled on the door. "Welcome to Trnka Manor. How may ... Oh." She stepped back to admit Sheriff Zasko and Deputy Gray.

Hat in hand, the sheriff said, "I just came to put your minds at ease. You are free to leave at any time, and I'm sorry your stay was so manic."

A small voice squeaked. "Me, too, Sheriff? Am I allowed to leave?"

"Yes, Ms. Bluestone. Reginald Chesterfield has been pretty close-lipped, but Ryker has no desire to be drawn any further into the murders. We know most of what happened."

I was dying to know more, but only Kahula had the nerve to ask. "What did happen, Sheriff?"

When the sheriff gave the go-ahead, Deputy Gray burst with the news. "Reggie had this planned for years."

Lauren raised one finger. "If this is going to take long, let's sit at the table and eat while my feast is still hot." She gestured to the dining room.

Gray continued with his tale after we were all seated, having helped ourselves to plenty, and the only sound he had to compete with was the clinking of the silverware on the breakfast dishes.

"Ryker and Reggie have the same father. He spent most of their childhoods behind bars. But Reggie played an important role in one of his dad's simplest cons. He played the part of a widow's husband's estranged sister's son ..." Gray nodded his head as he checked off each of the possessives. "And was rewarded with a bequest when she passed away. I think it stuck with him. When his mother died, he explored successful widowed women and hit on a few of them up until he came across Edith. He'd consulted records and had names and dates and even photos to show her. Apparently, Edith's husband had been estranged from his family when his older sister died. Reggie claimed to be her son, looking for family. Edith fell for it hook line and sinker. Of course, Ms. Bluestone, you were already here. He knew how she felt about you, and pardon my saying so, but he thought he'd have his cake and eat it too. He'd get his bequest, marry someone he thought he loved, and get your bequest too."

"Take a breath, man," Drew said.

Gray tucked into Lauren's tasty egg dish and rolled his eyes in bliss before continuing. "He'd seen an early will where the two of them had it all. He begged her to fund this ..." Gray circled the room with his fork. "But then Edith fell for Lauren's son Davy. His poisoning was accidental. Davy never should have eaten with Edith. Reggie hoped she would get a little sick from the glyphosate herbicide, and he'd be her superman by saving the inn. Then Ryker showed up and introduced himself. He knew all about Reggie and wanted in on the action. Reggie felt he had to act. Edith had to go."

When Gray stopped to take another bite, Sheriff Zasko broke in. "Willy's always been the curious sort. After you, Dr. Bluestone, explained why you'd come, Edith prepared to reunite you and Danica. She rewrote the will one last time, but Willy had raised enough questions for Edith to cut Reggie's inheritance down to a token. She figured Danica would be taken care of, so there was just Davy. Ryker took over Reggie's volunteer shift at the hospital desk early Friday morning, and he had a pretty good idea what Reggie had done so he's not off the hook. Luckily, he kept his guys close. He didn't trust Reggie and for good reason. Ostensibly, Reggie wanted to talk to Edith, but he'd already decided on an offensive confrontation and came prepared with the awl.

"You can thank Katie for being a royal pain or we might not be having this conversation." Pete cleared his throat. CJ nodded. Deputy Gray smiled and took one look at the sheriff. He cocked his head and continued, "That's what you said at the station, Sheriff."

The smallest smile graced Sheriff Zasko's lips.

FORTY-FIVE

We packed up and made a heartfelt farewell, wishing Lauren and Davy the best. Kahula and Paul planned to spend time in Columbia with their newish family and their truck rolled out after CJ, Danica, Carlee, and Galen. Drew took my place with Jane and after losing an arm-wrestling bet with Patricia, pretended to pout about having to drive the Edge home.

Maverick sat in the back seat, and I rode shotgun in Pete's Ram truck. "You never said how you were able to get out of the ER."

"We really were running ragged, and the nurses demanded the hospital hire locums so there wouldn't be any screw ups. They threatened to go to the paper. I guess all of the administrators were gone somewhere for spring break."

"Are you good?"

"I have to work tomorrow, but call is every fourth night. I came to rescue you, as if you needed it." I loved his low rumble when he chuckled.

I really wanted to ask about ZaZa, but instead I said, "Did you see the way Gray looked at Lauren?"

However, Pete read my mind. "That Frenchwoman." Maverick whined. "ZaZa sparks more drama than any five other females I've ever known, combined. After her last visit, Susie stuffed her in her taxi and told ZaZa she couldn't come back to the ER without a note from her primary care practitioner." He shook his head. "If you ever leave again without giving me a get-out-of-jail card to get away from her, I don't know what I'll do."

On the road, I texted but ended up calling Dad to check-in. He'd slipped on some ice and turned his knee, so they were on their way home, and I couldn't wait to see him. I saved the more critical info about the memorial trip for our face-to-face conversation.

Ida didn't answer a call but texted her curious response.

Can't talk now. Be home Saturday. Some serious issues to discuss soon.

I had no time to wonder what her cryptic message meant.

The second half of our spring break was spent recovering from the first half—reading, walking, talking, resting, helping Dad, dinners with Pete, and tiptoeing around the topic of Ellen. She'd taken a room at the motel, and I still didn't know how I felt.

Ida slept most of Saturday, recuperating from her week away too.

We met Pete, the Bluestones, and Danica's parents after Mass on Sunday, and Ida invited them to supper.

"Four thirty," she said. "For lasagna, and Katie's going to help." I think Carlee's wide eyes and open mouth duplicated my own. "I'm getting too old to do it alone."

Without turning our heads, we both glanced sideways to see if she was kidding. She wasn't, and suspicion clouded her good cheer.

Danica took a step forward and hugged her. "We'll be there ready to celebrate. What can we bring?"

I expected Ida's usual, "Absolutely, nothing," and was chagrined to hear her say, "How about a green salad?" She'd never let me make a green salad. I unclenched my teeth. Ida was finally releasing her grip on doing everything herself and sharing responsibility. The visit with her cousin had done wonders.

When Ida said *we* she'd meant *me*. She lounged on the chair in her kitchen with a cup of tea, giving orders. Fortunately, she kept her eyes peeled for my disastrous cooking calamities. Pete arrived and her concentration wavered. I avoided all other mistakes but charring the Italian sausage. Pete saved it from complete ruination.

We finished a fine supper, even if I do say so myself, and retired to Ida's living room. Danica sat at Ida's grand piano, and she tentatively noodled the keys, playing the song written especially for her seventeen years earlier—the song she'd performed the night Carlee was born. Carlee had grown up playing a version of the song and sat next to her. When she joined in, the piece swelled with love.

I looked at Pete, checking on my dad and Ida. CJ smiled from the tip of his nose to his toes. Even Ellen hadn't brought up our complicated background. "Family," I said.

Ellen heard me. She stepped close and laid her head on my shoulder. I tensed for a moment before I inhaled, wrapped my arm around her, and drew her close.

Family.

PINK LEMONADE MARTINI

Five raspberries
2 oz vodka
½ oz Cointreau
1 oz simple syrup
1 oz lemon juice

Muddle the raspberries in a shaker with ice. Add the remaining ingredients. Shake to chill. Pour through a sieve. Garnish with a cherry and/or mint leaf.

Thank you for taking the time to read *Creeps, Cache, & Corpses*. If you enjoyed it please tell your friends, and I would be so grateful if you would consider posting a review. Word of mouth is an author's best friend, and very much appreciated.

Thank you,

Mary Seifert

What's coming up next in Katie's life?

Months ago, Katie Wilk discovered she has a younger half-sister, Ellen, which means her mother had not died, as Katie had always believed; she'd left and started a new family. Ellen has not seen their mother in almost a decade, and Katie is struggling to reconcile this new definition of family. But meanwhile, her dear landlady, Ida Clemashevski, confesses to bouts of melancholia and forgetfulness, and Katie worries the symptoms are a prelude to dementia. With so much to occupy her time, Katie finds it easy to avoid her half-sister. But when Ellen begins a search for their long-lost mother and then is arrested for murder, Katie knows she can't sit idly by. It will be up to her to find the real killer.

* * *

Acknowledgements

Thank you to Stephanie Dewey and Lee Ellison, the driving force that keeps me heading in the right direction, on track, on time, and in line, with insight, wisdom, and guidance.

Even though New Prague is very real, if you've been there, you probably won't remember it as portrayed here, but even though this is a work of fiction, fiction won't make any sense if everything is made up. I have so many people to thank for keeping my fiction as true as it can be. My niece, Rachel Jarzombek, is a speech pathologist who helped me discover the capabilities of my character, Patricia, reminiscent of a former deaf student in one of my classes. Kids are truly amazing and resilient. Darlene Witt checked the accuracy of my description of the beautiful Catholic church in New Prague.

During the process of writing this book, there were readers who made comments about inconsistencies and unknowns, faulty descriptions, and possibilities. For advice along the way, thank you Dennis Oakland, Colleen Okland, Anne Eischens Bisek, Patty Gehlen, John Seifert, Tim Ellington, Kate Michaelson, Judy Jones, and L.C. Hayden, and our marvelous team of beta readers.

Note, the mistakes made under the guise of artistic license are all mine.

Friends never cease to amaze with their caring support and by sharing their views of the world. Thanks to Sandi Unger, Amy Ellingson, Joan Christianson, Eve Blomquist, Maria Hughes, and Deb Van Buren.

As always, my family gave terrific insight, comfort, encouragement, and unconditional love. Thank you, John, Kindra, Adam, Danica, Mitch, CJ, Emely, Thomas, Jack, and Leo. I couldn't do this without you.

Have you read all the books in the Katie & Maverick Series?

Maverick, Movies, & Murder
Rescues, Rogues, & Renegade
Tinsel, Trials, & Traitors
Santa, Snowflakes, & Strychnine
Fishing, Festivities, & Fatalities
Diamonds, Diesel, & Doom
Creeps, Cache, & Corpses

Get a collection of free recipes from Mary —Scan the QR code to find out how!

Visit Mary's website: MarySeifertAuthor.com/
Facebook: facebook.com/MarySeifertAuthor
Twitter: twitter.com/mary_seifert
Instagram: instagram.com/maryseifert/
Follow Mary on BookBub and Goodreads too!